JUST ONE YEAR

PENELOPE WARD

Edited by: Jessica Royer Ocken
Proofreading and formatting by: Elaine York
www.allusiongraphics.com
Cover model: Chase Mattson
Cover photographer: Derick Smith
Cover design: Letitia Hasser, RBA Designs
www.rbadesigns.com

JUST ONE YEAR

CHAPTER
ONE

Teagan

Ever have one of those days where everything seems to go wrong from the moment you wake up? Like someone up above just decided this was going to be a crappy day for you, and no matter where you go or what you do, you can't seem to avoid trouble? Today had been that kind of day for me. It was sophomore orientation day at Northern University, and everything that could go wrong today had.

First, I was informed that I didn't get into the chemistry class I'd wanted. They'd overbooked it and needed to oust the last few people who'd signed up. Instead, I'd have to suffer through physics, which I found boring and easy, because it was the only thing that fit into my schedule.

Then I found out Maura's request to have an international student live with us for the year had been accepted. The university had a housing shortage and gave stipends to people who lived nearby that were willing to house some of the students. My stepmother had specifically requested an international student because she wanted to teach my little sister about a foreign culture. We'd be welcoming a guy from China. Finding out we were about to have a stranger living with us put another damper on my afternoon. I really didn't feel like having to be "on" in my own house.

But that news was nothing compared to the worst part of my day: my current situation as I ran in search of a bathroom. I'd gotten my period unexpectedly while touring one of the newly constructed school buildings. As I rushed away from the science lab, the sound of my shoes hitting the ground echoed in the halls.

When I finally found a ladies' room, a sign on the door read: OUT OF ORDER.

Of course!

Since I couldn't afford to waste time searching for another bathroom, I made the hasty decision to use the adjacent men's room. Putting my ear to the door, I didn't hear any activity inside. Thankfully, it *was* actually empty when I went in.

There were two urinals on one wall and two stalls on the other. The first stall I entered looked like the toilet was about to overflow, so I opened the second one. The most horrid stench I'd ever smelled in my life emanated from it, but it did appear to at least be working. And I now had no choice but to use it. Holding my nose, I attempted to fish a tampon out of my purse with my remaining hand. Bending without touching the toilet seat, I took care of business as fast as I possibly could—but not before someone entered.

The door creaked as it opened. *Great. Just great.*

"Hang on!" I said from behind the stall door as I rushed to pull my shorts up. "Don't take your pants off yet. I'm coming out."

Don't take your pants off yet? I cringed at my choice of words.

"I'm sorry?" a voice said.

I busted out of the stall. "The ladies' room is out of order, and I really needed to use the bathroom."

He sniffed. "Evidently."

Shit! He thinks I'm responsible for the smell.

Don't do it. Acknowledging will make you look guilty.

But I couldn't help myself.

"I just want you to know—the smell...it wasn't me. It was like that when I walked in."

To make matters worse, this guy was pretty amazing looking, not the ideal person to have caught me in the men's room. *Was there actually an ideal person?*

My heart beat faster as I washed my hands.

"Hmm...curious, if you ask me," he muttered in his British accent.

"Curious? What does that mean?"

He smirked. "The whole thing is curious. You're not supposed to be in here. You seem guilty. And it smells like someone died. Suspicious. But it's none of my business."

I shook off my hands and grabbed a piece of paper towel, ripping it harshly. "You can't be serious."

He looked me up and down. "It's surprising a little thing like you could have created such a stench."

My heart raced. "It wasn't me."

I knew the more I denied it, the worse it made me look. I needed to get out of here.

He chuckled. "Relax. I'm kidding."

Is he? I rushed past him. "Have a good day."

"Smell you later, love," he called from behind me.

I headed through that door and down the hall like a bat out of hell.

———

My family lived about ten minutes from Northern's main Boston campus in the town of Brookline. Our house was a large, old Victorian with dark wood fixtures and a winding staircase. *Vintage* was the best way to describe it—bright purple on the outside with a red door. It looked like something that belonged in a children's book.

As beautiful as the bedrooms were, when I'd turned eighteen last year, my dad had allowed me to move downstairs. The basement had its own smaller bedroom and an adjacent bathroom. On my birthday, instead of partying or going out to redeem my complimentary Starbucks drink, I'd spent the entire day moving my belongings. My room now had its own door that led out to the yard. That made it easy to escape when I needed to. I liked being able to come and go as I pleased without having to talk to my father, Maura, or my twelve-year-old half-sister, Shelley. It wasn't that I hated being around them; I just needed my space. But it didn't make sense to pay for housing at the university when we lived so close. So the basement was my compromise.

Because we had so much room and lived so close to the college, Maura often offered one of our bedrooms to various people traveling through town or students needing to rent a room. Having strangers in my house had never bothered me when I was younger. But now that I'd be attending school with this latest international student, it was going to be weird having him around.

"You're back late," my stepmother said as I entered the kitchen that afternoon.

"Yeah. Orientation was stressful. I watched a movie after I left school to get my mind off things."

Syd's Theater, the small, independent movie house in my town, was practically empty during the weekdays. My stepmother was convinced the wrong kind of people lurked in there during slow times—like the middle of the day—but that was exactly when I liked going, when I was alone or nearly alone in the place.

She frowned. "I told you to stop going there."

"It's fine. No one's ever bothered me. In fact, I was the only one in there today. No one can bother you if you're alone. Aside from the floors being sticky, it's harmless."

"God knows what's on that floor that's *making* it sticky. And you were all alone? That's exactly what I mean. You're an easy target. I have a bad feeling about that place."

I changed the subject because I didn't need to have this dumb discussion again. "Did the exchange student arrive?"

Banging a metal spoon against the pot she was stirring, she said, "There's been a change in plans. Bo Cheng from China is no longer going to be living with us."

"Why not?"

"Turns out he's highly allergic to cats. He showed up earlier with all of his stuff and couldn't stop sneezing. He went back to the school and requested a reassignment."

My hopes were up. "So, no one's moving in?"

"They were able to find another student willing to switch with Bo. So now he's coming instead. He's supposed to be arriving tonight. I guess he's packing up his stuff."

I sighed. "What's his deal?"

"They didn't say. It'll be like unwrapping a present," she teased.

Feeling anxiety bubble up in my chest again, I headed down to my bedroom and lay on my bed, staring at the ceiling, once again appreciative of the sanctuary that was my own space. The screen door that led out to my yard let in a cool breeze. Listening to the rustle of the leaves, I drifted off into a nap.

———

My sister's voice woke me sometime later. "Come upstairs and meet Caleb!"

Rubbing my groggy eyes, I mumbled, "Who?"

"Caleb. The guy who's gonna be living with us!"

Ugh.

She plopped onto my bed. "He's really nice. He's already fixed my bike. He figured out how to loosen the stuck seat."

"He's been here for a while?"

"About an hour and a half. He's upstairs putting his room together, but Mom just called everyone for dinner. We're about to start eating. She made spaghetti."

I looked at the clock. *Jesus.* It was nearly eight at night.

After my sister skipped back upstairs, I forced myself out of bed and walked over to the mirror. I tied my long, light brown hair back up in a knot. I hadn't worn my hair down in ages, and makeup wasn't my thing. *Good enough.* I wasn't trying to impress anyone anyway.

Slowly, I made my way up the stairs. As I reached the top, a British accent began to register. I stopped just short of the dining room and lingered around the corner before entering. *Why does his voice sound so familiar?*

I leaned my head out to take a peek into the room.

No!

Just no!

Why?

It was the chiseled face of the guy who'd judged me in the men's room today. My stomach sank.

Not the bathroom Brit!

Anyone but him.

He was our new tenant?

My father caught sight of me, thwarting my attempt to hide around the corner. "Teagan! So nice of you to join us."

I took a few reluctant steps into the dining room.

Caleb turned to meet my shocked eyes. His mouth fell open before curving into an amused smile.

Maura introduced us. "Teagan, this is Caleb." She grinned. "Caleb, this is our daughter, Teagan."

"Nice to meet you," I forced out.

He smirked. "Actually...we've met before, haven't we?"

Maura looked between us. "You have?"

Caleb nodded. "We ran into each other today at orientation."

I narrowed my eyes at him. "Oh, that's right. I recognize you now."

"It was brief...but memorable." He winked. "Wasn't it?"

I wanted to smack him from across the table. But instead, I sat, vowing not to say anything further to him.

7

Throughout dinner, I played with my pasta and avoided making eye contact.

Maura pushed the serving dish closer to him, a silent encouragement to eat up. "So, Caleb, what brings you to the States? I mean, I know you're studying at Northern, but why did you decide to make that move?"

He took a swig of water. "Well, I took a few years off after high school. I wasn't sure what I wanted to major in. That's why at twenty-two, I'm a bit old for a freshman. My uni in England has a partnership with Northern. I was given the option to spend one year here. So, I chose the first year. I figured when else in my life would I get this opportunity?"

"Is this your first time in the US?"

He wiped his mouth and nodded. "Yes."

"What do you think so far?" she asked.

"I love it. But I'm definitely noticing some differences."

Maura leaned in. "Oh? We'd love to know more." She turned to my sister. "Shelley, pay attention. This is good for you to learn."

"Well, for one, the portion sizes here are more fit for a gorilla."

Everyone but me got a good laugh at that.

"Not that I'm complaining..." he added. "I think it's great. We just aren't served that much food back home."

Smiling, my dad crossed his arms and leaned back into his chair. "What else?"

"Well, thus far I'm finding there are two types of people here. There are extremely friendly ones who start talking to you on the tube for no reason. And then there are people who can't seem to take a joke or laugh at

8

things." He turned and looked right at me. "I feel like Brits are somewhere in between the two—more neutral, really."

Maura filled his glass with more water. "That's so interesting. So our personalities are more extreme."

"Perhaps." He smirked at me.

My stepmom continued to grill Caleb through dessert. He seemed more than happy to answer her questions. Meanwhile, I longed to escape but stayed since I didn't want to appear any ruder than he apparently thought I was.

After dinner, Caleb helped us clean up, despite Maura's insistence that he didn't have to. He definitely had good manners. I'd give him that.

It was late by the time everything was put away. Much to my delight, Caleb retreated to his room.

Relief washed over me, since I no longer had to avoid looking at him. I could momentarily forget he was living in my house.

———

The next morning as I was in the kitchen pouring coffee, I felt the vibration of his voice at my back.

"Morning, roomie."

I jumped and, with my back still turned to him, managed to say hello.

"You know, if we're going to be living together, you might as well learn to look at me. I can imagine it's a lot more work to avoid eye contact. It's sort of like playing dodgeball with your eyeballs."

That made me chuckle a little. I turned around to face

him. "We didn't exactly get off on the right foot. I guess I'm still trying to accept that you're here under our roof, given how we were introduced."

"You must have nearly crapped when you saw me."

I rolled my eyes as his mouth spread into a wicked smile, his white teeth nearly blinding me. He was painfully handsome, and I hated it. His thick, gorgeous head of hair was a beautiful mess in the morning, too. *Pretty-boy asshole.*

"Yeah. It was supposed to be Bo Cheng, not you," I said.

His eyes narrowed. "Bo Cheng?"

"The guy you replaced. That's his name."

"Ah. That bloke. I met him briefly when I was moving out of the other place. His eyes were all puffy."

"Yeah. He was allergic to Catlin Jenner."

"Who?"

"Catlin Jenner—the cat."

"Ah, that's her name?"

"Yes. Shelley named her after that Kardashians dad who's now a woman—Caitlin Jenner. Except ours is *Cat*-lin Jenner. Get it?"

"She's a clever one, your sister. And that makes sense about the allergies. That cat certainly has no lack of hair."

"She's Persian."

"She's beautiful. We slept together last night, actually."

I was certain it wasn't the first time he'd said that. "Be careful. She scratches sometimes."

"Scratches don't scare me."

Why did every word that came out of his mouth put my mind in the gutter?

He grabbed a mug from the cabinet. "So I have Catlin Jenner to thank for the fact that I'm now living in this awesome house?"

"Are you being sarcastic?"

Caleb closed the cabinet a little too hard. "Are you kidding? This place is brilliant. I've never eaten better, slept better. I love it here. I feel more at home than my own house in England."

"Oh. I couldn't tell whether you were joking."

"You don't feel the same?" he asked.

"It's different when something isn't novel. I guess I ju—"

"Take it for granted?"

I sighed. "Maybe a little. Yeah."

I looked down at my shoes—anything to avoid contact with those blazing green eyes of his.

"So...would you have looked Bo Cheng in the eyes?"

"Probably," I said, still refusing to look up.

"Should we bring him back, give him some allergy medication? Put you out of your misery?"

"That's not necessary. We won't see much of each other aside from meal times anyway."

"Oh, that's right. You hide down in the basement, hardly pay attention to your sister..."

What?

How dare he!

"Who said that?"

"Shelley seems to think you avoid her."

Now he's ganging up on me with my family?

Anger coursed through my veins. "She told you that? That's ridiculous! What are you doing talking to my sister about me?"

11

"I wasn't talking to her about you. She offered the information. I asked her how you two get on, and she informed me that you don't seem to have time for her."

That hurt. I didn't know what bothered me more— what she said or that she was talking to *him* about it. Or maybe it bothered me because it was true. I didn't so much avoid my sister as my family as a whole. I could do a better job of relating to everyone, but it pissed me off that he was interfering when he didn't even know me. He'd been living in this house less than twenty-four hours.

"I'm always here if she needs me, and she knows that."

"Really? When was the last time you initiated hanging out with her, helped her with her homework?"

I didn't have an answer. And that made me feel like crap. The past year, I'd retreated into my own world a lot. I *had* been a shitty sister. There was no denying it. I just didn't appreciate a stranger waltzing into my life and calling me out on it.

For the first time, I really looked Caleb in the eyes. "I don't know who you think you are, but my relationship with my sister is none of your business."

He took the last sip of his coffee before placing the mug in the dishwasher. "Very well then." He nodded. "Cheers. Good talk."

Then the critical bastard left the room.

CHAPTER
TWO

Teagan

The nerve of him.

Classes hadn't started yet, so I had nothing better to do with the rest of my morning than stew over judgmental Caleb. He didn't know me or anything about the issues I had with my family.

Then guilt over what he'd said started to set in.

Damn you, Caleb, for getting in my head.

Eventually I went with Maura to the store, but when my friend Kai came over early that afternoon, she could see I was still upset over something.

"What's going on?" she asked.

Kai lived a few doors down. She was a year older than me and commuted to Suffolk University.

"You know how I told you we were getting an exchange student to live with us?"

"Yeah. The guy from China—"

"No. That's Bo Cheng. I *wish* he were the one living with us. He had to move out because he's allergic to Catlin Jenner."

"Oh, bummer. Okay...so...what's the problem?"

"The university sent someone else, an infuriating guy named Caleb Yates from England."

I proceeded to tell her the story of meeting Caleb in the men's room.

She laughed her ass off. "Holy crap."

I rolled my eyes. "Yeah, literally."

"Okay, so what's the big deal? Life played a little joke on you. Get over it."

"I can totally get over the way we met. Truly. That's not my problem. My problem is that he took it upon himself to accost me in the kitchen this morning."

She wriggled her brows. "Sounds exciting."

"Nothing exciting about it. Sorry. He started asking me why I avoid Shelley. Can you believe that? I mean, really? You're living in my house for a matter of seconds, and you're questioning my relationship with my sister? Like...who *are* you?"

She deepened her stare. "You do avoid Shelley."

I blew out a frustrated breath. "Et tu, Kai? That's not what this is about."

"Alright, alright. I understand that's not the point here. The point is what you do or how you behave is not any of his business. What did you tell him?"

"I told him just that—that it was none of his business."

"What did he say?"

"He walked away."

She nodded. "And that bugged you even more."

"Well, yes, because isn't walking away about the worst thing you can do when you're in the middle of an argument with someone?"

"Actually, it's probably the smartest thing to do sometimes."

Blowing out a frustrated breath, I hugged one of my throw pillows. I needed her to be a friend and agree with me today, even if I wasn't in the right. Part of me knew I was overreacting. But I couldn't help how I felt.

I sighed. "I don't know why I'm letting him get under my skin like this. I really don't."

"What does this guy look like?"

I pulled on my ponytail. *Do I tell her?*

My words came out fast. "He's infuriatingly handsome and smells really good. It's annoying."

"A-ha! You know you've used the word *infuriating* twice to describe him." She laughed. "Anyway, I knew there had to be something fueling this reaction. He's good-looking on top of everything, and that's making this even weirder for you."

"My reaction would be the same regardless."

"No, it wouldn't. You wouldn't care so much if he didn't have some other kind of effect on you—the *effect* you're always trying to avoid when it comes to guys."

"Don't go there, okay? We're talking about him, not me."

"Alright, well, you know what you do? Send him something in writing, like an email. Nip this in the bud. Tell him that while you appreciate his concern, you *don't* appreciate him sticking his nose where it doesn't belong when it comes to your personal matters."

I raised my brow. "You really think that's going to help?"

"Written sentiments are more formal and show a certain level of seriousness. If you take the time to write him, you must really mean it."

———

After much consideration, I decided to do what Kai said. I took out some yellow-lined paper and began to write down my thoughts. After going back and forth and scratching things out, I finally determined what my message to Caleb would be.

I then went to find Maura to see if she had Caleb's email address with the information she'd received from the university. As expected, she did ask why I would write to him when he was just upstairs, but she gave it to me without prying too much.

I returned to my room and carefully typed out my message.

Subject: Unsolicited Advice

Dear Caleb,

While I appreciate your concern about my lack of interaction with my sister, I find the fact that you're inserting yourself into our business very intrusive and unbecoming of someone who doesn't know me.
You don't know all of the details of my life or my history with my family. Actually, you don't know me at all.
So, I would greatly appreciate it if you didn't offer unsolicited advice on matters you don't understand.

Regards,
Teagan

I read it over a few times and hit send before I could change my mind. Boy, that felt good.

I kept my computer open as I folded some of my laundry over the next several minutes.

Then I heard my email notification chime.

A message in bold showed a response from Caleb.

From: Caleb Yates
To: Teagan Carroll
RE: Unsolicited Advice

Dear Teagan,

I've edited your email. I believe this is what you meant to say:

Dear Caleb,

I don't like to be called out on my bloody awful behavior because it causes me to have to stop and look in the mirror. I don't like the fact that, even though you don't know the details of my life, you were still able to recognize something about me that I don't like about myself—thus the attitude I gave you. I want to change, to be better, but don't know how. You see, I've become very wrapped up in my own head as of late. If I hadn't forced you to walk away from our argument, maybe I would've figured out that you only had my and Shelley's best interests in mind. But since I have my head stuck up my arse at the moment, I chose to believe you're a tosser and write

you this note instead, even though you're right upstairs.

Fuck off,
Teagan

Oh my God.
Oh. My. God.
My blood boiled.
Are you kidding me?
This time, I started writing without thinking first. I tapped on the keys in anger.

From: Teagan Carroll
To: Caleb Yates
RE: Unsolicited Advice

Dear Caleb,

Are you serious right now???

Send.

Ten seconds later, a new email came in. The fact that he'd been waiting by the computer for my response annoyed me even more.

From: Caleb Yates
To: Teagan Carroll
RE: Unsolicited Advice

Dear Teagan,

You asked if I was serious. I am going to

assume that's a rhetorical question, and you don't actually want me to answer it. Let me know if I'm mistaken.

Caleb

Again, I typed without thinking it through.

From: Teagan Carroll
To: Caleb Yates
RE: Unsolicited Advice

No, it wasn't rhetorical. I asked if you were serious because I find your attitude unbelievable. I seriously want to know why you think it's okay to analyze someone you don't even know. Seriously!

Exhaling my frustration, I told myself this fruitless attempt at communication was finished—until my computer dinged again.

I clicked on his response.

From: Caleb Yates
To: Teagan Carroll
RE: Unsolicited Advice

Sounds like you seriously have a serious problem with me and a serious overusage of the word serious.

What?
I typed.

From: Teagan Carroll
To: Caleb Yates
RE: Unsolicited Advice

There's no point in continuing this email exchange.

Almost immediately, he responded.

From: Caleb Yates
To: Teagan Carroll
RE: Unsolicited Advice

Ding! Ding! Ding! She finally gets it. There was *never* any point to this email exchange. It never should have happened. Want to take a guess as to why?

I banged on my keyboard as I responded.

From: Teagan Carroll
To: Caleb Yates
RE: Unsolicited Advice

What are you talking about?

Again, his reply was immediate.

From: Caleb Yates
To: Teagan Carroll
RE: Unsolicited Advice

There was never any point to this email

exchange because...DRUMROLL...I'm right upstairs.
RIGHT upstairs, Teagan.
Why would you send me an email instead of coming to talk to me?
(Seriously!)

I slammed my laptop shut. I was done. *Done.*

Yet over the next several minutes, as I continued to put my clothes away, I did nothing but obsess. Why was I letting him get to me? I didn't want to react this way. He'd blown the whole thing out of proportion. The email was an attempt to get my point across without having to see him, but maybe I'd have to get in his face after all.

I stormed up the stairs and headed straight to my old room—his room. But when I got to the top of the stairwell, I swallowed the words I'd been prepared to unleash. The unexpected sight of Caleb doing pull-ups met my eyes. He used a bar affixed to the top of the door to lift himself up. He wore a T-shirt that rode up each time he rose. His hard abs were now staring me in the face, ripples of carved muscle. He had black wrist wraps on. He'd turned my old room into a home gym.

He was a bastard—but there was no denying he was beautiful.

I cleared my throat. "Did my father give you permission to put that thing in the doorway?"

The house shook as he landed on his feet. "Well, hello, Teagan. Amazing how easy it is to walk up the stairs, isn't it?" He grabbed a towel and wiped the sweat off his forehead. "And yes, in fact, your father did give me permission to put the bar up."

I came out with it. "You think you know it all, don't you? Who *are* you?"

He glared at me. "Who *am* I? Well, nice of you to ask, Teagan." He threw his towel down on the desk. "You've had no interest in getting to know me from the moment I walked in the door. But since you finally *did* inquire... Hi, I'm Caleb Yates. Happy to be here. I have no clue what I'm doing with my life and have a somewhat crappy family situation back in England. So, I came to a strange country for the first time to get away for a bit. I miss my mum, but the good news is, I've just moved into a house where everyone is cordial—except for the cranky girl in the basement."

Wow.

"That's a bit harsh, don't you think?"

He came closer, and the smell of his cologne mixed with sweat was...interesting. Couldn't say it was a bad thing, that's for sure.

"You didn't have to write me a snooty email, Teagan. You can come talk to me if I do something to piss you off. If you write me emails like that when I'm right upstairs, that's the kind of response you're going to get, each and every time."

He had a point. The email was a bit cowardly of me. Yet I'd still managed to convince myself it was a good idea. He was right. Anything I needed to say to him, I should be able to say to his face. Quite honestly, the benefit of that was also his face—getting to look at it, I mean. It turned out, looking at him was a lot more fun than avoiding eye contact had been. *Thank goodness he can't read my mind right now.*

Seeing that he actually seemed angry as opposed to amused caused me to change my tune—that and perhaps his scent going straight to my head as it followed my mind right into the gutter.

He held out his hand. "Give it to me."

I looked down at my empty hands. "Give you what?"

"The stick in your arse. Take it out and give it to me."

I crinkled my forehead. "What?"

He wiggled his fingers. "Come on. Hand it over."

Genuinely curious as to where he was going with this, I motioned with my hand, pretending to remove the imaginary stick from my derriere and throwing it over to him.

He pretended to catch it, then let it weigh him down. "It's bigger than I thought." Looking around he said, "I'm gonna find a space for it. Hang on."

I laughed, against my better judgment. He shoved the imaginary stick under his bed and wiped fake dust off his hands.

"Now that that's out of the way, why don't we start fresh?"

Do I really have a choice? This guy was going to be living with us for a year. It would be easier to get along than continue on the rocky path we'd started down—the rocky path I'd carved. As annoying as Caleb was, he'd managed to charm me just enough. I decided to try to let my anger go.

"Okay, Caleb."

He was all too amused by my change in attitude. "Wow. Didn't think it was going to be that easy."

"Well, it just hit me that you're not going anywhere."

"Ah. So I'm like an incurable disease."

"Or an allergy." I laughed.

"Quick. Someone tell that chap Bo Cheng to stay far away from me."

"Good ol' Bo Cheng. He doesn't realize he dodged a bullet with the cranky girl in the basement," I cracked.

Am I actually playing along here? What kind of a spell had this guy placed on me?

"Why *are* you down in the basement?" he asked. "This is such a beautiful house. And seeing as though I'm now in your old bedroom and can personally attest to how nice it is, I can't imagine why you'd give up this space for that little room down there."

His comment set off an alarm in me. "You've seen my room in the basement?"

"Yes. I ransacked it when you were out. And what I found explains a lot."

His smothered laughter gave him away.

"No, you didn't!"

"Relax. Your father gave me a proper tour of the property while you were gone to the store earlier. He took me down to the basement and showed me where the washing machine is. I happened to see your room while I was there."

"I see."

"I found it very strange, by the way."

"My room?"

"No. The washing machine in the basement. In England, we do laundry in the kitchen."

"Oh, that's weird. What about the dryer?"

"We don't have one. My mum just lines the clothes up outside."

"I can't imagine that."

"What, you can't imagine your knickers flying in the wind for all the world to see?"

I chuckled. "Pretty much."

He scratched his chin. "You're very conservative, aren't you?"

I probably should've responded to his question. Instead, I let my eyes travel down his chest, noticing the way his shirt clung to the sweaty muscles. I felt far from *conservative* right now.

I shook my head. "Why do you say that?"

"The way you dress—always covered up quite well from head to toe. Also, the way you reacted when we met in the men's room at the university. You were mortified at the prospect of me thinking you were responsible for that smell."

"Let's not bring that up, please. We're doing so well."

He chuckled and wandered over to the bookshelves, which housed dozens of my old books. I hadn't bothered to move them downstairs because I didn't have as much space.

Brushing his index finger along some of the spines, he said, "Nice collection, by the way."

My brow furrowed. "Is that sarcasm? I can't tell."

"No. You have some interesting books here. Eckhart Tolle. Deepak Chopra. It's like self-help central. I take it you're all...helped? Totally zen? No issues at all?"

"Not quite."

He picked one out of the lineup. "*Ten Secrets*. What's this one about?"

"It's a self-help book," I deadpanned.

"You don't say."

"The gist is that everyone is hiding at least ten secrets that keep them from truly progressing in life."

"Ten? Is that right?"

"Yeah. Sometimes we're not even aware we're suppressing them."

He looked down at the cover, then over at me. "I've got at least one, but I'm not sure about ten. You?"

"Of course. We all have secrets, things that fester."

He flipped through the book. "Tell me one of yours."

"If I told you, it wouldn't be a secret."

He pointed to the pages. "Yes, but according to this book, your secrets are holding you back."

"I'll live with the risk."

Caleb snickered. "I have a secret you'd be interested in knowing, one that pertains to you."

My heart fluttered. "Really?"

"Yup." He raised his chin. "Want to know what it is?"

"Yes, I would, if it pertains to me."

Caleb put the book back on the shelf and rubbed his hands together. "My secret is..."

He paused.

When I couldn't take it anymore, I said, "What is it?"

"You're definitely gonna want to hear this," he murmured.

I laughed. "Okay...then tell me."

He took a few steps toward me and leaned close to my ear. Chills ran through me as he said, "I know for a fact it wasn't you who made that smell in the loo."

I looked him in the eyes. "How?"

"Because I'd been in the men's room earlier that morning, and it smelled exactly the same."

"Why didn't you say that at the time?"

"Because it was too much fun watching you squirm." He winked. "It's a good thing I'm living here. I'll have a lot more chances to do that."

CHAPTER
THREE

Teagan

Later that day, I nearly fell off the chair I'd been standing on in the kitchen when Caleb came up behind me.

"Need some help?"

I trembled as I slowly climbed down. For some reason, I'd assumed he'd left the house.

It was late in the afternoon. My father was still at work, and Maura and Shelley had left for my sister's cheerleading practice. Classes didn't start at Northern until the following Monday, so apparently Caleb had nothing better to do than hang here. I suppose that shouldn't have annoyed me since he lived here now, but it did.

With Maura out of the house, I'd figured this was my opportunity to raid the candy shelf. I'd seen her stashing some bags up high the other day. She had been cracking down recently on Shelley's and my dad's eating habits, so I assumed she'd been hiding the sweets on the highest shelf in the kitchen. But because our ceilings were so tall and our cabinets so high, I'd underestimated the ability of this chair to get up there. Caleb had appeared in the midst of my botched effort.

"Trying to reach something?"

"Yeah, actually." I could feel myself breaking a sweat.

He pushed the chair back to the table and scratched his chin as he looked up. As tall as Caleb was, he couldn't reach the cupboard either.

To my shock, he knelt in front of the counter and pointed to his shoulders.

"Get on."

"What?"

"I'll give you a lift to get what you need."

He wants me to get on his shoulders? "That's okay."

He insisted. "Hop on."

I swallowed hard and did as he said, sitting on his shoulders and wrapping my legs around his neck. The feel of his hard muscles pressing against my clit was *interesting,* to say the least—pretty sure this was the ultimate cheap thrill. He rose slowly, and when he reached his full height, I was exactly where I needed to be to open the forbidden cabinet at the top.

It was hard to concentrate on what I'd come up here to retrieve, though. There was no light inside the cupboard, and admittedly, I wasn't paying close attention. All that registered was the heat of his body and the sensation of his strong hands holding each of my legs. And from up here, his musky smell was amplified. My heart was going a mile a minute as I grabbed any old thing.

"Got it," I said, assuming I'd found some sort of tart candy or chocolate.

Anything would do to satisfy my sweet craving. The bigger problem right now was the fact that my nipples were hard. I needed to get down off of Caleb because he'd be able to read my body's reaction if I stayed with the back of his head between my legs any longer.

Only my deprived body could get off on a piggyback ride.

He lowered himself to the ground, and I climbed off. "Thanks."

His eyes fell to the bag of candy in my hand. He squinted. "Interesting choice."

"What..."

I looked down at the package. *What the hell, Maura?* "Um...this...I don't even know what this is."

He nearly snorted. "You went through all that trouble for penis candy?"

The bag was filled with rainbow-colored tart candies in the shape of dicks.

I wanted to kill my stepmom. Then I remembered she'd been planning a bridal shower for her friend Darlene. She'd probably bought these as favors and had been hiding them from Shelley.

"Okay, full disclosure: I was trying to satisfy a sweet craving and wasn't really paying attention to what I grabbed. I just wanted something sugary. I had no idea Maura was hiding these up there. Pretty sure they're for a bridal shower she's planning for her friend."

He seemed confused. "Bridal shower?"

"Yeah. It's a party you have for a woman who's about to get married."

"Ah. Like a hen-do."

"Hen?"

"Yeah. A hen party. That's what they call it back home when they take the girl out before the wedding."

I nodded. "Bachelorette party—yeah, something like that."

He smirked. "So that's what you women do at those things? Sit around eating penis candy?"

"Not always." I shook my head. "Never mind."

Caleb reached for the bag. I handed it to him, and he examined it. Then he grabbed a chair so he could return the candy to the cabinet.

After several seconds up there, he announced, "Well, it's confirmed."

"What?"

"There's definitely a dick party in the works. Massive penis piñata stuffed at the back here."

I couldn't help but laugh. "Shit."

"Oh wait. I'm wrong. Not *just* a penis party. There are some pussy licker pops up here, too." He snorted. "That bag is open already. What does that mean?"

That I'm mortified. Just mortified.

"Do you mind just...getting down, please?"

"Sure, love."

He closed the cabinet and climbed off the chair.

He hadn't come down empty-handed, though. "Do you think Maura would mind if she knew I stole a peach pussy pop? It was a pack of one hundred."

My face must have been so red right now.

He pulled the wrapper off and licked it in one long swipe. That sent an unwelcome shiver down my spine that went straight to my loins. He popped it into his mouth.

"Your face right now?" He laughed as he sucked on it. "Priceless."

When it came to this guy, I had to be cursed. "I just wanted a piece of candy," I muttered.

He pulled the pop out of his mouth and handed it to me. "Well, here you go."

He winked and squeezed my shoulder before heading up the stairs.

I went down to my room feeling embarrassingly worked up.

I lay on my bed and sucked on the pussy pop, painfully aware that it was still wet from his mouth and disgusted with myself for being so turned on by that.

———————

Once classes started, I avoided Caleb when I saw him around campus. I wasn't entirely sure why it felt so awkward to run into him there, of all places. He'd lift his hand and wave from across the student union or go out of his way to say hello if we passed each other. I, on the other hand, would walk the other way if he hadn't spotted me yet.

Things with him had gotten better at home, though. No more arguments or awkward encounters to speak of. He'd eat with us a few times a week—always an entertaining addition to our dinners, and most of the time the center of our conversations. The initial shock of him being here had waned. Overall, having Caleb living with us was a lot different than I'd imagined it would be. He didn't spend his nights taunting me or trying to get to know me better. As the days passed, he kept to himself more and more.

And that was fine, right? I mean, I didn't need the complication of having to befriend him on top of everything else I had going on: adjusting to my classes and starting my new internship at the New England Aquarium. As a marine biology major, I was excited to gain hands-on experience that would help me toward a career as a research biologist.

So, given this cordial groove Caleb and I had found, it shouldn't have bothered me when a girl I recognized from my biology class showed up at the house one Saturday. And yet, an unwanted, visceral jealousy hit me like a ton of bricks.

I knew her name was Veronica. She was tall with long, brown hair and a gorgeous face. She hadn't knocked yet, but I spotted her approaching from the kitchen window. I could only assume she was here for Caleb.

"Hi. What's up?" I said as I opened the door.

She jumped back, surprised. "Oh, I'm sorry," she said. "He said he was coming down to meet me. I wasn't going to bother you. I'm here to see Caleb."

Big shocker there.

Before I could say anything, the sound of Caleb skipping down the steps registered.

"Hey, Veronica." He turned to me. "Sorry. I didn't mean for you to have to answer the door, Teagan. Veronica texted me she was here."

I shrugged. "Oh, no worries. I was right by the door anyway."

"Have you met my pseudo-sister Teagan before?" he asked her.

Pseudo-sister?

"Not officially. Although..." She squinted. "I think you're in biology with me, right?"

"Yup. Yeah, I recognize you now."

My eyes landed on his hand as it touched the small of her back, sending another pang of jealousy through me.

I cleared my throat. "Where are you guys headed?"

"Actually, we're gonna check out that theater around the corner—the shady one your stepmother mentioned over dinner. Syd's, is it? I've been morbidly curious about it."

It stung a little that they were going there. Not sure why.

"Oh." I nodded. "Well, have fun."

"Thanks." Veronica smiled. "We will."

Heading to the theater on a gloomy day sounded really good. But I could have done that on my own, if I wanted. I was officially irritating *myself*. Caleb was a good-looking guy, but there were a lot of good-looking guys. Did I believe I had some kind of territorial right to him because he lived here?

I watched as they walked away. Any pathetic doubt I might have had about whether they were a thing went out the window when I saw him pull her close on the sidewalk and plant a long kiss on her lips. My stomach churned as I watched them until they eventually disappeared from sight.

Shelley ran down the stairs, snapping me out of my thoughts. "Did you see Caleb has a girlfriend?"

"How do you know she's his girlfriend?" I asked, still looking toward the outside.

"Well, I don't, but I saw them kiss from the upstairs window."

"You should mind your own business instead of spying on Caleb."

I was just about to turn around and go downstairs when I stopped myself. It was typical of me to have these kinds of brief interactions with my sister and then immediately retreat to my room. Whether I wanted to admit it or not, Caleb noticing my behavior toward Shelley sort of hit me where it hurt. And I really did want to be better, even if my relationship with my family had always been challenging.

I forced the words out. "Would you want to maybe go to Coolidge Corner? Get a bite to eat?"

She wrinkled her forehead. "You just told me to mind my own business. Now you want to take me out?"

"I know. I'm sorry for saying that. It's natural to be curious." I smiled. "Anyway...I just figured maybe I should spend more time with you. Wanna go?"

"Heck yeah, I wanna go! Do I need money?"

"Nah. I got you."

Sometimes you have to force yourself to do what's right, even if it doesn't feel natural. Maybe eventually, it would get easier. *Fake it till you make it.* I needed to work on things with my sister—and my family, for that matter. But one step at a time.

———

Shelley and I ended up having a pretty good time that afternoon. We went for Japanese food. Shelley opted for hibachi while I ordered a few different maki rolls. The restaurant was one of my favorites. They had the best miso soup and shumai. It also happened to be just down the street from the theater. I couldn't help wondering which movie Caleb and Veronica had chosen. I also wondered if they were watching the movie at all.

As we ate the orange slices the waitress brought to our table along with our bill, my sister said something that completely floored me.

"Did you know Caleb's sister died?"

I stopped chewing. "What?"

"Yeah. I asked him if he had any siblings, and he told me he had a sister who died when they were younger."

The orange felt like it was coming back up as my heart sank. "Oh my God. That's terrible. I had no idea. Did he say how it happened?"

"No."

Right then it dawned on me why he might have felt so compelled to remind me not to take my sister for granted—he no longer had his.

The rest of that Saturday, my chest felt heavy. It was impossible to think about anything else.

The next evening, I was reading downstairs in my room when Caleb appeared at the door.

"Fucking Mensa, Teagan? How could you keep this from me?"

Feeling my cheeks heat, I closed my book. "Who told you about that?"

"Shelley." He entered and sat at the edge of my bed. "So it's true? You're a genius?"

I shook my head. "It's no big deal."

"It's no big deal that you're a genius—a flipping genius?"

A few years ago, I'd taken a test that qualified me for that particular high IQ society. Those who score at or above the ninety-eighth percentile on Mensa's approved intelligence tests are granted membership.

"It's nothing special. It just means I can pass a test."

"Bloody hell. You don't realize how impressive that is?"

I shrugged. "I mean...I never really think about it. I—"

"Let me tell you, then. It's *really* fucking impressive."

"Okay. If you say so..."

Blood seemed to rush to my head. I wasn't that used to compliments, apparently.

He lay back horizontally on the bottom of the bed, placing his hands behind his head and staring at the ceiling. "I knew you were more than just a house mouse."

"A house mouse?" I asked. "What's that?"

He laughed. "I'm not even sure. It's just the first term that came to mind. Maybe it's like...a creature that hibernates in the basement, gnawing on cheese occasionally. At least now I know you're doing brilliant things down here. I'd give anything to be able to ace tests."

"You strike me as someone who's very intelligent."

He continued to look up at the ceiling as he confessed, "I'm clever, not necessarily intelligent. I have the potential to be smart, but I get distracted very easily. That's my downfall."

I was currently *distracted* by his long, lean body splayed out on my bed, and by his intoxicating scent now saturating the air in my room and making my legs feel weak. My quiet sanctuary had been overtaken by his masculine energy.

"Distracted by what?" I asked.

"Everything. The smell of bacon. A pretty girl. A fly on the wall. Songs in my head. Random thoughts. Medication commercials at two in the morning. Pornographic imagery. You name it, it distracts me."

"So, like ADD?"

"Not *like* ADD. *Actual* ADD. I've always struggled with my attention."

"Oh, okay."

"Yeah. So, school has always been a challenge for me. It took me a few years to garner the courage to start university. It's part of the reason I'm late to the game. I feel like I might officially be the oldest freshman at Northern."

Because he was a freshman and I was a sophomore, I sometimes forgot that Caleb—at twenty-two—was three years older than me.

I was sorry he struggled in school. It was hard for me to imagine because academics had always come so easy to me. I realized I was lucky.

I suggested something I hoped I wouldn't regret. "Well, if you ever want to study together, let me know. I can quiz you or hold you accountable, make sure you're not goofing off."

Caleb's face lit up as he rose to a sitting position. "You're serious about that?"

Slightly unsure what I was getting myself into, I said, "I wouldn't have offered if I wasn't serious."

"I know, but sometimes people offer things hoping the person won't really take them up on it. Like when you see someone you haven't seen in a while and say, 'We should get together sometime.' Half the time, you know that's not going to happen, and you probably won't ever see them again after you walk away. I'm the type of person that if you ask me over for dinner, I'm texting you immediately to set a date."

"That's a little annoying." I laughed.

"It's called follow-through. More people should follow through with things in life instead of just talking about them. If life were nothing but empty promises, where would any of us be?"

"Oh, that's so deep," I joked.

"It is." He gave me a look. "So anyway, if you're serious about studying together, I'm gonna take you up on it. I think just having someone physically there who's also studying might help my wandering mind."

"Yeah, sure. Why not? You know where to find me."

"Down in your dungeon." He winked as he placed his hand briefly on my arm.

That single touch sent an electric current through me. Holy crap, I needed to get laid.

I sighed. "Will you stop making my need for privacy sound like some horror movie?"

"You know I'm kidding, right? I just like to tease you, because every time I do, your face turns red. If you had no reaction, it wouldn't be any fun, and I probably wouldn't do it."

"What brought you down to my dungeon tonight again?"

"I found out you're a genius and had to let you know, remember?"

"Oh, that's right. My little sister loves to talk, doesn't she?"

"She's a great kid. She means no harm." He grinned. "She told me you took her out yesterday."

"Yeah. We had a nice lunch at the Japanese restaurant."

"It meant more to her than you realize."

The fact that Caleb had lost his sister was still heavily on my mind. I wasn't sure if I should ask him about it... I suppose he would've mentioned it if he wanted to discuss it.

I moved on to another subject. "How was the movie yesterday...with Veronica?"

He shrugged. "It was alright. It was Italian with subtitles. But Maura was right about that place. There were some dodgy characters in there, and that was on a Saturday afternoon with plenty of normal-looking people around."

"Did you ever stop to consider that I might *enjoy* any potentially crazy people I find in the theater? Or that I might *be* one of them?"

"You bring up a good point." He winked.

After a moment of awkward silence, I said, "So...you and Veronica... You're dating..."

Thanks, Captain Obvious.

He hesitated. "Yeah. It's new."

A rush of jealousy hit me again. "She's really pretty."

"Yeah. Indeed, she is." He smiled. "What about you? Are you seeing anyone?"

"No, not at the moment. My last relationship ended a couple of months ago."

I'd dated a guy named Thad for a few months. While he was really sweet, I didn't want to have sex with him, so I'd ended it.

"What happened?"

"I just didn't see the point in continuing."

He laughed. "I guess that can be reason enough. You weren't that into him?"

"He was nice. We got along really well. But I wasn't that attracted to him physically."

He nodded. "Yeah. Physical attraction is important. People you get along with that you're not physically attracted to are called friends."

I chuckled. "That's true."

He clapped his hands together. "So when are we studying together?"

I guess he hasn't forgotten.

"Whenever."

"Alright. Eight tomorrow night after dinner sounds good to me, too."

CHAPTER
FOUR

Caleb

Shelley poked her head into my room Monday afternoon after I'd returned from class. I'd just started a set of arm reps when she interrupted me.

"Wanna see something funny, Caleb?"

I put down my weights. "What's up?"

She pulled up something on her phone.

"What's that?"

"It's this karaoke app where people can sing and record songs. If they make it public, strangers can sing the same song and join their performance. Then the app puts it all together like a duet."

I wiped my forehead with a towel. "That sounds wicked. You're into that, huh?"

She shook her head. "No. But look who is." Shelley giggled as she handed me the phone.

I hit play on the video. It took me a few seconds to realize I was watching...Teagan. Teagan singing! Teagan singing "Someone Like You" by Adele.

I was gobsmacked. Just when you think you have someone figured out... Her voice wasn't perfect by any means, but putting herself out there like that was impressive. I made a mental note of her username: teagirl888.

"Thanks for sharing. Better not to tell her I know, though. Okay?"

My phone rang right then, interrupting the conversation.

"I better take this. It's my mother." I winked.

Shelley left the room to give me some privacy.

I answered the call. "Hey, Mum."

"How's my baby?"

"Good. Everything okay back home?" I opened a bag of Hot Cheetos. I'd been addicted to them since arriving here.

"Yes. I just wanted to check on you. I haven't heard from you in a while."

"I know. I'm sorry. It's been busy here. Managed to get a job, though."

"Oh?"

"Yeah, I'll be waiting tables at this pub down the street from school."

"Very good. When does that start?"

"This weekend they train me. I'll have shifts during the week as well."

"That's excellent. And are you still liking the house you're living in?"

I popped one of the Cheetos into my mouth. "It's bloody amazing. My bedroom is bigger than half our flat back home."

"Brilliant. And the people?"

"The Carrolls are a really nice family. The father, Lorne, is a real man's man, you know? Like Dad. He loves to watch American football. He's a professor. The mum, Maura, is very sweet. And Shelley, their twelve-year-old, is hysterical."

"You said their oldest daughter goes to school with you, right?"

"Yeah..." I sighed. "Teagan. At first she was a bit narky with me, but we're getting along better now."

Mum laughed. "Why was she narky?"

"I'm not really sure. I think she found me intrusive. I haven't quite figured her out yet. She's part genius, part closet extrovert, apparently. But we're supposed to be studying together later. So, I suppose I'll get to know her."

"That should be...fun? Seems like she's a lot different from her sister."

"Teagan is not Maura's daughter, actually. No one's made mention of Teagan's mother aside from Shelley saying she's not around anymore."

"Meaning she's dead?"

"No, she's alive, I think, just not in the picture."

"Oh, that's interesting. Wonder what the story is on that. Poor thing. A girl, especially of that age, needs her mother."

"Yeah, that might explain why she's a little guarded. I like her, though. Seems like a good person."

"Auntie told me she saw a photo of you with a girl on Instagram—said she was pretty."

Great. I'd forgotten my nosy aunt stalked me on there.

"That's Veronica."

"You fancy her?"

"We've just been hanging out. It's new."

"Well, be careful." My mother's voice grew stern. "You know what I mean."

44

I rolled my eyes. "Yes, Mum, I do."

"Well, alright then. I won't keep you."

Before she could hang up, I caught her. "Hey—how's Dad?"

"He's good. Busy as always. You know how it is."

I sighed, suddenly feeling depressed. "Yeah."

It was always my mother calling, never my father. Not once had he come to the phone to check in with me since I moved to the States.

"Love you, my boy. Take care."

"Love you, too, Mum. I will."

———

I knocked in a loud rhythm on Teagan's door, which was halfway open.

She jumped and put her hand over her chest. "You scared me."

"You didn't forget our study date, did you?"

Taking off her headphones, she said, "No, I didn't."

I took a few steps inside. "You weren't at dinner, so I thought maybe you were blowing me off entirely tonight." I sat across from her on the chair by her desk.

"Yeah, my internship at the aquarium ran late, so I grabbed a bite to eat on the way home."

"How's that going?"

"It's okay—perfect for someone like me who likes fish more than people. I'm weird that way."

"I like that about you, that you're a little weird. Not very easy to figure out, either. It makes you interesting—and better to hang with the fish than pretend to like people in a disingenuous way."

She blushed, and that made me chuckle. I wondered if she was flustered when I walked in because I'd interrupted one of her karaoke app performances.

Teagan rushed to open her laptop. "Let's get going on the studying. Otherwise, talking defeats the purpose of why we're here."

Hmmm... As soon as you turned attention toward Teagan, she tried to move on to something else.

"Yes, ma'am." I said. "A disciplinarian. I like it."

We spent the next hour alternating between quietly studying and Teagan quizzing me on some history questions. She also helped me outline an essay I had to do for my English literature class. Some people were better at math and science while others excelled in writing. Teagan seemed smart at everything.

We returned to studying for a while, but being the master of distraction that I was, my mind started to wander. Well, actually my *eyes* started to wander. As she looked down at her laptop, I took some time to examine Teagan's face without her knowing. It was perfect, really. She had large eyes and full lips. A few freckles dotted her small nose, which had a tiny bump in the middle. Her hair was somewhere between the color of sand and caramel. She typically wore it up in a massive knot, but I imagined how it might look down. And I knew that underneath the layers of clothing she wore like armor, there must be a beautiful body as well. But she tried like hell to hide it all. I wondered why.

She suddenly looked up. "What are you doing?"

Shit. "Studying..."

"No, you aren't. You're looking at me."

"Okay. I was studying *you*."

She turned her head away. "Don't do that."

"Why not?"

"Because I don't like when people look at me." Her eyes darted to the side, like she didn't want to deal with my reaction.

"I can tell. That's why I was trying to do it when you weren't paying attention."

"Creeper."

In an attempt to *not* seem like a creeper, to assure her I wasn't ogling her, I added, "You're like a little sister I love to annoy."

A look crossed her face that seemed a little like... disappointment. Had my sister comment irked her?

"Well, stop being annoying and get back to studying," she demanded. "Your next quiz is in approximately twenty minutes."

"Shit."

She gave me a look and went about her business. I tried to get back into what I was supposed to be doing.

After about ten minutes of buckling down, I realized maybe hunger was the reason I was having so much trouble concentrating. I decided to text her, even though she was right across from me—just to mess with her.

Caleb: Whatcha doin'?

Teagan: Trying to study, which is what YOU should be doing.

Caleb: I feel like we've done enough tonight. Don't you? I'm gagging for a snack.

Teagan: Gagging?

Caleb: Yeah.

Teagan: You're choking? LOL

Caleb: No. It means, like really wanting something.

Teagan: Well, here it means something else. Like "Caleb makes me want to gag."

I laughed as I typed.

Caleb: I've definitely made a few girls gag before.

Her eyes widened as she looked up at me.
I snorted at her reaction.

Teagan: OMG. You're gross.

Caleb: LOL. You walked right into that one.

Teagan: So, you're "gagging" for what kind of snack?

Caleb: Well, not a pussy pop or a tart penis.

Teagan: Thank God. LOL.

Caleb: ;)

Teagan: If you want to be done studying, we can stop.

Caleb: How about I go upstairs and make us something? Then we can continue.

She closed her laptop and said, "I could eat. I had an early dinner."

"There's something I've been dying to try. I'd never heard of it before I came here."

"What?"

"It's called s'mores?"

She started to crack up.

"Are you laughing at me, Teagan?"

"Yes. The way you said it...like you didn't know if you were saying it correctly."

"I didn't."

"They don't make s'mores in England?"

"If they do, I've never heard of it."

"Well, I doubt we have the stuff to make s'mores right now."

I hopped up from my seat. "Let's go to the store then."

"You can't just *make* s'mores. You need to light a fire. It's not a snack. It's an experience."

"Then, let's light one."

"You call that a quick study break?" She laughed. "That's called camping. It's too involved."

"Well, then, we have a problem. Because once I get a craving for something, I can't get it out of my head. Literally. So, now we *have* to do it."

Teagan got up from her bed and placed her laptop on the desk next to mine before grabbing her jacket. It surprised me that she was going for this. I hadn't pegged her as spontaneous.

We hit up a twenty-four-hour store down the street that luckily had all of the ingredients stocked: marshmallows, chocolate, and graham crackers. The sell-by date on the graham crackers had passed, but they would have to do.

We brought everything back to the Carrolls' yard and gathered some sticks to make a campfire.

Once we got the flames going, I wondered if her sister might want to join us. "Shelley's asleep?" I asked.

"Yeah. She has school tomorrow. She's usually in bed by ten on weekdays."

"I feel kind of guilty doing this without her."

"Yeah," Teagan said. "I'm sure she'd love it."

"We can do it again with her sometime."

At that moment, Maura walked out to the yard.

She pulled her sweater close and shivered. "Oh, I didn't realize what the hell you guys were doing. I saw flames from the window and freaked out."

"Sorry, Maura," I said. "We probably should have told you we were making s'mores so you didn't think there was a forest fire in your yard."

"He's never had s'mores before," Teagan explained.

"I didn't mean to interrupt." She smiled, looking between us. "Glad to see you two getting along."

I raised my stick. "You want to stay and have some s'mores with us?"

"No, thanks. You guys have fun. My book and some hot tea are waiting inside for me by the pellet stove."

After she went back in, I threw more wood into the flames and turned to Teagan. "Maura seems surprised we're getting along?" I arched my brow. "Any particular reason that would surprise her?"

"I might have talked a little smack about you when you first moved in."

"Ah."

"I judged you, thinking you were being...judgy," she said. "I don't feel that way anymore, nor do I think your intentions were bad."

"I'm glad you can see that now."

After Teagan briefed me on the steps to making s'mores, I ripped open the bag of marshmallows and popped one into my mouth. I poked a stick into the next one and handed it to her. We spent the next several minutes quietly watching the transformation of our marshmallows from white to toasty brown.

I lifted mine. "It looks ready, yeah?"

"Any more than that, and it will burn. So, yup, that's perfect."

I placed the marshmallow over a flat square of chocolate and smooshed it between two crackers.

Taking a bite, I sighed before speaking with my mouth full. "Fuck, that's good." It was the perfect mix of flavors.

Teagan moaned as she devoured her own. It was the most enthusiastic sound I'd ever heard come out of her. And it turned me on a little. It was the first time my body had reacted to her like that, and it caught me by surprise.

I took the last bite. "So, how many of these are we allowed?"

"However many you want."

"I'll just keep making them unless you stop me, you know."

She smiled. "Go for it. It's your first s'mores experience. I get it."

After I'd consumed five consecutive s'more sandwiches, Teagan looked at me from across the flames. "We're not doing any more studying tonight, are we?"

"Seeing as though I'm about to turn into a marshmallow and combust, probably not."

The fire crackled as we sat in silence. It was so peaceful and serene, I could've fallen asleep out here. The slight chill in the air was the perfect complement to the fire. Some leaves on the trees around us fell as the wind blew them around. The Carrolls' neighborhood was quiet at night—definitely different from what I was used to back home.

My curiosity about Teagan increased with every minute I spent with her. I decided to ask a question I hoped wouldn't upset her. I just really wanted to understand her.

"What happened to your mother?"

Her eyes widened as they met mine across the fire, but she said nothing. Seconds passed as the flames continued to crackle. I had started to regret the question when she finally began to talk.

"I honestly don't know," she said, "aside from the fact that she left right after I was born." She swallowed, seeming uncomfortable.

Now I *definitely* regretted asking.

"You don't have to talk about it. I know it's none of my business. I've just been really curious. I've come to feel close to all of you very quickly. My observation is that Maura, Lorne, and Shelley are like one happy family, and you're sort of this...outlier, this mystery. It feels like there's a missing piece of a puzzle somewhere."

Teagan nodded and looked as if she were pondering my words. I suspected she might be preparing to open up, so I stayed quiet.

"My mother was a stripper," she suddenly announced. "Were you expecting me to say something different?"

I chuckled, my eyes wide. "Perhaps."

CHAPTER
FIVE

Teagan

I don't know why opening up to Caleb felt natural all of a sudden. But his eyes remained so intently focused on me that I decided he was just a genuinely curious person, not judgmental like I'd thought. Maybe my attitude had changed because of what Shelley had told me about him losing his sister. I wasn't sure.

"It feels so strange to admit the stripper thing aloud, but it's one of the few things I know about her," I said. "I find it fascinating, in a sense. But the stripper part is only the very beginning of a long and fucked-up story, one you probably don't have time for."

The light from the fire caused Caleb's green eyes to glow. "Look," he said. "I've turned into a marshmallow. I'm not going anywhere for a while. So I have the time, if you want to talk about it." He moved from across the fire to right next to me. That simple change of position was probably the difference in me trying to get out of this conversation or following through. Something about his nearness, that silent show of support, was enough to make me pull the trigger.

"I don't really talk about her, but I probably should sometimes."

"I have stuff like that in my life. Stuff I *should* talk about but don't," he muttered. "Believe me."

I wondered if he was referring to his sister. I paused, thinking he might elaborate, but when he didn't, I started telling my story.

"You know my dad is a professor, obviously."

"Yeah. Of course."

"Well, years ago, when he first started out, he fell in love with one of his students. Her name was Ariadne Mellencamp."

"Pretty name. Your mother?"

"Yeah."

"Alright."

"Anyway, they had a very forbidden and intense love affair."

His eyes widened. "Wait—affair? He wasn't married to Maura then, was he?"

"Oh, no. This was before he ever met Maura. My dad was only a few years into his career at the time. He was in his early thirties, and Ariadne was only about twenty."

"Okay..."

"As I mentioned, she was an exotic dancer. That was how she paid for school. My father thought she was the most beautiful thing he'd ever seen. He kind of became obsessed with her. When he found out where she worked, he went to watch her dance one night without her knowing. He stayed in the corner where she couldn't see him."

Caleb laughed a little. "Jesus, Lorne was a stalker?"

"Yeah." I chuckled. "Eventually, they started sneaking around together. He moved her into his house and took care of her. Their relationship was very...sexual."

Caleb blew out a breath. "I'm so fucking intrigued by this story, it's not even funny. Keep going."

I'd never told anyone this before.

I took a deep breath. "Well, the best part is pretty much over. Ariadne was manipulative. She convinced my dad to quit his job and travel with her—him footing the bill, of course. So they traveled the world for two years. One of the places they visited was England, actually."

"Sounds like a nice life."

"Yeah, except she got pregnant with me, and that sort of put a damper on their lifestyle."

His expression turned serious. "Ah... I see."

"My so-called mother didn't want me. She wanted an abortion. But my father begged her not to have one. He loved her so much, and the baby was an extension of that." I played with some grass. "They went back and forth for a long time about it, and at some point it was too late to abort the pregnancy. So, she suffered through those months while my father took care of her."

Caleb looked over at me. "And after you were born?"

"She stuck around long enough to give birth to me. And then she packed up and left."

"Just like that?"

"Yeah," I whispered. "My father was devastated for a few years after that. He somehow managed to return to teaching. He found childcare for me. He functioned, but his heart was broken. He truly did love Ariadne. And she was basically just selfish. She wanted nothing to do with her own child." I feigned laughter. "But she cared just enough not to abort me, I suppose."

Caleb stared off into the fire. "So after she left, your father did the best he could..."

"Yes, as time went on, the effect she had on his life lessened, although he could never really forget her."

"Where did she go when she left?"

"He doesn't know. She just disappeared. Nineteen years later, we still don't know where the hell she is."

"You never tried to find her?"

"For what?" I threw the pieces of grass I'd gathered to the ground. "She didn't want me. And seeing her again would likely only hurt my father. She knows where to find him—us—and she's never tried."

His eyes filled with sympathy. "Fair enough."

"Anyway, those early years of raising me alone were not easy on my dad. One day, he realized it would be more economical to find a live-in nanny than pay for the daycare where he'd put me. So he hired a woman full time to take care of me."

"How did that work out?"

I smiled. "Her name was Maura."

"Really...wow. Your stepmum."

"Yes."

"Okay. Makes sense, I suppose."

"I know."

"I think I know where this story is going now," he said.

"Yup. So that was that. My father made a life with Maura. And even though she's the only mother I've ever known, I still haven't given her the respect she deserves— by calling her Mom. I don't know why it's so difficult for me. I started calling her Maura when I was four, and she's always just been Maura. Even at that age, I knew the difference between Maura and a biological mother. Perhaps if she'd raised me from the time I was a baby, things might have been different. But I can actually remember the time when it was just me and my dad—before Maura. I knew she was my nanny from the very beginning, so it's always been hard to view her as my mother. Then when Shelley came along, watching their mother-daughter relationship, how close they are—it's just innate. The difference is clear to me. Maura is not my mom. I'm motherless."

Caleb blinked several times. "Is it innate with Maura and Shelley, or is it just the fact that you've always put a guard up and haven't allowed her to be your mum?"

I took a moment to think about that. A lot of it was my fault. "Maybe it's a bit of both."

He nodded. "And your dad? How's your relationship with him? I haven't been able to figure that out." He placed his hand on my knee. "I'm sorry if this seems like an inquisition. You don't have to get into it."

The brief contact of his touch felt good.

"It's okay," I said. "I have a very strange relationship with my father. He loves me, but I'm always afraid he sees *her* in me. He's never exactly *told* me I'm a painful reminder of Ariadne, but I guess I still worry that all he sees when he looks at me is her."

"Do you look like her?"

"I look *exactly* like her. He showed me a photo of her once. When I was thirteen, I threatened to run away if he didn't tell me the honest truth about my mother and what happened between them. He'd been so insistent on *not* telling me until that time. All of the information I have today basically came from one very long conversation."

"One and done."

"Yeah." I chuckled. "So, because I look so much like her, I know my father must see Ariadne whenever he looks at me. And that makes me sad. I don't want that."

Caleb stared up at the night sky. "Do you think that's why you're sort of...aloof around your family? It's like maybe you're trying to hide yourself in some way."

Caleb picked up on things in a way that astounded me. *Hiding* was a good way to describe what I did when it came to my family. In many ways, I felt like an outsider.

"I do think on some level I feel like an extension of Ariadne, even though I don't know her—especially since I'm practically the age now that she was when my father met her. It's odd because, as much as she didn't want me, I feel this strange connection to her—a connection to her need to flee. I just don't have the balls to leave." I knew then that I might have divulged more than I should. Shaking my head, I said, "I just told you way too much."

"I'm really fascinated, Teagan. Thank you for sharing the story with me. Honestly, it explains a lot."

I grinned. "Does that count for my first secret of ten?"

"The fact that you hide from everything because you feel like a reflection of your mother who abandoned you? Yeah, I'd say that counts for a rather big secret."

"Yeah," I whispered.

We sat in a comfortable silence. Then Caleb startled me when he jumped.

"Holy shit, Teagan!"

"What?"

"There's one last marshmallow in the bag." He smiled from ear to ear.

He had such a gorgeous smile.

"You scared me."

"I thought we'd finished them. Gonna char this sucker up now, unless you want it?"

"No. I'm good."

After a few minutes of watching him roast the last marshmallow, I realized my lips were upturned. And I didn't know how long I'd been grinning. He'd somehow managed to put a smile on my face tonight, even though I'd just unleashed my darkest secret.

"Alright, Caleb. Your turn. Now you have to tell me your first secret of ten."

"I already told you my first secret, remember?"

I squinted. "No."

"Sure you do. You know, that you weren't the one responsible for the smell in the loo."

"Ah. Well, that's sort of a waste of a secret."

"Still counts." He gazed into the flames for a bit before turning to me, his stare more incendiary than the fire. "Teagan, I do have secrets, and my biggest one is something that's very hard for me to utter aloud on cue. But maybe in time I can talk about it with you. Okay?"

Chills ran through my body. "Okay."

My mind began to race. *Is it about his sister?* He'd already told Shelley his sister died, so his biggest secret had to be something else.

I realized in that moment that my happy-go-lucky, witty "pseudo-brother" was far more complex than I had thought. Perhaps I was no longer the only one in this house with issues. That knowledge actually brought some comfort to me.

After Caleb polished off the marshmallow, he spoke with his mouth full. "This was fun. Like *really, really* fun. Thanks for going along with it."

"I don't want you to get the idea that I'm going to let you goof off like this all the time when you're supposed to be studying," I teased.

"Understood."

"I'm gonna have to start cracking the whip."

He grinned impishly. "Well, I didn't know you were into BDSM. But alright..."

Even in the dark, he must have noticed my cheeks turning red.

Oh, the images that conjures up.

CHAPTER SIX

Caleb

Veronica and I walked past campus toward the trolley platform so we could go to lunch in Kenmore Square after our classes had ended for the day.

She seemed anxious and hadn't had much to say, but she finally turned to me. "So, don't kill me."

"Uh..." I shook my head. "I don't have any intention of doing that."

"You might after you hear what I'm about to say."

I stopped walking for a moment. "What's up?"

"My parents decided to fly in for a couple of days. They're here. My dad has really wanted to see more of Boston, so they decided to kill two birds with one stone—come see me and do some touristy stuff."

We continued toward the platform. "That's brilliant. What's wrong with that?"

"When we get to the restaurant, they're going to be there. We're meeting them for lunch."

Ugh. Now I saw where this was going. "Oh."

"I know it's too early to be meeting my parents. But they saw my photo of you on Instagram and are just curious about who I'm spending my time with."

We stopped at the platform to wait for the trolley. This was a bit of an ambush.

Looking down at my ripped jeans and black hoodie, I said, "I would've dressed up or something if I'd known I'd be meeting your parents today."

She placed her hand on my chest. "You look fine. Just be your usual, charming self."

My mind raced during the trolley ride, which was only one stop. I had no idea what Veronica had told her parents about me. We'd never discussed exclusivity, either, though I hadn't dated anyone else since arriving in Boston. Did they think I was her boyfriend? *Was* I her boyfriend? *How do I explain myself?*

Veronica and I had been having a good time, just shagging and hanging out. But I was nowhere near the meet-the-parents point.

When we arrived at the restaurant, Veronica waved to an older couple, who were already seated. They both stood up at the same time.

"Mom and Dad, this is Caleb." She turned to me, looking almost as nervous as I felt. "Caleb, these are my parents, Lawrence and Virginia McCabe."

I extended my hand to each of them. "Very nice to meet you, Mr. and Mrs. McCabe."

Her mother smiled. "I just love your accent."

That was probably the thing I'd heard most since moving here. It was becoming a little annoying.

"Thank you."

We sat down, and things turned quiet as her parents waited for us to peruse the menu. After we ordered, the inquisition I'd feared commenced.

Mr. McCabe crossed his arms. "So, Caleb, what is your major?"

I took a sip of my water. "Right now, I'm in general studies. I haven't quite figured out what I want to do with my life."

He took a moment to let that sink in. "You're reluctant to commit."

Here we go. "I suppose."

"Sometimes in life, son, you have to make a choice and stick to it."

I straightened in my chair. "Yes, I understand that. Life is all about choices. But I'm reluctant to make a decision about my career right now. So, I'm trying to find my passion so I can really focus on that in grad school. I'm hoping it comes to me soon, though."

"What made you decide to go to school in the States versus back home?" Mrs. McCabe asked.

"Well, my university has a partnership with Northern, so I was able to study for a year here. And then the other three years will be back home."

She seemed surprised. "Oh, you're not here for the full four years?"

"No, ma'am. The plan is to go back home after this year."

Veronica tensed. "Do you have the option to stay beyond this year if you wanted to?"

I wasn't sure of the answer to that, but I wished Veronica hadn't put me on the spot. We hadn't discussed this before, and the first time should not have been in front of her parents.

"I haven't really inquired, but my plan has always been to return home. I think my mum would have my arse if I stayed longer than a year."

Veronica's mother addressed her. "Are you prepared for Caleb to leave?" She turned to me. "Because you're not taking our daughter to England."

She said it in a joking manner, but I knew she meant it.

After the food arrived, I did my best to bury my face in my fajitas, hoping the questioning had stopped. I even fantasized about going to the men's room and slipping out the window.

After her parents left to see Fenway Park, I breathed out a huge sigh of relief and immediately ordered a beer, thanking fuck that I was of legal age to do so right about now.

Veronica cringed. "I'm sorry they were so tough."

It took me about a minute to respond, my frustration building with each second. "Whatever made you think it was a good idea to bring me here to meet them? Surely you knew how your parents would react toward me."

"I never thought it would be *that* awkward."

"Your father thinks I'm a dim idiot because I have no career path, and your mother expects me to relocate here permanently if I want to keep seeing you."

Veronica looked like she was about to cry. I hadn't meant to upset her; I was just baffled by her behavior.

I took a long swig of my beer. "Let's just forget about it, okay? I'm sorry for getting upset."

She sat and watched as I continued to sip my drink. As much as I'd urged her to forget it, I was still stewing as I looked out the window at the hustle and bustle of Kenmore Square. Mr. McCabe reminded me a lot of my own father—his critical nature. Perhaps that was why I was having such a tough time letting it go.

I remained in a contemplative state until my phone chimed, signaling a text had come in. It was probably the last thing I ever expected: a message from Maura.

Maura: Teagan is okay. But she was attacked at Syd's Theater today. She stopped the guy before anything terrible happened. I can't believe my worst fear came true.

What?

I got up from my seat. "I have to leave. Something's happened back at the house. No time to explain. I'll text you soon." I didn't even fully make eye contact with Veronica as I dashed away.

My pulse raced as I exited the restaurant and ran down Beacon Street toward Brookline. I would've hopped a trolley, but there was none approaching that I could see. So at this point, the fastest way home was to run.

When I got to the house, everyone had surrounded Teagan in the living room. Aside from one bruise on her face, she seemed fine—physically, at least.

I panted from my sprint. "Are you okay?"

Rather than answer, Teagan asked, "Did you run home?"

"Yeah. I heard you were hurt, so I got here as fast as I could."

Maura smiled at me sympathetically. Lorne looked angrier than I'd ever seen him, and Shelley seemed downright scared.

I wanted to ask Teagan exactly *what* had happened, but I wasn't sure she'd want to rehash it again. Instead, I sat down next to her and said nothing. She must have seen the many questions written all over my face because she started to talk.

"So, I was sitting in my usual seat. I thought I was alone for the longest time. But apparently there was a man somewhere in the theater. Either he spotted me outside and followed me in, or he was already in there. He came up next to me and put his hand over my mouth. I started to kick and scream, but my voice was muffled. He said he had a knife, but it was too dark to tell if he really did. Thankfully, I had the panic button I always keep with me. It makes a loud sound. I was able to reach into my pocket and grab it. When I activated it, a clerk ran into the theater, and the man let me go."

My heart was palpitating. Teagan and I hadn't known each other very long, but I'd grown to care for her and everyone else in this house. The thought of someone trying to hurt her brought out a protective rage in me.

"When he ran away, I ran after him," she continued. "All I could think was that if I didn't catch him, he'd be out there doing this to other people." She looked over at her sister. "I thought about Shelley."

She ran after him?

"So I ran as fast as I could, and the theater employee ran with me. When we caught up to him, we were able to tackle the guy to the ground until the police came."

"Holy shit, Teagan. You caught him?"

She managed a slight smile. "They took me to the precinct for questioning. And now he's in custody. Apparently he's a registered sex offender."

Teagan had come so close to being raped in that theater. And instead of running away when she had the chance, she ran *toward* him. Her courage overwhelmed me. I was so fucking proud of her.

"I will personally do whatever it takes to see that he stays behind bars," Lorne said.

"Thank you, Dad," she whispered.

"Can I get you anything?" Maura asked her.

"No. I'm fine. Maybe I'm still in shock. I don't know."

Shelley hugged her sister. It was nice to see that at a time like this, Teagan wasn't pushing her family away. But I knew she had a limited tolerance for being smothered.

After several minutes of sitting with everyone in quiet shock, she excused herself to her room.

I joined the rest of the family in giving her space, but I couldn't concentrate on anything for the rest of the afternoon.

Later, Teagan didn't want to come upstairs for dinner, so everyone just ate in silence. I felt certain every person at the table was reliving the events of the afternoon in their minds.

In a continued attempt to let Teagan rest, I returned to my room after dinner. I was shocked when she sent me a text.

Teagan: Don't forget, tonight is our study session at 8.

What? Is she serious?

Caleb: I assumed you wouldn't be up for it.

Teagan: Anything to get out of it, eh, Yates?

Caleb: You got me. Always the slacker. I'll be down in ten.

It hadn't been quite ten minutes before I made my way downstairs. Teagan clearly hadn't expected me this soon, because when I stood in the doorway, I found her wiping tears from her eyes. Perhaps I'd walked in at the moment that what had happened today finally hit her.

When she saw me, she wiped her eyes again and sniffled. "I'm sorry."

"Fuck, Teagan. Don't apologize." I moved to sit at the edge of her bed, putting my laptop down next to me. My chest felt tight, and the right words wouldn't come out.

She spoke before I had a chance to figure out what to say. "You know what I'm the most pissed about?"

"What?"

"The fact that Maura was right. Do you know how long I defended that damn place, argued that it was safe?"

"I told you I thought it was dodgy, but I never imagined something like this would happen, either."

She stared down at her bedspread for a while, and then looked up at me. "You caught me crying...because I let my mind go to that 'what if' place for a moment, but I can't do that. The worst didn't happen. I just need to be grateful."

"You were smart to have that panic button in your pocket. You saved yourself."

"I got lucky. It doesn't matter how smart you are, how rich or poor, what you look like, if someone is attacking you, you're only as good as your physical strength—your will to risk your life to get away." She shook her head, as if to stop herself from thinking too deeply about it. "Anyway, let's get to work."

Studying at the moment didn't quite feel right. "Are you sure you want to study tonight?" I asked. "We can just talk or hang out. You've had quite a day."

"I actually think studying will help me get my mind off things."

"Alright. Good enough."

We dug right into our homework. And I did my best to concentrate. As usual, she stopped at a certain point to quiz me. This time, I flubbed up, but I didn't want to admit it was because I couldn't stop wondering about the 'what-ifs' of today either—the very thing I'd told her not to do.

"I'm sorry. I'm particularly bad tonight, aren't I?" I finally said.

"It's okay. I think we can pretty much throw away this day." She closed her laptop. "You know what else really sucks? I loved going to that stupid theater. It was my place. Now I don't think I can go back without thinking about what happened today."

The fact that she'd even consider going back there baffled me. But if there were some place I loved to go, and someone had taken that from me, I might have felt the same way.

"You might be able to go back someday."

She exhaled. "Where were you today when Maura texted you about me?"

I laughed a little, remembering my miserable encounter with Veronica's parents. It was the first time I'd thought about it since arriving home.

I rolled my eyes. "Oh, that's a story for another day."

"No. Tell me."

I sighed. "Well, Veronica and I had lunch plans in Kenmore Square, only she didn't tell me they included meeting her parents. It was sort of an ambush."

Teagan narrowed her eyes. "I didn't realize you guys were that serious."

"We're not. I mean, I guess we're not seeing other people, but in my opinion, meeting the parents was premature."

"How were they?"

"Like my biggest nightmare. Her father questioned my decision to major in general studies, and her mother basically said I might as well break up with her daughter now if I planned to move back to England."

"Ouch."

"Yep. They ended up leaving to go sightseeing. So I ordered a beer and downed it just before I got Maura's text about you. Then I took off and left Veronica sitting there."

Her eyes widened. "Did you tell her what happened? Why you left?"

"No. Just that something happened at home. I texted her later to explain and apologized for booking it out of there."

"You ran all the way from Kenmore Square?"

"Of course. I was freaking out, thinking you were hurt."

What I neglected to mention was how pissed off Veronica was after I left her at the restaurant. She didn't understand my reaction. I wouldn't have expected her to, considering she and I had never discussed my friendship with Teagan.

Teagan blinked. "Thank you for caring so much."

"Of course. You guys are like a second family to me. I couldn't imagine anything happening to you, Teagan."

I meant that. Teagan had no idea about the issues I dealt with at home. Being here with the Carrolls was like a breath of fresh air.

She stared off. Again, her mind seemed to slip into a contemplative place. I supposed when you experienced a traumatic event, the realization came in waves.

"I do everything in my power to hide my sexuality," she finally said. "And yet just being a woman, I'm a target. It's so scary."

"Even if you were flaunting your sexuality, it wouldn't have been your fault. It's never someone's fault when a sick person decides to attack them."

We sat in silence for a bit.

"Can I tell you a secret?" I finally said.

"This would be your second secret out of ten, so make sure it's a good one." She smiled.

It's good to see her smile.

"Okay, then I should clarify that it isn't officially a secret, because I've sort of hinted at it before, mostly when talking about your intelligence, but today it applies more to your overall character. I'm not sure if anyone's told you this, but you should know it."

"What?"

"You're a badass, Teagan."

"That's your secret? That I'm a badass?"

"Yes."

Her mouth curved into another smile. "Well, thank you."

"You really are. And I think we need to celebrate that fact tonight."

"How are we going to do that exactly?"

"Spoiler: not by studying."

"Well, that's a given."

"I'll give you a hint at what I'd like to do to celebrate your badassery. It begins with an S and rhymes with floors."

She took a second to ponder. "You want to celebrate with s'mores."

"I thought you'd never ask."

"Didn't we just make s'mores the other night?"

"I can't help it. I think I'm addicted—to s'mores and Hot Cheetos. Two things I don't have back home. I need to get my fill while I'm here."

"You can make s'mores back home."

"I suppose. Although I don't see myself lighting a fire outside our flat with no real yard. Quite sure that's not allowed."

"Yeah, that probably won't work."

I hopped up. "What do you say?"

"I say you're crazy." She shrugged. "But let's do it."

CHAPTER
SEVEN

Teagan

A week later, I was in my room when I noticed I'd missed a notification that someone had joined one of my performances on the singing app. That rarely happened to me.

I cracked it open and saw the user's name: S'moresDude.

My heart sped up as I clicked into it and saw Caleb's smiling face in the preview.

Oh my God!

No, he didn't.

How did he know about this? It had to be Shelley. She always used to sneak my phone before she got one. *I'm going to murder her!*

After I pressed play, I couldn't help laughing like a fool as I watched our duet, a split screen of Caleb and me singing Adele's "Someone Like You." Our voices blended well, his deep baritone complementing my soprano. It was kind of great, actually.

The exaggeratedly serious expression on his face as he sang cracked me up, and Caleb's voice was pretty good. I was no professional, but I could carry a tune, and apparently so could he. I'd even venture to say his voice was better than mine. I'd always done these for fun, to let loose, not because I thought I had something to offer in the singing department. Oddly, though I tended to be uncomfortable expressing myself around people I knew, I had no problem interacting with strangers. No one knew me on the app—until now. It had been a place I could let my inhibitions go and not be judged or recognized. *Or so I thought.*

I exited the app and clicked on my text icon.

Teagan: I'm not even going to ask how you found out about the singing app.

The dots danced as he typed out a response.

Caleb: It took you bloody long enough! I've been dying for your reaction for two days.

Teagan: You're nuts. And I hate you for doing it. But it cracked me up.

Caleb: I think we give Shawn Mendes and Camila Cabello a run for their money, don't you?

Teagan: I wouldn't give up your day job just yet, S'moresDude.

I was still smiling from ear to ear when Kai came over for a visit a little while later.

We were just hanging out in my room. I chose not to tell Kai about the attack at the theater because I didn't want to deal with her reaction. I hoped she hadn't seen the story on the news, although my name wasn't mentioned. Between talking to the police over the past week and rehashing everything to my family, I didn't want to relive it again. So, we were doing what any two girls with nothing major to discuss would be: mindlessly scrolling our phones and ignoring each other.

"I saw Caleb making out with Veronica over by Coolidge Corner yesterday. He had her pinned against the wall of a brick building. I guess they're still going strong."

I looked up from my phone. "Why are you telling me this?" My tone was definitely defensive.

"I don't know. I'm just gossiping, I guess. Normally you're down for that."

"Yeah, well, I don't need to know about Caleb."

She narrowed her eyes. "Are you...into him now or something?"

"Of course not. Why would you say that? He's basically like my brother at this point," I lied.

There was nothing about Caleb that made him seem like a brother. But pretending was my way of hiding any feelings I might have had for him.

"Why would I say that?" she asked. "Because you just snapped at me for telling you something I observed."

"I get that it was just an observation, but it's one I don't need to be told about."

Kai stared at me for a few seconds. "Because you like him."

My pulse started to race. "No."

"Why else would it upset you so much?"

"It doesn't upset me."

"Look, I get it. He's super hot, and from everything I can tell, pretty sweet and personable. You told me you guys have been getting along lately. Why wouldn't you be a little jealous?"

"It's just not *news*. I know he's with Veronica. I know he has sex with her. The fact that they were kissing is just... not anything new."

Kai squinted at me and smiled. "So how long have you been in love with Caleb?"

I felt sweat form on my forehead. I instinctively wiped it. "I'm not in love with him." Realizing that my physical reaction might be giving me away, I decided to concede. "But I am starting to care for him."

"Define *care* for him."

I stood and walked over to the window to hide my face from her. "It doesn't matter. He has a girlfriend."

"What if he didn't?"

"Then I would still keep my feelings to myself because he's leaving to go back to London at the end of the school year, and nothing good could come from getting attached." I turned to face her. "But here's why we *really* shouldn't be having this conversation: Caleb doesn't like me that way. He calls me his 'pseudo-sister' and while he may like being around me and might be a little protective, he wouldn't be *interested* in me."

"Well, you do nothing to hint that you might be open to anything. When was the last time you let your hair down or wore something feminine?"

"Feminine is not my style. I'm a jeans and T-shirt kind of girl. You know that."

"You're gorgeous, Teagan. And the only reason you aren't with someone right now is because you *choose* not to be."

"I was with Thad for three months."

She tilted her head. "And how did that turn out?"

"I ended it because I wasn't sexually attracted to him."

"Okay, but you knew there wasn't sexual chemistry before you guys started dating. I think you intentionally choose people you're not sexually attracted to, because you don't want to have to worry about sex or all of the feelings that come with it."

"I've *had* sex."

"One time in high school 'just to get it over with', as you put it, doesn't really count, Teagan."

"Sure, it does."

"Did you have an orgasm?"

"No."

"Sex without an orgasm is like a candle without fire. Useless. It doesn't really count."

————

The following day, I was just leaving campus when Caleb came running across the lawn.

"Teagan, wait up." He was a bit out of breath by the time he got to me. "Hey!"

I grinned. "Hi."

He flashed a wide smile as he fell into step with me. "You heading back to the house?"

"Yup."

"Me, too."

"I thought you worked on Wednesdays after class," I said.

"I switched with a friend of mine tonight. I'll be working the late shift instead."

"I just saw Veronica hop the trolley."

"Yeah," he said. "She's going shopping on Newbury Street with some friends."

"Oh. Fancy."

"She does like to spend money."

"She comes from money, doesn't she?"

"Her parents are wealthy, yeah. So naturally they love the fact that she's wasting her time dating a skint bum who's leaving the country in less than a year."

I hated that he said that. Personally, I felt like Veronica was the luckiest girl on campus—maybe in the world—to be with Caleb.

"She could have her choice of almost any guy here," I said. "But she chose you. You're charismatic and interesting compared to the cookie-cutter options. So, obviously, she doesn't agree that being with you is a waste of time."

"Are you trying to make me feel better about myself, Teagan? You're supposed to be deflating my ego, not making it bigger." He winked.

"As enjoyable as it can be to hurl insults at you, I also have to be honest, sometimes."

He nudged his shoulder into mine. "Well, thank you for that compliment. Truly."

Feeling flushed, I changed the subject, remembering a story I wanted to tell him. "Oh my God. You're never going to believe who I ran into today."

"Mark Wahlberg."

"What?" I chuckled. "No! Why did you guess him?"

"Because I heard he was in the area filming a movie."

"Really? Damn. I wouldn't mind running into him, but no."

"You like Marky Mark, eh?"

"Yeah, I do. But unfortunately it wasn't him I ran into. It was Bo Cheng."

"Ah, good old Bo Cheng. How's my mate doing?"

"Get this—I was standing in front of this guy in line at the salad takeout place in the student union. And he started sneezing repeatedly. You know how when someone sneezes, you say 'God bless you'?"

"Yeah."

"Well, I had to keep saying it over and over, until it was just dumb to keep going because he was sneezing so much. Then they called his name to pick up his order. It was *Bo*. And I realized it was THE Bo Cheng."

"The myth, the legend!"

"Yes. Not only that, but it hit me that the reason he was sneezing was *me*!"

Caleb cracked up. "You're a walking allergen, Teagan. Fucking hysterical. Did you tell him who you were?"

"Nah. No point. But I must have cat germs all over my shirt, which makes sense since I was snuggling with Catlin Jenner this morning."

Practically crying, he wiped his eyes. "That's some good shite right there."

I'd been looking forward to telling Caleb this since it happened. His reaction was even better than I'd anticipated.

Caleb towered over me as we walked along Beacon Street. I wasn't sure I'd ever realized how much taller he was than me. It was rare to be walking with him like this. Normally we were sitting across from each other.

We were about to pass the theater—my now-forbidden old stomping grounds. And damn it, they were playing a movie I really wanted to see. Caleb probably assumed the look on my face as I saw the sign was due to the attack. But it wasn't.

"You okay?" he asked.

"Yeah. It just pisses me off. I want to see that movie."

He stopped walking. "Really? Fuck it, then. Let's go watch it. I don't think you should go in there alone, but I'll be with you."

I hesitated. "I don't want to make you sit through it just to protect me."

"Are you kidding? I love movies about..." He paused and looked up at the sign. "Love in Prague."

"That's not the one I want to see. The murder one."

"Same difference." He smiled and gestured with his head. "Come on."

An uneasy feeling came over me as I followed Caleb into the theater. But with each second that passed, that feeling was replaced by empowerment. I settled into the seat next to him, and it felt good to be back and to have my friend with me. It was the best of both worlds: being able to enjoy the movie and also feeling safe. The chances of being attacked twice here were probably pretty slim, but there was no way I would have taken a chance.

I also didn't mind the chance to sit with Caleb for a couple of hours. When we studied together, we were never this close. But he always smelled so good, and the closer I was, the better to breathe him in. I pondered sneaking into his room when he wasn't home to see what cologne he wore. I could buy it and still be able to smell him after he moved back to England. I'd never admit that to anyone, of course. I hated myself for even thinking like this. Nothing was going to come of my attraction to Caleb. Even if he weren't leaving, he was completely out of my league. I just needed to be grateful he was sweet enough to accompany me here today.

The movie got going, and he seemed into it.

About midway through the film, though, I noticed that Caleb's body language had changed. During a scene where the heroine was kidnapped and stuffed into the trunk of a car, Caleb started to fidget, and his hand, which had been resting on the arm of the chair, shook a little. His breathing became ragged as the character in the movie began to scream for her life.

"I need to leave," he suddenly said.

What's happening?

Without questioning, I followed him out of the theater.

Caleb panted as we made our way out to the sidewalk. He took a seat on the ground and said nothing as I sat down next to him.

That scene had apparently triggered this awful reaction, and I couldn't begin to understand why. I suspected it had something to do with the big secret he'd said he might be able to tell me someday. Had Caleb been abused? Had someone once tried to kidnap him and put him in a trunk?

"I'm not gonna make you talk about what happened in there. But if you want to, I'm here. I'm not leaving you. Whatever it is, you're okay. Everything is going to be okay."

He blew out a breath and nodded, still trying to gain his composure.

Then he took my hand and looped his fingers with mine. It wasn't a romantic gesture; I knew that. He had reached to me for support, because I was there. But also because he trusted me, as I did him.

We stayed there on the sidewalk for an indeterminable amount of time, Caleb resting his head against the brick wall of the theater and me alternating between watching him and giving the evil eye to onlookers who turned their noses down at us for sitting on the ground. I was sure some assumed we were about to ask them for spare change.

Caleb finally turned to me. "I think this fucking theater is cursed."

He managed to laugh, so I followed suit. We were still holding hands when he stood and pulled me up along with him. Only then did he let go of me. As horrible as what happened had been, I certainly had enjoyed his touch.

"Let's go home," he said.

I nodded.

We walked together in silence as the autumn leaves crunched under our feet on the sidewalk.

Once back at the house, Caleb went straight to his room, and I spent the remainder of the afternoon in my own room, unable to stop thinking about his freakout. It pained me to know something had traumatized him.

———

Caleb wasn't at dinner that evening, which didn't surprise me, since he'd told me he had to work until closing at the restaurant.

Later, past 11PM, he showed up at the outside door that connected to my bedroom. Rather than enter the house from the front with his key, he'd chosen to come through the yard. He'd never entered through that door before.

I got up to let him in.

"Did I wake you?" he asked.

Returning to the bed, I said, "No, not at all. I was just watching a show on my laptop."

He proceeded to lie right next to me on the bed—another first. He leaned his head against the headboard and closed his eyes.

After a minute, he turned to me. "I'm so sorry about today, Teagan. It was all I could think about tonight at work. I was supposed to be supporting you, and I completely fucked it all up."

I moved to face him. "Are you kidding? You don't owe me an apology. Clearly the movie triggered a memory for you. I understand that. You couldn't help it."

"You were supposed to be the traumatized one in that theater, not me. I feel a bit ashamed for how I acted. I'm so sorry."

"Caleb, seriously. Please stop apologizing. You have nothing to be ashamed of."

"But I do, Teagan. I really do, and you don't even know the half of it."

84

When he looked at me again, the pain in his eyes was so palpable, I could practically feel it squeezing at my chest.

"I did a terrible thing," he said.

My heart sank, but for some reason, none of this alarmed me. I knew from the look of pain on his face that he couldn't have intentionally done anything terrible. Whatever it was, it clearly filled him with sorrow and regret.

"You can tell me. I promise I won't judge you. I don't care what it is." When he remained silent, I said, "I've done some terrible things, too."

He looked at me as I proceeded to vomit out the first thing that came to mind.

"One time, when Maura was eating a chicken wing, I wished she'd choke on the bone. I didn't really mean it. But I had the thought, nevertheless."

He cracked a slight smile, and that alone made my ridiculous confession worth it. That brief reprieve from his pain, though, did nothing to prepare me for what he said next. Nothing could have.

"Teagan..." He paused. "I killed my sister."

CHAPTER EIGHT

Caleb

I'd never uttered those words aloud. I hadn't planned on ever admitting it to anyone here, least of all Teagan. But after what happened today, I felt I owed her an explanation. A part of me wanted to tell her, not only to explain things, but because her own honesty had inspired me to want to open up to her, too. It just didn't happen as organically as I'd hoped. What took place in the theater had robbed me of that opportunity, leaving me no choice but to force it out.

"Okay," she said after a moment. "Still not judging you, by the way. Just so you know."

I loved her for saying that, because it gave me the courage to continue speaking.

"It's hard for me to talk about, because talking forces me to have to *think* about it. And when I think about it, I shut down."

"It's okay if that happens," she said. "There's no rush."

I took a deep breath and exhaled until there was no more air left in me. "My little sister's name was Emma. She and I, we were thick as thieves as toddlers. We were only one year apart. Even though I barely remember her, I have little glimpses—enough to know she was really there and I really loved her."

Despite the tightness building in my chest, I continued. "My parents left us with a sitter one afternoon. We were four and three years old at the time. The two of us were typically easy kids to watch. We had each other, so we just played together."

Teagan clung to every word, a look of fearful anticipation on her face. She nodded silently.

"We had this toy chest, a large wooden box my mother had inherited from her grandmother." I closed my eyes briefly. "I thought it would be funny if I emptied out all of the toys and my sister got in while I closed the lid. Then she could jump out like a jack in the box. And we'd laugh about it. We had so many toys inside that the chest always remained open."

Teagan blinked faster as she seemed to understand where this might be going.

"I assumed I'd just be able to open it and let her out after a few seconds." I swallowed. "But once she got in, the heavy chest locked, and I couldn't get it open."

Teagan gripped my arm as I closed my eyes. There was no turning back now. I had to tell the rest.

My voice cracked. "My sister was kicking and screaming, and there was nothing I could do because it was just...locked."

Teagan squeezed my arm.

"I panicked—ran to find the babysitter. Because we were supposed to have been napping, the sitter had gone outside for a ciggy. I screamed and screamed until she finally heard me and came back in." I paused. "We ran back upstairs, and she couldn't get the chest open, either. By that time, my sister had stopped..." My words trailed off.

She squeezed my arm again. "You don't have to say it."

Feeling exhausted, I nodded, accepting her permission not to continue.

We sat in silence for a bit until I said, "There's no way of predicting when something will trigger the memory. That scene in the movie obviously did it. But I've seen similar things before and haven't had a problem. For some reason, I couldn't control my reaction today."

"I completely get it now."

"I try so hard to block it out and not think about it. Even after years of therapy, it's not something I can get over."

Teagan looked into my eyes. "I know on some level you know this...but it wasn't your fault."

I'd heard that before, but I could never accept it.

"I closed the lid. I told her to get in. Even though I didn't intend for her to die, I caused it. It was my idea, and so it was indeed my fault, Teagan. It wasn't my intention, but it will *always* be my fault."

She seemed at a loss. How could anyone argue? I couldn't blame them for trying, but the fact that I'd caused my sister's death was not up for debate.

"For the longest time as a child, I wasn't able to look at photos of Emma," I told her. "Part of my therapy was to learn to tolerate it. I would sit there and cry and suffer through every agonizing second of having to look at her beautiful smile, realizing I had caused the end of her. I was never able to handle it outside the therapist's office. Eventually, my mother gave in and took most of the pictures down. I only hope wherever Emma is now, she can forgive me."

"Did you stop therapy?"

"I went from the time I was five until around twelve. It got to be too expensive. But I'm starting to think going back might do me some good."

"It's not really something you get over, I would imagine. Just something you learn to live with," she said.

I nodded. "It's not just the loss of the person, you know? But the lasting effects on those left behind. My father resents me, whether he realizes it or not. He's always treated me terribly, and I believe it's because on some level he can't forgive me. He knows it wasn't my intention to hurt my sister, but he can't see beyond what I did. If I hadn't made that stupid decision, she'd still be alive. And he can't let that go. Neither can I."

"I'm sorry to hear that about your dad."

"I've spent my whole life trying to make it up to him, but it's never good enough, because nothing I do can bring my sister back. He avoids me mostly, distances himself from my mum and me, in general."

"Are you and your mother close?"

"Yeah. My mum's great."

"She must miss you."

"She does. But she checks in a lot. Coming here was as much about escaping the situation with Dad as it was experiencing a new place. Here, I feel wanted. As much as my mother loves me, I just don't feel wanted back home because of my father."

Teagan continued to look at me, soaking all of this in. Bless her for being such a good listener and dealing with this crap tonight.

I forced a smile. "See? You thought you were the only one with issues, Teagan. You were so wrong."

"I don't think there's any comparison..."

"Exactly. I'm much more fucked up than you."

She shook her head. "That's not what I meant—just that we're fucked up in different ways."

"Welcome to the fucked-up-by-parents club. Have a seat. Stay a while." I smiled and looked into her eyes. "Thank you for listening."

"Of course. I was super worried about you all day. I'm glad you came to talk to me."

I definitely felt better now that I'd let it out. "Me, too."

She hesitated. "Does Veronica know?"

"No. I told her my sister died in an accident, but I haven't told her the circumstances. I haven't really wanted to go to *this place* in front of her. Not sure why. I guess I'm more comfortable in some ways around you. I don't feel like you're judgmental."

She nodded. "I'm more defensive than judgmental."

I lifted my brow. "Perhaps."

"But seriously, Caleb, you'll never have to worry about me judging you over this. Ever. Okay?"

I didn't deserve her acceptance, but I took it. "Thank you, Teagan."

I looked over at the time. It was late. Yet I had no desire to move from this spot. But considering I had made myself comfortable in *Teagan's bed*, it wasn't cool for me to stay here indefinitely.

Forcing myself up, I said, "Anyway, I'll let you get to sleep."

"You don't have to go," she countered.

I don't want to go. But I need to.

"I'd better. It's late."

She got up from the bed, too. "Okay…"

We stared at each other for more than a few seconds, and I got the sudden urge to hug her. It felt like the natural thing to do after she'd let me pour out my soul.

So, I did.

The moment I leaned in, she fell into me, welcoming it. Her soft breasts pressed against my torso. The nonjudgment she spoke of manifested itself through her touch. In her arms, I felt truly accepted. It felt good. Too good. Too good as in "more than a friend" good. "More than a friend" *great,* in fact. Thus, dangerous.

Her heart beat against me, and I was sure she could feel mine beating as well. The top of her head was right against my chest. I took a long whiff of her hair and forced myself back.

We looked at each other for a few seconds more before I waved and walked out of the room.

As I went upstairs, my heart continued to race.

CHAPTER
NINE

Teagan

Even after a few days, I couldn't get Caleb's admission out of my mind. It was probably the most heartbreaking thing I could have imagined.

Then my mind would wander to the hug he'd given me. Though it was innocent, the warmth of his chest pressed against mine had lit a fire inside of me, one that still seemed to be simmering. Such a simple thing, and my body had taken it completely out of context. I wondered if he'd noticed the way my heart was beating out of control. My reaction was completely inappropriate given the sad circumstances, but I couldn't help how attracted I was to him. Despite my not wanting to fall for Caleb, that seemed to be exactly what was happening.

I'd been hoping to run into him, but he hadn't been around as much lately. I went upstairs to see what I could find out.

"Is Caleb home?" I asked Maura.

She shook her head. "I caught him as he was leaving for Veronica's. He said he was going to spend the night there. He wanted to tell me so I wouldn't worry. He's so considerate."

My stomach sank as I tried to seem nonchalant. "Oh. Okay. He doesn't normally do that—spend the night there."

"I know. Things must be getting serious between them." Maura cocked her head. "How do you feel about that?"

"How am I supposed to feel?" I responded defensively. "Why would I feel anything about that?"

"You and he seem to get along really well. I just wondered if maybe you..."

When she hesitated, I finished her sentence. "If I have feelings for him?"

"Well, yeah. I mean, he's obviously a very handsome guy. And I don't know... Ever since that night I walked out and found you two making s'mores, I've thought there might be...something there."

My mouth welded itself shut. I sure as hell didn't want to admit to Maura that I had a crush on Caleb. But I feared denying it would somehow make it more obvious. So I said nothing. I was really good at that.

"You have always resisted opening up to me," she said. "There's not much I can do to change that because the more I try, the more you retreat. But I want to remind you again that I am on your side. You can tell me anything, and I'll listen, Teagan. I didn't bring Caleb up to embarrass you. I just sense something between you and thought maybe you would want to talk about it. I know it's none of my business. You're nineteen now—an adult. At the very least, if you won't let me be your mother, let me be your friend."

There was no reason I had to keep shutting Maura out. I just didn't know *how* to let her in.

"I'm sorry, Maura. It's me, not you."

"I've been worried about you," she admitted.

Because of Caleb? "Why?"

"I feel like you might be harboring your emotions since the attack. Are you sure you don't want me to find you a therapist?"

Oh. "If I were going to go to a therapist, I probably should have gone a long time ago for reasons other than what happened in the theater. I really *am* okay."

I didn't understand why I hadn't been more traumatized by the attack. I'd had one good cry that night—the night Caleb walked in on me sobbing—but I hadn't experienced anything like it since. Lately I'd mostly been thinking about Caleb, wondering if he was okay, because he'd seemed to be avoiding me since the night he told me about his sister. He'd canceled our last study session for no real reason. I missed hanging out with him but also recognized that my feelings were dangerous.

I needed to end this conversation. "Thank you for always being there, Maura. I know you mean well. And I'm sorry if I come across as unappreciative."

"I just want you to be happy, Teagan. You're at a tough age. As long as you know you can come to me about anything..."

"I do. Thank you."

———

Later that night, Caleb texted, which was odd considering he was sleeping over at Veronica's.

Caleb: So, when you imagined Maura choking on a chicken bone, was it barbecue or perhaps a buffalo wing?

Oh my God.

Teagan: I was hoping you didn't remember that admission.

Caleb: I remember everything. So you're out of luck.

Teagan: Great.

Caleb: So was it buffalo? Maybe some bleu cheese on the side?

Teagan: Teriyaki. LOL

A few seconds later he responded.

Caleb: Sorry I haven't been around to study lately.

Teagan: Excuses. Excuses.

Caleb: I'll get back on track this coming week.

My stomach did a little dip at the prospect.

Teagan: What are you doing right now?

Caleb: Veronica's sleeping and I'm bored. Figured I'd taunt you.

Teagan: Why aren't you sleeping?

Caleb: Why aren't YOU sleeping?

Teagan: I had two cups of coffee after dinner.

Caleb: I'm just wired for no reason.

He texted again before I had a chance to respond.

Caleb: I also wanted to say thank you for listening the other night.

Teagan: I was worried that maybe you were avoiding me because you felt ashamed or something.

Caleb: That's not it. I guess I just needed some time. I know the second I look at you, I'll start to feel some of those emotions again. Because now you know, and there's no hiding from it. It's complicated, I guess. I needed a few days.

The confirmation that he'd been intentionally staying away made me a little sad, but I understood.

Teagan: I get it.

Caleb: I've missed studying with you.

I wanted to slap my own face for feeling tingly. I liked hearing that. Once again proof that I couldn't control my feelings—about a guy who viewed me like a sister. Then I started to overanalyze. It hit me that maybe he liked me because I reminded him of what it would have been like if his sister were alive. She was younger than him. So was I.

I wished I could see him as a brother. It would make things much less complicated. I hated feeling jealous over his sleeping at Veronica's. But I couldn't help it.

Caleb: How's the internship going?

Teagan: I have a new task at the aquarium, but I'm reluctant to tell you about it.

Caleb: Why?

Teagan: Because you'll laugh at me.

Caleb: I promise I won't. Tell me.

Just typing the words made me laugh.

Teagan: I have to dress up as a dolphin and give out tickets to the dolphin show.

He didn't immediately respond. So I typed again.

Teagan: Stop laughing. You said you wouldn't.

The little dots danced around as I waited for his response.

Caleb: It turns out laughing is involuntary.

Teagan: Sigh.

Caleb: I must come see this.

Teagan: Please don't.

Caleb: You're a good sport.

Teagan: I have no choice!

Caleb: You could have fought it. But I'm certain you went with the flow.

I'd been accused of hiding my femininity. But I now knew that nothing makes you feel less feminine than a furry dolphin suit. I definitely didn't have to worry about getting hit on at work now.

I decided to send him a photo my co-worker had snapped of me in the costume.

Teagan: I figured I'd save you the trip.

About a minute passed. Then he responded.

Caleb: I think I nearly woke Veronica up. That is hysterical.

Teagan: Glad I could make you smile.

Caleb: You always make me smile, even when you're not dressed in a ridiculous costume.

I wanted to strangle my heart for beating so fast. My own opinion of myself didn't line up with that.

Teagan: Why do I make you smile? In general, I'm a pretty miserable person.

I waited forever for his response.

Caleb: I don't buy that. You like to keep to yourself, but that doesn't make you miserable. When you do smile, it's genuine. A genuine smile is worth more than a thousand fake ones. You're not capable of being disingenuous.

He clearly saw something in me that I didn't.

Teagan: What about you? How often are your smiles real? How often do you pretend?

Caleb: I've pretended less since arriving here.

Caleb: And I've never pretended around you.

My heart fluttered.

Teagan: I'm glad.

Caleb: I'm not sure I want to go home, but I know I have to. My mind doesn't wander as much to dark places here.

He'd only been here a few months, but the idea of Caleb leaving already made me anxious. He made me feel less alone, like there was finally someone in this house who understood me a little.

Teagan: My mind wanders to dark places, too.

After several seconds of nothing, he responded again.

Caleb: Tell me your darkest thought, and I'll tell you mine. Murky waters are less scary to navigate when not alone.

I didn't have to think about it. My darkest thought was recurring.

Teagan: My darkest thought is that my mother was right—that she shouldn't have had me. Whenever I feel out of place or detached from everything around me, I think maybe that's because I wasn't supposed to be here.

I could see he was typing something.

Caleb: Our darkest thoughts have a similar theme. Mine is that I wish with all of my heart and soul that it had been me who climbed into that chest instead of Emma. So, you and I are two people who wonder whether we belong here. We have that in common.

Wow. I guess we do.

Teagan: I definitely feel less alone since you arrived.

I hadn't intended to be so candid. I wished I could take it back until his response.

Caleb: You're not the only one, Teagan.

CHAPTER
TEN

Caleb

It was about seven in the evening, just before dinner. I'd been looking forward to spending my first night back at the house in a few days and resuming my study sessions with Teagan tonight.

The doorbell rang, and Maura went to answer it. Then I heard my name being uttered by someone with a British accent. I went downstairs to check things out, and the sight of my friend from the UK standing in the doorway nearly knocked the wind out of me.

What the hell is he doing here?

Archie spotted me at the top of the stairwell and held his hands out wide. "Surprise!"

I ran down the stairs. "What's going on? Why are you here?"

"It's good to see you, too, mate."

Maura smiled wide, probably thinking this was a pleasant surprise. It really wasn't. This was weird.

"I'm just shocked. You didn't tell me you were coming."

"I know. It was supposed to be a surprise. Your mum gave me the address. I applied for a three-month work assignment here in the States and wasn't sure if I was going to get it. I finally got confirmation a couple of weeks ago. And here I am."

"Who's this nice young man, Caleb?" Maura asked.

He answered before I had the chance. "I'm Caleb's best friend, Archie."

Best friend? That was a bit of a stretch. Archie and I had known each other since childhood, yes. But I'd never referred to him as my best friend. I had a friend back home called Charlie who'd always been given that distinction. Archie was more of a person who always happened to be in close proximity, one I couldn't get rid of—sort of like a wart.

"You must stay for dinner," Maura said.

Archie looked between Maura and me. "Are you sure? I don't want to intrude."

Sure, you don't.

———

Everyone gathered at the table for Maura's famous spaghetti and meatballs.

I'd just walked into the dining room with Archie after showing him my room and the rest of the house.

"Nice to meet you, Archie," Shelley said before I had a chance to introduce him to anyone.

"Who's this lovely lady?" he asked.

"This is my pseudo-sister, Shelley," I said before looking over at Teagan, who was already seated. "And this is...Teagan." I didn't know what Teagan was to me at the moment, just that she meant a lot more than she had when I first moved in.

Teagan nodded and smiled but didn't bother to get up or extend her hand. Typical Teagan—guarded and aloof, just how I'd grown to like her. Especially now. I was perfectly fine with her keeping her guard up around this guy. I didn't want Archie anywhere near her.

Once we were situated in our seats, Maura began asking him questions. The friendly inquisition reminded me a bit of my first night here.

"So tell me about what brings you to Boston, Archie."

"I graduated from uni last year and got a job working for a biomedical company. We have a client here in Boston. It's a three-month assignment to help them with the design of a new product." He looked over at me. "I was really hoping to get it since I knew my mate was here."

Lorne spoke with a mouthful of pasta. "Where are you staying?"

"Well, my company gave me a stipend, but I'm still trying to work that out. It's not easy to find something for only a few months. I'd arranged to rent a room from a girl in Dorchester, but she's having trouble getting her previous occupant out."

Maura shook her head. "Nonsense. We have an extra bedroom upstairs. It's just wasting away as my sewing room. You can stay free of charge and keep the stipend."

I loved Maura, but right now I sort of wanted to kill her—with a chicken bone, perhaps.

Archie looked like a kid on Christmas morning. "Are you sure?"

"You're a friend of Caleb's, so you come preapproved, right?"

He turned to me. "That okay with you, Caleb?"

What am I supposed to say? "Yes, of course," I offered reluctantly.

He looked back over at Maura. "This is amazing. I can't thank you enough."

I sighed internally. Being in the States was my escape from home and all of the people there. Archie had blown in here like an unwanted storm. He'd stolen a bit of peace I might never get back.

"So how long have you guys been friends?" Shelley asked.

"We grew up on the same street," Archie answered. "Lived near each other our whole lives."

Which was precisely why I didn't need to be living with him *now*. I took a deep breath. It wasn't that I perceived Archie as an enemy. But he was always competitive, constantly trying to upstage me. If my mother enrolled me in a sport, he'd have his mum sign him up for the same team, and then he'd outperform me. It seemed anywhere I went, I couldn't escape him. And the current situation was no different.

"So I bet you could tell us some fun stories about our boy Caleb." Maura winked.

"I've got some photos from our childhood I could certainly blackmail Caleb with, particularly our tap dancing days."

Great. Here we go.

Teagan cracked a smile. Figures she'd light right up with that one.

I felt the need to explain. "Archie's mother was a dance instructor. She always complained that there weren't enough boys enrolled in the tap classes. She asked my mother if I'd be interested in classes free of charge. My mum thought it was a brilliant idea, so she registered me. Archie's mum enrolled him, too. So there you go."

Shelley's eyes nearly bugged out of her head. "You tap danced? I have got to see this."

Archie winked. "That can be arranged."

Teagan, while still quiet, looked more amused than ever.

Archie noticed her softening up and took it as his cue to start talking to her. "Teagan, where do you go to school?"

"I go to Northern with Caleb."

"Ah. Okay. So obviously you chose not to go too far for university."

"I considered moving for school, but in the end, Boston just has so many great options, and to not have to worry about paying for housing—this situation made the most sense."

Archie's eyes moved down to her chest, and my pulse raced. Teagan was wearing an open plaid shirt with a black tank top underneath. A tiny amount of cleavage peeked through the top. A mole that sat right between her breasts entered my awareness for the first time ever. Of all nights for her to show the most skin I'd ever seen, it had to be tonight?

"I'd love for you to show me around the city one day... since you grew up here," Archie said. "You probably know where the action is better than my mate here."

I felt my blood pressure rise. He certainly wasn't wasting any time trying to get into Teagan's pants.

She paused, seeming unsure whether to agree. Then she shrugged. "Sure."

Archie looked over at Maura. "Again, I can't thank you enough for the offer to stay here."

"My mom loves to rent rooms to strangers," Shelley said.

"Don't misinterpret that," Maura said with a laugh. "They have to come carefully vetted. But if we have the space, why not? This city is full of international students and people passing through who need a place to stay." She smiled. "Anyway, you're not a stranger like some of the people who have rented a room here."

"It used to be stray cats. Now it's stray people," Lorne cracked.

Archie smiled. "Meow?"

Everyone laughed except me.

The comfort level I'd found here, the feeling that I'd somehow stepped into an oasis away from England, was over. But my hands were tied. What was I supposed to tell Maura? To renege on her offer, because even though Archie and I were friends, he irked me? I couldn't put her in that position. She'd already offered him a room. He'd already accepted. So now my job was making sure he didn't lay a hand on Teagan.

———

That night when I went to Teagan's room for our study session, she immediately asked, "So what's the deal with you and Archie?"

"What do you mean?" I asked as I took a seat in her chair.

"You seem uncomfortable with him staying here."

Here I was thinking I'd done a good job of hiding it. I didn't want to throw Archie under the bus, so I made it more about me than him.

"It just took me by surprise. I've been enjoying the break from home—and all the things that went with it."

"And you feel like *home* walked in our door tonight."

"Yeah." I sat back in my seat and kicked my legs up on the end of her bed.

"That would piss me off, too."

It was a relief that she understood where I was coming from. I suppose if anyone could relate to the need for space, it was Teagan.

"Where is he now?" she asked.

"He went to meet some of his colleagues for drinks downtown." I opened my laptop. "Anyway, enough about him. We're behind in our studies, thanks to me."

"That's because you're spending more nights at Veronica's lately."

Her voice held a hint of disdain. Or maybe it was my imagination.

"Does that bother you?" I asked.

"No. Why would it bother me? She's your girlfriend. I was just pointing it out. If you're there, you can't be here, thus the lack of studying."

Despite her claim, her face turned red.

"Of course," I said.

Teagan got up shortly thereafter and opened the window in her room, though it was freezing out. I found this a little bizarre and wondered if she was lying to me.

Thankfully, after a few awkward minutes we returned to normal. Teagan quizzed me on my history questions, and things seemed as comfortable as they usually were. However, deep down I was still fixated on how red she'd turned before. Did Teagan have feelings for me that went beyond our friendship? I felt an uncomfortable excitement. I knew nothing could ever come of it, but the thought of being with someone unattainable was arousing in its own forbidden way.

We managed to keep our noses in our books for a while. Then I gave incorrect answers to nearly half the questions on the second round of quizzing.

"You're off your game tonight, Yates."

"I'm sorry. I'll do better next time. This day has thrown me off course."

"Well, your exam is tomorrow, and it unfortunately doesn't care what kind of day you had."

"Can I borrow your brain?" I asked. "I promise I'll take good care of it."

"Hmmm. I don't know if it wants to spend the entire day in your head. I might end up having a little too much fun and get in trouble for being overly snarky or something."

"Very funny, Dolphina." I crumpled up a piece of paper and threw it at her.

"Oh, is that my name?"

"It is now, yes. In fact, I think I might have an uncontrollable urge to get to the dolphin show this Friday so I can see you in that getup. That *is* the day you hand out the tickets, yes?"

"Yes. I hand them out to actual people who want to see the show, not to annoying friends who want to make fun of me in my costume."

"How much money would I have to pay to get you to let me take you to dinner in the North End dressed in your dolphin suit?"

She laughed. "Seriously? I can be bought."

I lifted my chin. "How much?"

She scratched her head. "A thousand dollars."

"Really?"

Teagan bit her bottom lip and smiled. "Yes."

"That's somewhat doable, at least."

"You're not serious, are you?"

"I don't know. I might be."

She shook her head and returned her attention to the computer screen. "You're crazy."

If she only knew all the ways I was scheming to come up with that money.

CHAPTER ELEVEN

Teagan

I hadn't intended to spend Saturday afternoon out with Archie.

When I woke up this morning, I realized Caleb had once again spent Friday night at Veronica's. Archie had been eating breakfast in the kitchen alone when I walked in. He'd asked me if I felt like showing him around. Unsure of how to get out of it, I'd agreed.

I took him to all of the typical places: The Public Garden, The Museum of Fine Arts, Copley Square. As I talked to him, I realized he was just as charismatic as Caleb. Maybe there was something in the water where they grew up that made them that way. Archie made me laugh a lot. Not to mention, he and Caleb were equally gorgeous— Archie in a slightly darker, more mysterious way.

The only difference, I suppose, was that I didn't quite trust Archie the way I did Caleb. I mean, sure, we'd just met, but it was more than that. I couldn't put my finger on why. Sometimes it's just a feeling you get. Oddly, spending the entire day with his friend had made me miss Caleb.

By the time we returned to the house, it was late.

"Thank you for agreeing to be my tour guide," Archie said.

"No problem. Anytime."

He ran a hand through his thick mane of black hair. "Yeah? I'd love to go out again sometime then."

Is he asking me out?

Unsure of what to say, I answered, "Maybe, yeah." I turned to walk away. "Well, I'd better go check on my... room."

My room? Did I just say my room?

"Ah, yes. The *room* can be very needy." He grinned.

I smiled and went downstairs, feeling like a total moron.

———

The following morning, I knew my dad, Maura, and Shelley had gone to an early church service. My family wasn't particularly religious, but a few years back, Maura had started volunteering at a liberal congregational church and began attending services there as well. My dad and Shelley went along with her.

Sundays were therefore typically quiet in the mornings. I was just about to head upstairs to grab some breakfast when I overheard two voices in the kitchen— two British voices. Caleb must have come home from Veronica's either late last night or early this morning.

"Didn't expect to see you this morning..." I heard Archie say.

Caleb's tone was bitter. "Why is that? I live here."

"You've spent the past couple of nights at the girlfriend's place. I didn't think you came home last night."

"Yeah, well, I did. It was late."

"I must have been asleep. I was tuckered out after a long day of sightseeing."

"Sightseeing with whom?"

"Teagan showed me around Boston."

I braced for his response, but it didn't immediately come.

"Did she now..." Caleb finally said.

"Yeah. She took me to a few of the touristy places. It was a really nice time. She's a great girl."

Caleb said nothing to that, and without seeing his face, it was difficult to surmise whether he was angry or unaffected.

"How come I haven't met your girlfriend?" Archie asked. "You hiding her from me or something?"

"No. I just don't bring her to the house. I don't invite friends here."

Not sure if Archie understood that was a dig, but I certainly did.

"We should go out sometime," Archie said. "I'd love to meet her."

"Oh yeah? You like being the third wheel?" Caleb taunted.

"No. I'll ask Teagan if she wants to come along."

Again, another pause.

"I'm not so sure that's a good idea," Caleb said.

Oh?

"Mind telling me why?"

"Teagan is not your type."

What the hell does that mean?

"Not my type?"

113

"That's right."

"She's beautiful and sweet. Why is that not my type?" Archie asked.

Before Caleb could answer, I heard the sound of additional voices. My family had returned from church, interrupting the conversation.

Damn it!

Why wasn't I Archie's type? Was I not pretty enough... sexy enough? Why wasn't I dateable?

———

That entire afternoon, I obsessed over the answer to Archie's question. I couldn't exactly ask Caleb what he'd meant when I wasn't supposed to have heard their conversation.

But I was hurt. I was hurt that he'd discouraged his friend from asking me out—not because I wanted to go out with Archie, but because I cared how Caleb felt about me. And if I wasn't the *type* of person who was worthy of being asked out on a date, what type was I? The type of person you befriend but don't covet, don't respect, don't love? What did he mean?

Kai knocked on the outside door to my bedroom just as I'd nearly been swallowed by my own anxiety.

She frowned when I opened the door. "What the hell is going on, Teagan?"

After I told her the story of what I'd overheard, she seemed adamant that there was only one next step.

"If Archie asks you out, you go."

"But I don't like him that way. He's handsome, but—"

"It doesn't matter whether you actually like him or not. You need to prove Caleb wrong. You *are* the type of person Archie would want to date."

The more she spoke, the more worked up I got. I had never cared much about what people thought of me. But for some reason, I cared what *Caleb* thought. Did he really see me as undateable?

"And who exactly is the type of person Archie would want to date?" I asked.

Kai twirled her long, black hair. "Oh, I don't know. Perhaps someone who lets her hair down once in a while, someone who doesn't hide her body. Someone with sex appeal?"

I waved my hand dismissively. "You know that's not me. That's not who I am."

"I'm quite aware of that. But this isn't about your norm. It's about stepping out of your comfort zone and proving a point at the same time. Any guy would be lucky to date you. Anyone who says otherwise is a damn fool."

———

Kai had gotten me all riled up. I'd never admitted the true reason for hiding my sexuality to her. She didn't know how deeply rooted my issues were and how hard I'd always tried not to resemble my birth mother who abandoned me.

It wasn't that I didn't want to experiment with my sexuality. Even though nothing was going on between Caleb and me, just having him around made me feel more connected to my feminine side—the sexual side. His presence meant there was a sexual energy in my life whether I liked it or not. And I mostly liked it. Okay, I loved it—when I wasn't pissed at him for potentially insulting me, that is.

Looking in the mirror, I wondered if maybe I could play around a bit. I took down my hair and brushed through it. It was very thick—long and straight, light brown with natural blond highlights. I could probably count on my hands the number of times I'd worn it down since the age of about fifteen.

And there was nothing in my wardrobe that could be considered sexy or revealing. That was intentional— though some items were more appealing than others. My typical garb consisted of roomy T-shirts, jeans, and Chucks. I grabbed one of the few fitted shirts I owned before slipping off my T-shirt and changing. The ample breasts I tried so hard to hide were now completely outlined by the thin, clingy fabric. Changing out of my jeans, I replaced them with a pair of black, curve-hugging leggings. Kicking off my sneakers, I put on a pair of black ballet flats Maura had bought me one Christmas, probably hoping I'd take the hint. But alas, the box had never even been opened up until now.

Looking at myself in the mirror, I tilted my head. "Well, whaddya know? She does clean up nice."

Remembering that I had some old makeup in my bathroom, I went in and opened the drawer, feeling clueless. *What to do. What to do.* After a moment I realized I didn't know how to apply eyeliner. So, I turned on one of those YouTube tutorials and watched a girl who had over two million views apply her eye makeup until I felt confident enough to try her technique. It took about twenty minutes and some trial and error, but my eyes were now fully lined and my lips plumped up with a mauve color. The finishing touch was a little rouge on my cheeks. Initially, I put on too much and had to wipe some of it off. By the time I finished, I'd managed to achieve the thing I'd always tried to avoid: I looked even more like Ariadne.

Having second thoughts, I hesitated before heading upstairs for Sunday dinner. But it wasn't going to get any easier, so I gave myself a mental nudge and made my way up the stairs.

When I entered the dining room, every head turned in my direction. Time seemed to stand still as they took me in. Was it that drastic?

My father looked stunned, probably to see the spitting image of the woman who'd broken his heart. Maura looked almost proud, like she was saying to herself *finally*. Shelley looked envious, and I assumed she'd be ransacking my room as soon as possible, looking for the makeup. And Archie and Caleb? Well, let's just say if there were a competition for jaw dropping, I'm not sure which guy would have won.

CHAPTER
TWELVE

Caleb

C *hrist.*

What had she done to herself?

Her eyes, her lips, her breasts—everything was magnified. She looked different, but absolutely beautiful. I'd always recognized Teagan's natural beauty, though, even when she tried her hardest to hide it. But now she was flaunting it. And I didn't know what to make of that, except that I suspected it had something to do with Archie. That angered me for so many reasons.

Shelley's eyes were wide. "You look beautiful, sister."

"Thank you." Teagan batted her lashes and looked down at her feet.

Tongue tied, I couldn't stop staring at her.

"What made you get all dolled up?" Maura asked.

"I felt like a change."

You could see the pride in Lorne's expression. "You look lovely, honey."

"I second that," Archie said.

Of course you do.

I was the only one who hadn't said anything, mainly because I was speechless. Teagan's cheeks turned redder, and it wasn't the makeup. She clearly wasn't used to being bombarded with so many compliments at once.

God, she really did look gorgeous. It was like she'd gone down to her room a girl and come upstairs a woman. I'd never realized how much hair she had, either. She normally kept it tied back in a ponytail or up in a knot. The makeup she wore brought out the green in her eyes. And it was hard not to notice her ample chest in that fitted shirt.

Over the past several weeks, I'd begun to view her in a sexual way—as much as I tried not to. She always hid behind her clothing, but seeing the effort she made tonight scared me. I actually needed to worry about her and Archie, and that didn't settle well in my stomach. I could see now how complicated my feelings for Teagan really were. I just didn't know what to do with that realization.

She finally sat down, and everyone's attention went from her to the food in front of them. Aside from my continuing to steal glances at her, dinner went as usual until Archie spoke.

"Teagan, this might be a dumb question, but do you have a curfew?"

My fists tightened.

"I'm nineteen. Curfew ended when I turned eighteen."

"Ah. Very good. Remember that bowling place you were telling me about yesterday, the one that stays open late?"

"Yeah?"

He cocked his head to the side. "Would you want to go tonight?"

A breadstick I'd been holding snapped in my hand.

"Sure. That sounds like fun," she said.

Clearing my throat, I asked, "What is this place?"

"Wonder Bowl," she answered. "It stays open really late. After ten at night, it's half off to bowl. And they have six-dollar pitchers of beer." She looked at her father. "For those who are legal, of course."

"When she was showing me around the city, Teagan said she felt like sort of a dork for liking bowling," Archie explained. "I told her I was in a league back home for a while."

I rolled my eyes. *Of course he was.*

No way was I letting her go out alone with him tonight.

I glared at him. "Sounds like fun. I'll ask Veronica if she wants to join us. We can all go."

Archie forced a smile. "Brilliant, then."

He was definitely on to me. But I didn't care. Looking after Teagan was my priority.

———

We borrowed Lorne's car to drive to the bowling alley.

Veronica wasn't thrilled. She'd apparently never bowled in her life and had no interest in coming. But I made it sound like I really wanted to go, and eventually, she gave in and agreed.

As we waited in line for those nasty bowling shoes, Veronica made small talk with Teagan. It seemed forced. I suspected Veronica still held a grudge about my ditching her at the restaurant to check on Teagan the day of the attack.

Veronica looked her up and down. "I almost didn't recognize you when I first saw you tonight."

Teagan glanced down at her feet. "I was just playing around with hair and makeup."

"You look pretty."

She smiled shyly. "Thank you."

We got to our lane and settled in to bowl. Every time Teagan bent over to swing her bowling ball, Archie's eyes landed on her bottom. I watched him so much that I couldn't concentrate on the damn game when it was my turn.

My score was pathetic. I kept throwing gutterball after gutterball, which had never happened to me before. Naturally, Archie outscored me, as he tended to do in competitive situations.

Veronica made it quite obvious that she had never bowled before. Every time she stepped up to the lane, she held the ball with two hands, scooted down, and swung the ball between her legs. It took everything in me to avoid completely losing it in laughter every time. Teagan made eye contact with me whenever Veronica was up, and I knew she was thinking what I was: that Veronica's bowling technique was absolutely ridiculous.

At one point, Teagan leaned in and whispered, "Nice granny roll."

At the feel of her breath, I knew my attraction to her was far more than mental.

Then came the part of the evening that really tested me. Teagan got a strike, and Archie ran over and lifted her up, wrapping her legs around his waist while his hands landed on her butt. He spun her around, and it felt like my head was spinning at the same time.

"They make a cute couple, huh?" Veronica said. "She's definitely changed for him."

"Changed? What do you mean by that?"

"Look at her. She typically dresses like a guy. I almost didn't recognize her tonight. She's working hard to impress him."

I swallowed. "Yes, I suppose."

It was my turn to bowl, and this time my stress was put to good use. Apparently, all I had to do was imagine the ball was Archie's head. I hit three strikes in a row.

What annoyed me the most about my reaction tonight was that I had no ground to stand on. There was no reason Archie and Teagan couldn't or shouldn't date each other. My feelings were my own problem, and I'd have to deal with them.

Eventually the four of us stopped playing for a while and sat down. Archie brought a pizza and a pitcher of beer over to the table.

"What time does this place close?" Veronica asked.

"Midnight," Archie answered.

Teagan blew on her pizza slice. "It's so cool that they stay open. I can't remember the last time I was out this late, which is pretty pathetic." She laughed. "Maybe I shouldn't admit that."

"Well, that's unacceptable," Archie piped up. "We need to get you out more often, Teagan. I volunteer as tribute."

When he began to pour beer into Teagan's cup, I held my hand out. "Whoa. What are you doing?"

Archie momentarily stopped pouring. "What do you mean?"

"She can't drink. She's underage," I scolded.

"You're kidding me, right? Did we not drink from the time we were, like, fifteen?"

122

"That doesn't matter. If someone comes around and IDs her, she could get in trouble."

Teagan shrugged the whole thing off. "It's fine. I'm not a big drinker anyway." She slid the cup back toward him.

Archie stared at me incredulously.

Veronica slapped my leg. "Since when did you become such a disciplinarian, Caleb? You don't bat an eyelash when I drink, and I'm underage. You even buy it for me."

Shit. She's right. I'm a hypocrite.

The truth was I didn't want Teagan drinking because I knew it would mess with her inhibitions. I was supposed to be spending the night at Veronica's, while Teagan would head back to the house with Archie. I knew he'd try to weasel his way to her room. Still, I needed to come up with an answer for my behavior that Veronica would find suitable.

"I feel responsible for her because her parents have been very good to me. She can do what she wants, but it's just stupid to give someone underage alcohol in a public place."

"That's what fake IDs are for." Veronica winked. "Then you never have to worry about it."

"It's baffling what a goody goody you've become, Caleb." Archie laughed. "I could tell you so many stories about the trouble Caleb used to get us into."

Veronica smiled. "I'd love to hear some of those. I only get to see his bad boy side in bed."

It could have been my imagination, but Teagan suddenly looked a bit uncomfortable. This whole outing was *very uncomfortable* for me, too.

"Are you going home for Christmas?" Archie suddenly asked me. "I'm sure your mum misses you."

Christmas was coming up in a couple of weeks, and I had no plans to leave Boston.

I shook my head. "No."

"Why not?"

"Funds are a bit tight right now."

While money was a partial issue, that wasn't the reason I wasn't going home. This would be the first Christmas I'd spend away from my parents, and that was fine with me. Christmas was probably the most painful time of year. My mother always hung Emma's stocking on the mantel alongside mine. My father withdrew into himself even more than usual. And my mother always insisted on wrapping a present for my dead sister, one that would have been age appropriate were she still alive. Then once she opened it, she'd donate it to charity.

Christmas wasn't just sad, it was excruciating. And this year was the first opportunity to forego that pain.

"I'll lend you the money to buy your ticket if you want to go home," Archie said.

Of course he'd use this opportunity to seem like a martyr, to flaunt the fact that he held a full-time job and had some money.

"Thank you. But I'm actually looking forward to experiencing Christmas here in Boston. It will be my only opportunity to do that."

Veronica looked disappointed. "I thought you said you'd think about coming home with me to Minnesota."

The last thing I wanted was another inquisition from her parents, this time lasting an entire week or more.

"I think it's best if you spend time with your family alone," I said.

When she didn't say anything else, I knew this would come up again later and turn into an argument about how she believed I planned to ditch her. I'd never actually told Veronica one way or the other what my plans for us would be when the school year was over. But wasn't it obvious? Going back to England *of course* implied that we'd be splitting up. Yet she still seemed to treat things as if we were serious. Case in point, wanting me to join her in Minnesota for Christmas. Ultimately, I supposed I *was* planning to ditch her. But she seemed determined to change my mind about leaving or that we could make it work long-distance.

"The place is going to close in fifteen minutes," Teagan said. "We'd better get going."

Teagan drove Lorne's car on the way back. I knew everyone at the house would likely be asleep, and Archie and Teagan would be alone together when they got there.

The first stop would be Veronica's dorm. After I directed Teagan there, my gut led me to make a split-second decision.

As Veronica was about to exit the car, rather than follow her out I said, "I think I'm going to head back home tonight."

She pouted. "You said you were spending the night at my place..."

"Yes, I know. But I realized I told Shelley I would fix her bike again so she could take it to school tomorrow. It's the same issue that keeps happening, and I'm the only one who knows how to fix it. I totally forgot."

This wasn't a complete lie. I'd told Shelley I'd fix her bike "sometime this week." That changed to tonight now because I really wanted to keep an eye on Archie. He'd given me the impression that he wasn't anywhere near done with Teagan this evening.

"Okay, whatever," Veronica huffed as she stalked away.

I'd pay for this tomorrow, but I wouldn't be able to sleep if I let Teagan return home alone with Archie.

At the same time, this was a little crazy. He'd be here for three months. Would I be able to intercept every opportunity he had to be alone with Teagan? Likely not. If she liked him, I'd have to accept that. But I knew him. Archie liked to use girls for sex and move on when he got bored. And I'd be damned if he made Teagan another notch on his belt. Bloody fucking damned.

Things were quiet for the rest of the ride home. Tension definitely lingered in the air—there was my slightly volatile goodbye with Veronica, and I was also sure Archie was starting to sense my feelings about this situation.

He'd try even harder to win Teagan over if he felt he was in some sort of competition with me. I had to tread carefully, keep an eye on her without him thinking I had feelings for her myself. I would have to go back to using the pseudo-sister card. I *was* trying to keep her from being hurt by him. My complicated feelings were just an extra part I'd have to hide.

When the three of us entered the house through the main door, my suspicions were confirmed.

"Care to continue hanging out, Teagan?" Archie asked.

I stiffened.

Before she could open her mouth to answer, I said, "Great. What are we doing?"

Archie's eyes darted to mine. "I was thinking...just Teagan and me, actually."

"That's not going to happen."

He squinted. "What is your problem?"

He'd said it loudly, and I feared he'd wake the family.

"Lower your voice," I demanded.

"Then let's go outside."

Teagan looked pissed off and followed us back out the door.

Archie and I faced off on the front lawn.

"Now that we're out here, tell me what your problem is, Caleb."

"My problem is you've been here a mere minute, and you're already up to your games."

"Games? What the hell are you talking about?"

Teagan interrupted, "Excuse me. Don't I have a say in this?"

Both of us turned to her.

She crossed her arms and looked straight at me. "If I want to hang out with Archie, if I want to invite him to my room, that's my choice. Not yours."

She was right, but even hearing her mention him in her room made me sick to my stomach. I nodded slowly as Archie smirked.

"But you know what?" she added. "I'm tired, and I'm going to bed. So I'm not hanging out with anyone tonight. I suggest you both do the same—especially you, Caleb, because you have class in the morning, and my sister's bike to fix, in case you've forgotten." She turned to Archie. "Goodnight. Thank you for a great time. It was really fun."

We said nothing as Teagan entered the house. Then it was just us guys left on the frosty grass.

Archie shook his head. "Where is this coming from?" Cold air billowed from his mouth. "You have a thing for her or something? Because if you do, that's really unfortunate for your *girlfriend*."

I looked down at my feet. "I'm protective of her. I don't have to have a *thing* for her to care about her and not want her to become just another one of your conquests."

"You've had plenty of conquests yourself. That doesn't mean I go around warning your new girl not to trust you. People change. They mature. They want different things than they might have wanted a couple of years ago."

"You're trying to convince me you don't have your sights set on fucking Teagan while you're here?"

"I genuinely like her. She's as sweet and intelligent as she is attractive."

That admission bothered me just as much as the thought of him trying to sleep with her.

"You're leaving in three months, so why bother?"

"Well, I could ask the same of you about Veronica. How is that any different?"

I ran my hand through my hair. I'd walked right into that one and had no answer, because there was none. It was no different. I was passing the time with Veronica with no long-term future plan, whether I admitted that to her or not. But in my mind, Teagan was different. Veronica would get over me in no time, move on to someone else. But Teagan? She was vulnerable, special, and she deserved to be with someone who would stick around. Maybe Archie had matured in the past couple of years, but I couldn't trust that he wasn't going to hurt her.

Walking back toward the door, I muttered, "It's been a long day. Let's just end this."

"Figures you don't have any answer for me."

I whipped my head around. "I don't owe you any answers."

"Nice. Real nice. Good discussion, Caleb." He shook his head. "What the hell has got into you?"

I waited in the kitchen until Archie finally went upstairs to his room. I didn't trust that he wouldn't detour to the basement. But when I returned to my room, I couldn't sleep for the life of me.

———

When I woke up in the morning, I checked my phone to find an email from Teagan. She'd written it just a few minutes earlier. It had been a while since she'd sent me an email. This probably wasn't good.

From: Teagan Carroll
To: Caleb Yates
Subject: You've got some nerve.

Caleb,

The more I think about it, the more I can't hold this in. I'm really confused as to why you're acting the way you are. You have zero right to dictate who I can and cannot

spend time with. If I wanted to hang out with Archie last night, that was my choice and not your place to intervene. Who do you think you are?

It wasn't the first time she'd asked me that question. Right now, I was a jealous bastard.

I should've apologized, but instead I did the opposite.

CHAPTER
THIRTEEN

Teagan

A few minutes after I sent Caleb the email, which I knew was his least-favorite means of communication, I checked my phone to find he'd responded.

That was fast.

My heart pounded as I clicked on his message.

From: Caleb Yates
To: Teagan Carroll
RE: You've got some nerve.

Dear Teagan,

Since you're clearly mistaken about my intentions last night, I'll happily re-write your message.

Dear Caleb,

The longer I think about it, the more I've come to realize your actions last night were for my own good. At first, I was confused as to why you acted the way you

did. I thought perhaps you felt you had the right to dictate who I could and could not spend time with. But then I decided, if you were acting so belligerent toward your own friend, you must know something I don't. You must be doing it to protect me. You must have a DAMN GOOD reason. Originally, I was going to ask, "Who do you think you are?" But I *know* who you are: a good friend, who's only looking out for me.

My blood pressure rose. He's back to this again?

I wanted so badly to write him back, but I didn't have enough time to come up with the right response since I was already late for class. So instead I grabbed my backpack and headed out the door, obsessing the entire way to school.

———

Before our testy email exchange this morning, Caleb and I had had a study session scheduled for tonight. Given the Archie situation, I wasn't sure now if our plans were still intact.

Neither Archie nor Caleb was at supper. Archie apparently had a business dinner with some colleagues, and Caleb had told Maura he'd picked up a shift at the restaurant.

Given that, I was shocked when he appeared at my bedroom door at 8PM sharp.

My heart beat faster. "I wasn't expecting you tonight."

He entered and sat down in his usual spot at the desk across from my bed. "Why not? We need to study." His tone was a little pissy.

"Yeah, but given our falling out this morning, I just thought—"

"It wasn't a falling out. It was a clarification."

"Well, let me *clarify* something, then. I don't appreciate it when you twist my words and send them back to me."

His face turned angry. "Do you remember what I told you when I first moved in about writing to me instead of talking to me when I'm home?"

"It was early. I wasn't sure if you were up yet, and I didn't want to wake you. I needed to get it off my chest."

When I said chest, his eyes fell to my breasts briefly. I'd put on a shirt similar to the one I'd worn bowling, one that hugged my curves. I'd continued wearing my hair down, too, and wore a little makeup, albeit not as much as that first night. My need to make Caleb eat his heart out had trumped my fear of looking like Ariadne, it seemed. And I was rethinking that fear anyway, as my dad hadn't seemed bothered by my new look. He'd been only positive and supportive. So maybe my worries about triggering bad memories for him had been just that—*my* worries.

"Teagan, hopefully this is the last time I have to remind you that if you have something to say to me, *say* it, so we can *talk* about it. I don't play the email game."

Fine. I'll say it.

"Why did you tell Archie I wasn't his type?" I blurted.

Caleb's forehead wrinkled in confusion. "What are you talking about?"

"I overheard you talking in the kitchen the day after I took him sightseeing. He expressed interest in asking me out. You didn't warn him not to mess around with me. Instead you said I wasn't his *type*. You never clarified what that meant. And I've been left wondering."

Caleb's lip twitched. He finally let out a deep sigh. "I didn't know you were listening."

"Clearly," I huffed.

"Honestly? I don't even know what I meant by it, Teagan. I would've said anything at that point to discourage him from pursuing you. Saying you weren't his type was my way of getting around having to tell him I didn't think he was worthy of you. It was not a dig at you, if that's what you thought. Just the opposite."

I looked at him for a moment, still perplexed. Even if he was trying to protect me, he had no right to intervene.

"What if I *wanted* him to pursue me?"

Caleb's face reddened. "I can't stop you from doing anything. He's my friend, but he treats women like absolute rubbish."

"He seems to think you were the same way back in England."

"I was," he said without hesitation.

"And you're not now?"

"I'm a bit older and wiser."

"Then why can't you say the same about Archie?"

"I'm just venturing my best guess, based on past experience, that Archie isn't right for you. Do you want to get involved with someone who's leaving in less than three months?"

"You won't be here all that much longer than that. Why are you bothering with Veronica?"

Caleb leaned his head back and exhaled. "Archie asked me the same thing last night, and I didn't have an answer for him. I still don't."

"You're being hypocritical. That's the answer."

"Maybe. But I don't care, if it means protecting you." He rubbed his temples. "Look...I just don't want you to get hurt. That's all it comes down to. If you want to date Archie, I can't stop you. I've warned you. That's all I can do. I won't interfere anymore."

I had no intention of dating Archie. It wasn't worth it—not only because Archie was leaving soon, but because I knew it would upset Caleb. He was my friend, and I would never do anything to hurt him. Now, to ruffle his feathers a little? Maybe. But it was time to come clean.

"When you said I wasn't his type, it angered me. I wondered if you meant I wasn't...sexy enough, desirable enough. That's when I started playing around with the hair and makeup. I feel stupid even admitting that to you."

Caleb's eyes went wide. "I assumed you were doing that to impress him. I never imagined it had anything to do with something I said." He closed his eyes for a moment. "Fuck, Teagan. You don't need that mud on your face. You look ten times more beautiful right now than you did last night."

He immediately looked away. I wondered if he regretted saying it. But it was too late. Those words would forever be happily ingrained in my memory.

"I agree on the makeup." I smiled. "But I do like my hair down. I might stick with this look."

"You have beautiful hair," he whispered, almost like he didn't want me to hear it.

I felt my loins heat up. "Thank you."

What was happening between us right now? I honestly didn't know. Nothing had changed. Caleb still had a girlfriend. And I was still the awkward girl in the basement. Yet the vibe somehow felt *different* than it had before.

"Teagan," he said. "Not everyone would've admitted what you just did—that I made you feel insecure. I love how honest you are. There are very few people in this world I can count on to be honest. That's why it makes me so angry when you email me when you're pissed off. I know you're capable of so much more. We both are." He looked up at the ceiling. "I've really come to value you as a friend. And my behavior over the past couple of days has everything to do with that. I don't want you to get hurt. That's all." His eyes met mine again. "I've grown to care about you very much."

He looked conflicted.

I didn't know what to say. My body buzzed with an excited energy, likely fueled by some insane hope that his feelings for me might go beyond friendship.

As much as we'd just opened up to each other, I felt no closure. He was being more honest than I was. My feelings for him had evolved way past an innocent point. But I didn't see what good it would do to admit that. Aside from the fact that he had a girlfriend, I had no clue if his feelings for me were truly platonic or not. Did he care for me like a sister, or was he starting to feel more? I was terrified to ask directly. I wasn't prepared for the answer, no matter what it was.

I decided to change the subject altogether. "So, you're staying here for Christmas?"

"Yeah. I hope that's okay."

"I was happy to hear that, although I think your mom might be upset. Can your parents really not afford to fly you home, or do you just not want to go?"

His jaw clenched. "I didn't want to get into it at the bowling alley, but there's more to it than cost. Christmas is a difficult time of year for my family. My sister died around Christmas, so the fact that she's gone just becomes magnified. I'm giving myself a break from it this year."

I nodded, not surprised by his explanation. "Well, I hope you'll have a good time here. Maura does a great job making everything festive. We have a party on Christmas Eve, and she invites the entire neighborhood. The house is so cold from the door opening and closing constantly with people coming and going."

"Will there be a penis piñata?"

"Fortunately, no." I laughed.

Caleb smiled. "I can't wait."

"My situation is nothing compared to yours, but I get more depressed around the holidays, too. It's funny how that works. It's supposed to be such a joyous time, and yet for so many people, it's the opposite. It's a weird feeling."

"Well, we can feel weird together this year." He winked.

I smiled wide. The idea of having him here for Christmas made me so happy—giddy, even, the total antithesis of how I normally felt as the holidays approached. Caleb had changed my outlook on life. The fact that he'd endured so much pain and still had the ability to laugh, to charm people, to bleed charisma, made me realize even if you sometimes feel dead inside, you can live. You can fake it till you make it. You don't have to live like you're dead.

I didn't want to think about how I would feel when it came time for Caleb to leave. I only knew this year with him was something I would never forget.

CHAPTER
FOURTEEN

Caleb

The following afternoon, Archie rolled a suitcase into the kitchen as I was making a snack. "Can I talk to you for a second, mate?"

I looked down at his luggage. "What's going on?"

He parked his suitcase in the corner. "Look, I haven't felt like you wanted me here from the moment I walked in the door. At first, I thought my sudden appearance had just taken you by surprise, but then I realized it was something more than that."

I closed my eyes briefly. "You're right. But it's *my* issue more than anything. I'm sorry if I—"

"Don't worry about explaining. A true friend wouldn't stick around if it made you uncomfortable, regardless of the reason. Our friendship might not be perfect, but I value it too much to fuck it up for a free room. You clearly want your space. And you want me away from Teagan. Whatever your reason, I need to respect that."

This should have been the part where I told him he was wrong, that I was sorry, and asked him to stay. But I didn't. I was relieved.

Specifically dodging the Teagan part of his comment, I asked, "Where will you stay?"

His mouth curved into a smile. "That girl in Dorchester finally got her boarder out. I went today to check out the room—which is brilliant." He winked. "And it turns out, so is she."

Ah. Well, it certainly didn't take him long to move on.

"You're leaving because the girl in Dorchester is fit?"

He laughed. "That's not the only reason. I disturbed your peace here. And I didn't mean to do that." He shrugged. "It just happened to work out that the room opened up at the same time I had that realization. I'll still be in the city. You'll still get to see me, just not right under your nose."

"Did you tell Maura?"

"Yes. I thanked her profusely for her hospitality. She's a great lady. You hit the jackpot with this place."

I blew out a long breath. "I'm sorry for the way I've acted."

"Can I give you a piece of advice?" he asked.

"Sure. What is it?"

"Save yourself the trouble later. Break up with that girl of yours. It's not going anywhere. She doesn't make your face light up the way Teagan does. It hit me after we parted ways that night—what was really going on, how much you fancy her. You do realize it's Teagan you want, right? Because if you don't see it now, you eventually will." He smiled. "I'll call you soon."

While I said nothing, he patted me on the shoulder, rolled his suitcase away, and walked out the door.

A few days later, my stomach was in knots as I watched Veronica pack for her trip home to Minnesota for the holidays.

If there was one benefit to Archie's recent stint at the house, it was that he'd pushed me to do something I'd known I had to. I was about to end things with Veronica— not so I could start something with Teagan, but because I didn't want to lead Veronica on anymore. Being with Teagan wasn't an option. I would still be leaving at the end of the year, and it wasn't wise for me to get involved with anyone at this point, least of all Teagan, regardless of whatever undeniable feelings I might have.

Veronica zipped her carry-on bag. "I'm gonna miss you."

That was my cue to rip the Band-Aid off. Knowing what was about to happen while she seemed to have no clue was excruciating. My heart pounded. I did care for her. I just wasn't falling in love with her and didn't think I ever would be. She deserved better.

Rubbing my sweaty palms together, I came out with it, "We need to talk, Veronica."

She'd just opened a drawer when she froze and looked at me. "I don't like the sound of that. I don't like the look on your face, either."

Spit it out. "I don't want to hurt you. You've been so good to me. And being with you has been a highlight of my life. But I have to be honest, and I just don't see this working out long term."

She placed a hand on her chest. "Oh my God. What are you saying? I knew you were going to do this to me!"

Her reaction only made things harder. "I'm going back to London at the end of the school year, and it's not going to work out between us. I think it's best if we end things now. It's only going to hurt more the longer we're together."

"So that's it? You're breaking up with me right before Christmas? You knew all along that this was our fate?"

"It's not like that. I only recently realized this needed to happen. My intention is not to ruin your Christmas. I figured this was the best time to part ways. You'll have your family around you as a distraction, and when you come back, the new semester will be like a fresh start."

"How thoughtful of you," she said facetiously. "So you had your fun with me this semester, fucked me repeatedly, and this is my Christmas present?"

Sometimes, you needed to know when to shut up. That question was not meant to be answered. I couldn't blame her for being upset.

"I know this sucks. I'm sorry, Veronica."

"Yeah, me, too." She started throwing a bunch of her clothes in the suitcase. "Go. Just go. There's nothing more to say here."

I wasn't going to feed her a line of bullshit, like we should keep in touch or remain friends. I knew better. That wouldn't benefit either of us.

"Take care of yourself," I said before leaving.

Despite feeling like crap for hurting her, I walked home from her dorm with a sense of freedom I hadn't experienced since landing in Boston.

Relief.

Veronica and I had started dating almost as soon as I arrived. While I'd always look back fondly on my time with her, it had been too much too soon.

Breathing in the cold winter air, I felt euphoric for the first time in a long time, completely unsure of the future and perfectly okay with that.

———

Archie may have left the Carroll residence, but he didn't go quietly.

Bugger.

When I arrived back at the house after leaving Veronica's, taped to my bedroom door was a photo of Archie and me taken when we were about ten years old. We wore matching sailor costumes and had on our tap shoes. Our hands were sticking straight out in the same pose.

Shelley giggled behind me.

I ripped the photo off the door. "Did you put this here?"

"Archie gave me that before he left. He said I could do whatever I wanted with it. You guys were so cute."

Teagan called up from the bottom of the stairs. "What's so funny?"

Great.

"Nothing," I shouted.

Shelley yelled down. "You have to see this, Teagan!"

Teagan rushed up and caught sight of the photo in my hand. "Oh my God. Is that you and Archie?"

"Afraid so."

"You were adorable. Both of you."

"I suppose I have to own it now, don't I? I was quite good, actually. Tap dancing was probably the one area where I outperformed Archie, even though it technically wasn't a competition."

Teagan arched her brow. "So, if I were to go out today and buy you a pair of tap shoes, you'd be able to tap? Like Fred Astaire?"

My brow furrowed. "Is that a dare, Ms. Carroll?"

Shelley clapped her hands and jumped. "Do it! Do it!"

A brilliant idea came to me in that moment. "I'll tell you what. I'd be willing to display my tap dance skills publicly through the streets of Boston if you forego your one-thousand-dollar requirement and have dinner out with me dressed in your dolphin costume."

Teagan's mouth went agape.

I thought she'd never go for it, but then she said, "Oh...this is tempting."

"Think about it."

"Actually, I don't have to. Provided they let me take the costume home with me this Friday, you have a deal for dinner on Saturday night. Unless you have plans?"

"Nothing more important than getting to see you walk around the city as a dolphin." I smiled. "I'd better find tap shoes in men's size twelve before then."

Shelley stuck out her bottom lip in a pout. "Can I come?"

"Of course," I said. "The bigger the audience the better."

It was funnier than I ever expected. Teagan looked absolutely ridiculous as we walked down Hanover Street. She was supposed to be a dolphin, but she could also have passed as a gigantic blue banana.

She turned to me. "Why am I doing this again?"

I loved when she turned to look at me because she had to turn her entire body. It was hysterical. Teagan's face was the only part of her not completely covered in blue fur. She was perpetually peeking through a hole.

Children would stop us occasionally to take photos, and I'd have my camera ready, too.

The whole thing was crazy, but perhaps the best part was getting to see Teagan and Shelley bonding over the ridiculousness. I'd never seen them laugh more together than today. That alone made it worth it.

We'd decided we were going to the most exclusive restaurant in the entire North End. Dinner was on me, of course. A two-hundred-dollar meal was a lot cheaper than the one-thousand dollars this experience was originally going to cost.

My tap shoes, which I was able to rent from a local dancing school, were in a black bag I'd slung over my shoulder. Our plan was to have dinner and then visit one of the famous Italian pastry places for dessert before I topped off the night with a tap dance routine somewhere on the streets of Boston. I hadn't tapped in over a decade, so I couldn't be sure if the steps would come back to me.

Shuffle, ball change. That was all I could remember.

When we arrived at the restaurant, the hostess didn't seem too amused.

She gave Teagan a once-over. "Can I help you?"

"I have a reservation," I said in my most serious tone.

"The name?"

"Dolphina."

Teagan chuckled.

The hostess looked up our name in the computer. "Um...I'm not sure she can come in here like that."

"Why not?"

"Isn't it obvious?"

I had to stop myself from laughing. "Are you discriminating against her? Dolphins are mammals. We're all mammals. What's the problem?"

Teagan snorted, and Shelley was practically crying.

The ever-so-polite hostess with no sense of humor rolled her eyes and hesitantly grabbed a few menus. "Follow me."

Once seated, the waitress was a lot more gracious than the hostess had been, seeming to get the humor in it all.

After I explained that I'd put Teagan up to it as part of a bet, the server said, "I might do anything you asked me to as well." She winked.

Okay. I hadn't been expecting that—or the eye-fucking that went with it.

The dirty look Teagan flashed her was priceless, even though the waitress hadn't noticed. Teagan's little face poking through the opening was ten times cuter when it wore a frown.

I ended up ordering the steak, while Shelley got a loaded burger. Teagan insisted on sticking to what dolphins eat, so she ordered mackerel. I also got a beer, hoping it would help me unwind a bit before my dance performance later.

We amused ourselves by laughing at all the strange looks Teagan received, and when the food arrived, it was phenomenal. I knew every last morsel on my plate would be properly demolished.

A little while later, the waitress came back and placed another beer in front of me.

I looked up. "Oh, I didn't order another."

"I know." She smiled flirtatiously. "It's on the house."

She seemed to hope I'd give her at least a massive tip, possibly more.

Even Shelley picked up on it. "I think she likes you. Too bad you have a girlfriend."

That comment gave me pause. I hadn't yet announced that I'd ended things with Veronica. Now she'd given me a good opportunity to bring it up.

I cleared my throat. "Actually, I don't anymore." My eyes immediately went to Teagan, who I found looking down into her mackerel.

She whipped her head up. Her mouth was full. "What?"

"Yeah...we broke up."

"She broke up with you?" Shelley asked.

Maybe it had been a mistake bringing this up. I didn't want to get into the details in front of Shelley. But Teagan's eyes were locked on mine now, awaiting my answer, so I had to explain further.

"I was actually the one who ended things."

Shelley looked almost sad. "You broke her heart?"

How am I supposed to answer that? "I hope it's not totally broken. But it was the right decision, all things considered."

"Wow. I wasn't expecting that." Teagan said, the look on her face contradicting the silliness of her attire. "Are you okay?"

"Yeah. I am."

We returned to eating dinner, but over the course of the next several minutes, Teagan's face turned redder than I had ever seen it.

"Are you alright?" I asked her.

"Honestly, I think I need to get out of this fur. I'm burning up."

"Well, you've more than paid your dues. You should've said something sooner. Go get out of that thing."

She got up out of her seat. "I'll be right back."

Shelley and I made small talk, but my mind was preoccupied. I kept looking back toward the restrooms; Teagan was taking an unusually long time. It began to concern me a little, so I told Shelley I'd be right back, that I was going to check on her sister.

I knocked on the ladies' room door. "Teagan, are you okay?"

"Yeah."

For some reason, I didn't quite trust that.

"Are you alone?" I asked.

"Yes."

I opened and entered the bathroom, where she was at the sink, splashing water on her face.

"You can't be in here," she said.

"It's empty. Besides, are you forgetting how we met?"

Her breaths were heavy. "Good point."

She'd hung the costume on the hook of an open stall.

"Give me that thing. I'll carry it back to the table."

She handed it to me before turning on the faucet again and splashing more water on her face. She looked in the mirror for a few seconds before she turned around to face me.

"How come you never told me you broke up with Veronica?"

"It just happened a couple of days ago. You and I hadn't hung out until today. I was going to tell you."

She still seemed flushed. I stepped forward and placed my hand on her forehead. "You look like you're burning up. Are you sure you're okay?"

"Yeah. I'm just hot from the fur. I'll be fine."

I examined her face for a few seconds and decided to give her space. "Okay. I'll go back to Shelley then. Just wanted to make sure you were okay."

"Thank you."

I returned to our table, but I still wondered if there was more to Teagan's reaction than the heat of the costume.

CHAPTER
FIFTEEN

Teagan

You'd think Caleb's news would've brought me relief, rather than cause me to panic. But I guess his relationship with Veronica had meant I didn't have to face my feelings for him or wonder how he felt about me. The prospect of him being free to date whomever he wanted was a little scary. Rather than one girl, there could be many. As jealous as his relationship with Veronica had made me, there was a certain stability and safety to it—and that was gone.

What happens now? I guess I was about to find out. After splashing a last bit of water on my face, I returned to the dining area and sat back in my seat.

A look of worry crossed Caleb's face. He'd stuffed my gigantic costume into the fourth seat at our table.

"Feeling refreshed?"

"Yeah." I breathed out. "I'm good." I downed the glass of water in front of me, which the waitress must have refilled while I was in the bathroom—probably another excuse to come back and ogle Caleb.

Thankfully, I was able to finish my dinner without incident, and once we left the restaurant and got back out into the cold air, I felt ten times better. Maybe the heat of the fur really had gone to my head, affecting my reaction to Caleb's news.

We went over to Mike's Pastry for their famous cannoli, with Caleb carrying my massive costume. I went inside and waited in the long line, then brought the pastries out to Caleb and Shelley. We devoured them outside the shop before making our way down the street to find an appropriate place for Caleb's tap dancing performance. Giddiness swept through me at the prospect of watching him dance.

Finally, we came across a man with long dreadlocks; he sat on the sidewalk, playing an electric guitar and belting out Bob Marley's "No Woman, No Cry."

The song and the style of music were completely inappropriate for tap dance. Nevertheless, Caleb stopped next to the guy and proceeded to change into his shiny black shoes.

After the street musician finished his rendition of the song, Caleb whispered something into the man's ear and slipped him some money. The guy nodded.

The man started playing some reggae song I didn't recognize, and Caleb began tapping right next to him. The taps on his shoes clicked away on the pavement as confused passersby stopped to watch. The pace of the tapping was a bit too fast and didn't match the rhythm of the song.

The funniest part was the goofy smile on Caleb's face. The musician just kept playing and singing, seeming to ignore Caleb's antics. The whole thing was bizarre. Shelley and I died laughing.

Caleb was pretty good, only a little uncoordinated and definitely worthy of performing in, say, a middle school dance recital. Tap dancing and reggae music certainly didn't go together, but that was precisely what made it so entertaining.

We go through so many days in our lives that we won't remember. But this day I knew would stay with me. I'd not only connected with Caleb, but also with my sister. And that, to me, was the entire point.

———————

A few days after our North End outing, it was Christmas Eve. Maura had the whole house decked out for our open-door neighborhood party. She'd spent the week prepping the place—plaid pillows on the couches in the living room, garland draped along the tops of the windows, and of course, the tree fully dressed and lit. The pellet stove was on full blast because it was freezing out, and it was rumored that we might get a few snowflakes tonight.

As usual, Maura and my dad had invited all the neighbors to pop in this evening. The only thing Maura ever asked was that they bring a food or drink item to share. We always ended up with more than we knew what to do with. We usually ate leftovers for a week or even longer.

Whereas many people waited until Christmas morning to open presents, my family opened ours on Christmas Eve. So that was always something to look forward to after the guests left—although Shelley often started opening hers earlier in the evening.

Caleb seemed really happy to be here. He'd spent the entire day hanging lights inside and outside the house and helping decorate. He said his parents never bothered with too many Christmas decorations, so that was a new experience for him. He'd looked even more handsome with lines of Christmas lights draped across his body.

That's one Christmas tree I wouldn't mind climbing.

Caleb found me in the kitchen shortly before people were scheduled to start arriving. I had been stirring some hot apple cider for the drink station when I caught him watching me.

Wow.

He looked good—smelled good, too. And he'd done something different to his hair. It was parted to the side, seeming more formal, maybe. A maroon sweater with a green stripe across the chest hugged his muscles and made me want to curl up into him. I suddenly forgot what I was supposed to be doing. I stopped stirring the cider.

"You look nice," I said.

He smiled. "So do you."

I had to look down to remember what I was wearing: black leggings, a red, fitted shirt, and those trusty black flats Maura had bought me. Once again, I wore my hair down.

Caleb peeked into the cider pot. "Can I help?"

I resumed stirring. "No, I've got it."

When he smiled at me again, I felt my pulse react. This was the best Christmas I could remember in a long time.

Once guests started arriving, though, I considered swallowing those words. For a while I stayed busy in the kitchen, helping Maura chop up vegetables for the veggie and cheese platter. When I finally returned to the living room, I spotted Caleb talking to Bethany Grillo, one of our neighbor's daughters, who'd been away at college. She was very attractive, and her body language was flirtatious.

I stayed in a corner watching them. All I could think was: *it's happening.* That didn't take long. He'd end up having a fling with her over the holidays, which would mark the official beginning of his new era of freedom.

My father interrupted my thoughts when he came up behind me.

"Hi, sweetheart."

I forced my eyes away from Caleb and Bethany. "Hey, Dad."

"Why are you standing here in the corner all alone?"

Well, I'm not going to admit to stalking Caleb's conversation.

"Just chilling for a bit."

He smiled. "You look beautiful tonight."

"Thank you."

His compliment gave me mixed feelings. I'd never discussed my hang-up about looking like Ariadne with him. But maybe now was the time. "You know, I always used to think if I wore my hair down or dressed a certain way, it would upset you."

Dad nodded and seemed to know exactly what I meant. "Because you look like her?"

"Yes."

He sighed. "The resemblance is uncanny. She was beautiful, as are you. But looking at you could never make me upset. You're not her. You have a good heart and a pure spirit. I'm glad Ariadne gave you her one good quality: her looks. But other than that, you're nothing like her."

Hearing that brought me some comfort, though I still didn't feel totally sure I wasn't somehow like her.

"Pretty sure most of my other good parts came from you," I said.

"I won't argue with that." He winked.

I grinned and glanced over in Caleb's direction. A few seconds later, his eyes met mine. Instead of continuing the conversation with Bethany, he immediately excused himself and came right over. Suddenly, everything was right again in the world.

"There you are. I was wondering what happened to you," he said.

My father placed his hand on my shoulder. "I'm gonna see if Maura needs anything."

As my father walked away, I turned to Caleb. "You didn't have to leave your conversation."

"Eh." He shrugged. "I was looking for an excuse."

Relief washed over me. "I'm surprised."

He cocked his head to the side. "Why is that?"

"She's really pretty. I thought maybe you were into her."

"Nah. Not my type. Nice girl, though. Seems really smart. But not as smart as someone else I know." He winked.

I looked at his red Solo cup. "What are you drinking?"

"Spiked eggnog. You want some?"

"I thought you were against underage drinking."

He leaned in, and his warm breath grazed my cheek. "We're not in public tonight."

Feeling a tingle down my back. "I know. I'm just kidding. Actually, Maura and my dad don't care if I have a few drinks, so long as I'm home where they can keep an eye on me."

"Your parents are really cool," he said. "I hope you know that. You're lucky to have them."

"I do know that." I smiled. "Speaking of parents, did you call your mom tonight?"

He looked into his cup. "Yeah...it's late there now. So I called her before the party started. I wished both my parents a happy Christmas. Even talked to my dad for a bit for the first time in a long while."

"How was that?"

"The usual tense small talk. Obligatory, mostly."

That made me sad. "I'm sorry."

His mood always shifted when he mentioned his dad.

I changed the subject. "By the way, is there something wrong with your phone?"

"Why do you ask?"

"Earlier when you were out and texted me, asking if I needed anything from the store, it sent me your same question like twenty-five times. It wouldn't stop."

He narrowed his eyes. "Shit. That's not good. I'll have to power down." He reached into his pocket for his phone and pressed the off button. "There. Let's see if that helps."

"Yeah, it was sort of funny. Until it wasn't."

"That could get annoying."

Our attention turned toward Shelley, who'd started opening some of her presents. She still got tons of gifts, and Maura marked them all from "Santa" even though Shelley had found out the truth a few years back.

When she opened her latest package, inside was a Target gift card and a framed photo. She ran to Caleb and gave him a huge hug. Then she showed me the photo.

"Look, Teagan."

She handed me the frame, and I examined the image. It was the three of us, taken when I'd first put on my dolphin costume the other night. It really was a fantastic photo. Caleb had become like a part of our family. Honestly, since his arrival, so had I. I'd never spent more time with my sister, or even Maura and my dad. Because of his own loss, Caleb appreciated the things I had always taken for granted. And he'd taught me to appreciate my family more. His stay here would leave an imprint on my life.

After Shelley returned to her spot on the couch, Caleb seemed uncharacteristically nervous. "Can I give you your present?" he asked.

"You didn't have to get me anything," I said. "I have your gift downstairs. I wrapped all my presents, but I haven't had a chance to bring them up yet."

"I'd like to give you yours in private," he said. "Only because I want to explain it without everyone listening."

Now he had me intrigued. "We can go downstairs," I suggested.

"Let me just run upstairs and grab it, and I'll meet you down there," he said.

As I ventured to my room, I felt my nerves tingle.

A few minutes later, Caleb came downstairs holding a small, red and green gift bag. "For you." He grinned as he handed it to me.

After lifting the tissue paper and putting it aside, I took out a little stuffed dolphin. I smiled. So cute and thoughtful. Then I noticed a silver chain hanging from it. Attached to the end was a charm.

Upon closer inspection, I realized it was a little snail peeking out of its shell.

I looked up at him. "This is so cute."

"You're probably wondering...why a snail?" He chuckled. "I saw this and wanted to buy it for you, because you've really come out of your shell since I've known you—just like a snail. It reminded me of you. I hope when you wear it, after I leave, it reminds you of *me*."

I doubted I'd need a reminder of him after he was gone. "I don't know what to say. This is the most meaningful thing anyone has ever given me."

"I'm glad you like it."

He fidgeted. Caleb seemed almost...shy about the whole thing.

"Were you nervous to give this to me?"

"A little. I'm not even sure why."

Looking down at it, I smiled. "I truly love it. Thank you."

"You're welcome."

"My present to you is not nearly as good," I warned.

Walking over to my desk, I picked Caleb's gift from the pile.

With a huge smile on his face, he ripped open the paper. His smile only grew when he realized what it was.

"Are you kidding me? It's brilliant! I didn't even know such a thing existed."

I'd bought Caleb a stainless steel s'mores maker. It featured a flameless electric heater for the marshmallows in the middle and a surrounding tray for the crackers and other accompaniments.

"I figured you could use it when you go back home. You mentioned you couldn't light fires outside where you live. This way you can make s'mores whenever you want. It might be a pain in the ass to pack though."

"I'll find a way to fit it, don't you worry. This is the best thing you could have got me." He looked over at me. "Thank you."

"You're welcome."

He examined my face. "What are you thinking right now? You look sad."

I decided to be honest. "I am sad—a little. This school year is already half over. Before you know it, you'll be packing up and heading home. I've gotten used to having you around. And I'm just...gonna miss you."

He shook his head. "I really can't stand to think about leaving. This feels like my home now. The time here is going by way too fast."

I'd looked away, but felt Caleb's hand on my chin, lifting it to meet his eyes before letting go. My body stirred.

"Who am I going to study with?" he asked. "Who am I going to taunt?"

My breathing quickened. "I'm sure you'll find someone."

"It won't be the same," he whispered.

"There's no chance you could stay, right? Even just another year?"

I immediately wanted to slap myself for asking.

He blew out a long breath. "I don't think so. I haven't inquired, but the exchange program is only supposed to be for a year. But even if they did let me stay, I'd feel a bit guilty leaving my mother. The situation with my dad is not good. I promised her I'd be back."

"Yeah. I'm sorry. That was dumb to even ask."

"No, it wasn't. It's crossed my mind many times." His tone was insistent. "And it's not that I don't want to. I'd give anything to stay."

Taking the necklace he'd given me into my hands, I asked, "Will you put this on me?"

He smiled. "Of course."

I lifted my hair and turned my back to him. The warmth of his hands as he put on the necklace made my body tingle with an excitement I tried hard not to feel.

I turned to him and rubbed my fingers over the charm.

"It looks nice on you," he said.

"Thank you again."

"Thank *you* again for my s'mores maker. Don't be surprised if I bring it down to study session."

"Oh gosh. What have I started?"

We were both laughing when Maura peeked her head into my halfway open door. For some reason, I jumped at the sight of her—as if she'd caught us doing something wrong. It definitely felt like we were hiding from everyone down here.

"Oh, there you are." She paused. "We...have some presents for both of you to open upstairs."

Caleb nodded. "Sorry, Maura. We just came down here to exchange our gifts." He headed toward the stairs and left without saying another word.

Maura's eyes lingered on mine, a mix of suspicion and amusement in their depths. She might have been the only one in this house that was truly onto my feelings for Caleb.

CHAPTER
SIXTEEN
Caleb

The month that followed Christmas flew by. Things were busier than ever. I'd taken on extra hours waiting tables at the restaurant, and the new semester was kicking my arse.

As a result, I was certain the rest of my time here was going to evaporate before I knew it. There was still so much I wanted to do and see in Boston, I hardly knew what to do with myself. I couldn't bear to think about it.

But the thought of leaving the Carrolls made me even more anxious. I wasn't ready for this reprieve from real life to end. It was truly amazing to be looked at with kindness and respect instead of resentment.

But what messed with my head the most were my feelings for Teagan, which had been evolving in a slow burn I couldn't figure out how to extinguish. Since breaking up with Veronica, I hadn't dated anyone else. I'd vowed not to make the same mistake again—leading someone on, only to have to break the news that it couldn't go anywhere because I was leaving.

Between work and school, any free time I had was spent studying with Teagan or occasionally hanging out with Archie, whose company I could enjoy now that he wasn't living under our roof. He'd started dating Angela, the girl he was living with in Dorchester. He, too, was spending a lot of time wondering what would happen when his time in the States ran out. But Archie had more freedom than I did to potentially relocate. He was finished with school and didn't have a mother dependent on him for her mental well-being.

I'd given Teagan no inkling that my feelings for her had crossed the line beyond friendship, but that didn't stop me from thinking about her when I lay down in bed at night or while I was in the shower. It didn't stop me from wanting her. Basically, anytime I had a moment to breathe, my mind wandered to forbidden thoughts of Teagan, and what it would be like to have her just once.

———

My little problem became impossible to ignore one night when Teagan skipped dinner. That wasn't all that unusual. She wasn't always at the family meals, and neither was I. But on this particular evening, the reason behind her absence caught my attention.

"Teagan's on a date," Shelley announced.

I stopped chewing my chicken and perhaps a bit too urgently, asked, "How do you know?"

"I saw her getting ready to go out. She wouldn't tell me where she was going, so I got suspicious. I looked out the window and saw her get into a car with some guy."

Some guy?

"Interesting," Maura said.

"Yeah, interesting," I muttered.

Lorne sighed. "Well, Teagan doesn't have to tell us everything. I just hope she's not getting into cars with the wrong people."

Maura gave me a slightly sympathetic look. I suspected she'd picked up on my feelings for her stepdaughter some time ago.

To my knowledge, Teagan hadn't been on a date the entire time I'd known her, aside from the bowling night with Archie—if that even counted. It shouldn't have surprised me that she'd gone out. You know, the whole coming out of her shell thing and all. That had certainly backfired, hadn't it? Anyway, I needed to get over it.

My chair skidded against the hardwood floor as I got up. "Dinner was delicious. Thank you, Maura," I said before excusing myself.

In my room, I did several repetitions of pull-ups to try to expend my nervous energy—anything rather than having to deal with my feelings.

My phone rang, interrupting my workout. It was my mother.

I wiped the sweat off my forehead with a towel as I picked up the phone. "Hey, Mum. It's late there. Everything okay?"

There was a slight delay in her response.

I started to panic. "Mum?"

"Hi, honey," she finally said.

"What's going on?"

After another short delay, she said, "Your father's been drinking again."

My stomach felt like it had been punched. My father had been sober for the past ten years or so. He'd started drinking after Emma's death, and the problem got progressively worse until my mother and his brothers staged an intervention. Everyone in the family had saved money in order to send him to rehab, and by some miracle, after those months away, he seemed to have left drinking behind all these years.

"How did you find out?"

"He'd been staying out a lot more than usual, and tonight he came home smelling like beer and slurring his words. It was the first time I noticed it, but I'm sure it's been going on for some time."

Sitting down on my bed, I rested my head in my hand. "I'm so sorry, Mum. What can I do? Do you need me to come home?"

"Don't you dare. I'll handle it from here. I'm not telling you this to interrupt anything. You'll be back home before you know it. I just needed to let you know."

"If things get out of hand, you have to tell me. I need you to keep me updated."

"Well, right now, he's asleep. So nothing is out of hand yet. But I imagine I'm going to have to figure out a way to get him back into a program."

"I'll send you money."

"No," she insisted. "I'll see if your uncles can help."

Back when Dad's drinking problem first came about, I was obviously too young to earn a living. But I remember feeling helpless, because I believed the whole thing was my fault. If Emma hadn't died, my father wouldn't have started drinking. Now that I was older, I had to find a way to help pay for it.

"I don't care what you say, Mum. I'm going to request more hours or get another job so I can send you something."

"You need to pay for school. Your loans are big enough already. We'll figure it out."

I didn't know what else to say, except, "I'm sorry."

She knew my apology had more than one meaning.

"Caleb, I don't want this to get you off track. That's not why I'm telling you. Please stay focused on school. That's how you can help—stay focused so I'm not worrying about both my boys at once. Okay?"

"Okay," I said reluctantly.

After I hung up with my mother, I couldn't rid myself of the terrible feeling her news had brought me. I wished Teagan were home. But of course, she was out on a date—where she should've been. Emotions ran through me: jealousy, guilt over my father. At the moment, I didn't want to feel anything. But turning to alcohol wasn't an option. My mother didn't need me developing a drinking problem, too.

I finally took a shower to calm my nerves, and then I ventured down to Teagan's room to see if by some chance she'd returned from her date. She hadn't. Blowing out a long breath, I lay on her bed and kicked my feet up. I longed for her company. I knew she would've said something to make me feel better, at least for a moment.

Grabbing her pillow, I took a deep breath of her scent—a mixture of rain and something all her own.

I lay there for several minutes, pining for a girl I could never have.

Pathetic, Caleb.

I reached for my phone and scrolled down to the number of one of my co-workers, a waitress named Simone. She was older, in her late twenties, and had made it clear to me one night after my shift that she was interested. I told her I wasn't looking to get involved with anyone while I was here in the States, and she'd insisted that getting involved was not something she wanted, either. Basically, she wanted to fuck me, and she'd invited me over to her place. At the time, I'd shrugged off her proposition, making some sort of joke, although I knew she'd been dead serious. She'd then taken it upon herself to enter her number into my phone. Until this very moment, I hadn't considered using it.

I texted her.

Caleb: Wondering if you're free tonight.

She responded almost immediately, a few seconds later.

Simone: What a surprise. And for you, yes.

Caleb: Are you home?

Simone: Yup. Wanna come by?

Though it didn't feel right, I typed the words anyway.

Caleb: Yes. Text me your address.

CHAPTER
SEVENTEEN

Teagan

I was relieved to be home. Jacob had taken me out for sushi and a movie—not the creepy, desolate kind I normally enjoyed, but the mass-marketable, packed-theater kind. It was a nice evening, but I felt nothing more than friendship for Jacob. That was likely the reason I'd agreed to go out with him. As Kai had pointed out, that was my MO. He was safe and didn't require any emotional work—or sexual work, for that matter.

I just wanted so badly to get Caleb out of my head. The sooner I did that, the better. So I had to make an effort to put myself out there. It didn't feel natural, but I tried. Still, I couldn't stop thinking about Caleb. Maybe he needed to be gone for that to happen. I hated the fact that going out with Jacob had only made me more focused on Caleb. I was well on my way to being crushed when he left to go back to England.

Kicking off my shoes, I lay down on my bed and curled into my pillow. My heartbeat accelerated when I realized I was breathing in his scent, strong and masculine. So Caleb.

Wait.

Caleb?

Caleb had been in my bed?

I'd just changed my sheets the night before. So there was no way this was residual from one of our study sessions. Hugging the pillow tighter, I continued to bury my nose in it, overwhelmed by longing—and confusion. What was he doing in my bed? Had he come down here to look for me?

I reached for my phone and texted him.

Teagan: Are you home?

Several minutes passed, and there was no response. I decided to go upstairs to see if he was in his room.

Maura was in the living room, watching one of her shows on Bravo.

She caught me before I had a chance to go upstairs. "Hey! How was your date?"

I stopped just short of the first step. "How did you know I was on a date?"

She lowered the volume on the TV. "I guess I didn't. I just took Shelley's word for it. She mentioned seeing you get into a car with a guy."

I sighed. "His name is Jacob. He works at the aquarium with me. We just went for sushi and a movie. It was okay. Nothing to write home about." I glanced up at the stairs and then back at her. "Have you seen Caleb?"

"He's not here. I saw him leave a while ago."

My heart sank. "Did he say where he was going?"

"No. He sort of rushed out of here, actually."

"Damn," I muttered.

A look of concern crossed her face. "Is everything okay?"

"Yeah. I just needed to ask him something."

She paused a moment. "You should know that Caleb was at the dinner table when Shelley announced you were out with a guy. I wasn't sure if you'd been keeping that from him intentionally or not. He didn't seem to know."

Shit.

It wasn't that I'd planned to lie to Caleb if he'd asked me where I went tonight. I'd simply chosen not to advertise it. I knew I would've been jealous if the roles were reversed.

I wished Maura goodnight and returned to my room.

Still no response from Caleb, and I suspected he must be out with a girl. That gave me an upset stomach.

A little while later, I checked my phone again. An hour had now passed since I'd texted him. It was unlike him not to respond at all. I was desperate to know where he was, to ask him why he'd been in my bed, but sending him another text would have been pushy. I knew I didn't owe him an explanation for my whereabouts. But we normally told each other our plans if one of us wasn't going to be home at night.

As more time passed, I realized Caleb might not be coming home at all. I was just about to turn off my lights and resign myself to falling asleep when there was a knock on the outside door to my bedroom.

I jumped up. "Who is it?"

His voice was low. "It's Caleb."

169

When I opened the door, he looked tired, and his hair was a bit disheveled. He still looked handsome as ever, just a bit worn.

"Are you okay?"

He shook his head. "Not really."

I followed my instinct and pulled him into a hug. He gripped me tightly, almost as if holding on to me for dear life. To be in his arms like this, to be held like this, was so different from the casual hugs we'd had in the past. His heart beat so fast against my cheek. The warmth of his hard muscles consumed me, and I wanted nothing more than to stay like this all night.

Even though I was afraid, I asked, "Where were you?"

He pushed away from me to look at my face. "How was your date?" There was a hint of disdain in his tone.

"It was okay." I swallowed.

"You usually tell me your plans if you're not going to be home." His eyes lingered on mine for a few seconds. "But I understand why you didn't this time."

He does? "You do?"

After a long silence, he said, "Our relationship is complicated, isn't it, Teagan?"

I sighed. "Why were you in my bed tonight?"

His brow lifted. "How did you know I was in your bed?"

"I can smell you all over my sheets."

Instead of answering, Caleb climbed onto my bed and put his head on the pillow. It was too tempting not to go after him. We lay on top of the bedding, facing each other. He rested his head on his hand as he continued to look at me.

"I was worried about you tonight," I said. "How come you didn't answer my text?"

"I didn't get it immediately. Then by the time I did, I figured I'd just come home." He let out a breath that I felt on my cheeks. "You asked why I was in your bed. I needed to talk to you, and I came down to see if by some chance you'd come home early. I knew it was a long shot. When I realized you weren't back yet, I just laid down for a while."

"What did you need to talk to me about?"

"I was upset after talking to my mother." He exhaled. "I don't think I ever told you, but my dad is a recovering alcoholic. He hadn't had a drink in over a decade." Caleb sighed. "But he's relapsed."

I squeezed his hand. "Oh no. I'm so sorry I wasn't here."

"It's not your responsibility to be at my beck and call. I just needed to talk. It was a moment, and it passed."

"Is your mother okay?"

"She sounds like she thinks she can handle it. But I'm not so sure. She's going to need my father's brothers for support. If I were home, it would be different, even though she insists my coming back early won't help."

The pain in his eyes was transparent. Caleb blamed himself for all of this, and that killed me. It all went back to what had happened with his sister.

He played with some lint on my comforter. "Anyway...I don't really want to get into it now. I've thought about it way too much already tonight, and my need to talk has passed. But that's why I was in your bed."

"Well, even if I shouldn't apologize, I really am sorry I wasn't here. I would much rather have been here tonight."

My emotions bubbled up inside of me, and I felt my eyes start to water. That was not good. I just felt so much for him right now. Not only because of his pain, but because my being out with Jacob tonight had been so *not* like anything with Caleb. That scared me.

"Who was this guy, and where did he take you?" Caleb asked.

"His name is Jacob. I met him at the aquarium. He works at the gift shop. He took me out for sushi and a movie. It was nice...but there was nothing there. Pretty sure I knew that before I accepted the date. But I went anyway, because I really wanted to...get my mind off things."

My words had backed me into a wall. I was torn between wanting to tell Caleb how I felt about him and wanting to keep it inside.

He cocked his head to the side. "Get your mind off *what* things?"

I took a moment to search for the words. "I feel like I can talk to you about anything...except my feelings for you. I feel stupid for letting it get to this point."

That was too much. Now he was staring at me like he didn't know how to respond—until he did. And his words completely shook me.

"You asked me where I was tonight, and the reason I hesitated to tell you is because in order to properly explain it, I have to talk about my feelings for *you*. And like you, it's not easy for me to do that...because I never want to do or say anything that might change what we have, which is the kind of friendship that's rare."

My palms grew sweaty as he continued.

"When Shelley said you were out on a date, I got extremely jealous—and a little angry. I realize that's ridiculous. But nevertheless, it's hard to control your emotions. At first, I went upstairs to my room and worked out to expend some of that negative energy. But nothing was doing the trick. Then my mother called and gave me that news about my father's relapse. That's when I came down to see if you were home."

While hearing he'd been jealous made my heart sing, I couldn't fully appreciate it because I was scared of what he'd say next.

I braced myself. "And then? Where did you go?"

"I didn't want to be alone, so I...texted this girl I work with. She'd made it clear she wanted to fuck me—no strings attached."

His words sliced through me, and I pushed back a bit.

He fucked someone tonight?

"Teagan, all I cared about tonight was forgetting everything: my unreasonable jealousy about you, my father's relapse and the blame I placed on myself—all of it. So I went over to that girl's flat...hoping to...forget."

"You don't have to tell me the rest. I really—"

"Yes, I do," he said. He took a deep breath. "One thing led to another. This girl was practically attacking me—ripping my clothes off, digging her nails into me—and instead of feeling turned on, I felt the opposite. I felt sick. I couldn't even get hard. It was the most bizarre almost-sexual experience of my life."

Almost?

"You didn't sleep with her?"

He shook his head. "No. I just wanted to come home. And that's what I did. I saw your text on my way back and decided that rather than answer you, I needed to see you. So here I am."

I reached out and ran my fingers through his silky hair. It was the first time I'd ever touched it, and it was even softer and thicker than I'd imagined. Watching the way his breathing changed as I did it gave me a sense of power. This simple movement might have been the most brazen thing I'd ever done in my life.

Caleb shut his eyes, and I kept massaging his hair— until he fell asleep in my bed. And that's where he stayed.

CHAPTER EIGHTEEN

Caleb

The vibe between Teagan and me definitely changed after the night I spent in her bed. And I didn't quite know how to handle it.

We hadn't been alone since, but the one time we were both at dinner, Teagan caught me staring at her. Instead of looking away, she kept her eyes on mine and smiled. I smiled back and inwardly cursed at myself for being so damn transparent. I'd been fantasizing about what her lips would taste like all through the meal.

It had felt good to sleep next to her, though we'd never talked about it. The morning after, she'd still been sleeping when I slipped out of the bed.

Tonight would be our first study session since then. As much as I wished for a repeat—to lie next to her again—I planned to repeat my mantra instead: protecting her was more important than whatever selfish desires I had.

Good luck with that.

Later, everything seemed normal downstairs in Teagan's room—at least, at first. There was no mention of our night together, no discussion of what it meant or whether we would do it again. Instead, we dug right into our homework. I wrote out some math formulas while Teagan studied for her physiology test.

At one point, I looked up to sneak a glance at her. And I found her already looking at me. *We must stop meeting like this, Teagan.* I wondered how long her eyes had been on me and not her computer.

"Are you attracted to me?" she asked.

She said it so quietly, it barely registered.

Did I hear that right? I swallowed and tried to buy myself some time. "Hmm?"

She shut her eyes, shaking her head. "Never mind." She buried her face in her computer again, her cheeks turning red.

Fuck. How could I ignore that question? I needed to admit I'd heard it the first time.

"You asked if I was attracted to you..."

She lifted her head. "So you did hear me."

"It just took a moment to process."

"Or you had to think about how to let me down easy."

Is she kidding? I hadn't been able to focus on anything besides my attraction to her lately. "Fuck no, Teagan. You've got it wrong."

Her face grew even redder. "Forget I asked. Please. It was a mistake."

I put my notebook aside and walked over to her bed, sitting on the edge—close but far enough to be safely out of reach. She had her legs crossed and licked her lips nervously. My dick twitched. *Fuck.* I was such a lost cause.

The truth was dangerous. But I was tired of denying things. It had been so much damn work for so long.

"Let's be real for a few minutes," I said. "I'll tell you my thoughts, and you tell me yours. Be brutally honest. Alright?"

Her chest heaved. "Okay..."

"I am extremely attracted to you, Teagan," I said softly. "That's the truth." I let out a shaky breath. "It wasn't instantly as strong as it is now. When we first met, I definitely looked at you more platonically. But something changed along the way. And now I constantly dream about what it would be like to be with you."

She licked her lips again, and my dick stiffened even more.

"But you know why I haven't done anything about it, right? There's only one reason, and that's that I don't want to hurt you when I leave."

"I get that." She shifted on the bed. "Lately I've been catching you staring at me. I can't help staring at you, too. I've always had a crush on you, but recently I haven't been able to stop thinking about what it would be like, either."

I gripped the sheet of paper in frustration. She'd made her position clear, but I still needed to confirm exactly what she meant.

"You mean, you can't stop thinking about what it would be like to *be* with me...sexually?"

She bit her lip and nodded. I was about to come undone.

Teagan looked tormented. "I don't like feeling this way—very out of control," she said. "Whenever you're near me, my body reacts. Sometimes I feel like I'm going to explode if you don't touch me." She closed her eyes. "Oh my God. I can't believe I just said that."

My heart raced, and it took everything in me not to leap forward and take her lips. Still, I managed enough willpower to stop myself. I wanted to know something I couldn't figure out without asking her directly.

"Can I ask you a personal question? And feel free to tell me to go fuck myself."

"Yeah...okay."

"Have you had sex before?"

She nodded.

For some reason, I thought she might be a virgin. Now that I knew she wasn't, it made me wildly curious about the circumstances.

"Only one time," she clarified. "I had sex on my senior prom night. I'd basically planned to lose my virginity—to get it over with. It was stupid, and I didn't even...enjoy it."

Enjoy it. "You didn't come..."

She shook her head. "No. It hurt. And it was fast and over with before I knew it. He basically broke my hymen, and that was it."

Her terminology made me chuckle. "Did the hymen breaker have a name?"

"Zach."

"Zach is wack. A two-pump chump."

She laughed. "I'm not sure it really counted."

"It didn't," I insisted.

"How many girls have you slept with?"

Blowing out an exasperated breath, I closed my eyes, genuinely trying to recall. "Don't laugh. But this is my best estimate."

"Okay…"

"Fifteen."

Her eyes widened. "Wow."

"Approximately two per year since high school. A few were girlfriends. Most were just one-night stands, though. And I used a condom every single time, even with my girlfriends, because I don't trust anyone."

"Good to know." She grinned. "I guess I have a lot of catching up to do."

"No, no, no, no, you don't." The thought of her "catching up" made me ill. "But I *am* curious as to why there was never anyone else after the hymen breaker."

Teagan stared off. "I've had a tendency to choose people I know I'm not going to lose my mind over. That ensures I never really get hurt. But in turn, I'm not attracted enough to anyone to sleep with him. It's a fucked-up result of my background—somehow not wanting to be like my deadbeat mother, or worse, end up hurt like my father. I've fucked up every halfway normal relationship I've ever had because I wasn't attracted to the person. And I've always shied away from people I *am* sexually attracted to." She blinked a few times. "Guys like you."

Shit. I tried to make light of it, though I was freaking out inside. "I make it hard to avoid me."

"That's the difference. I don't *want* to avoid you. You make me feel safe, Caleb—like I could let myself go with you, like you wouldn't judge me if I took a chance and fucked it all up." Teagan rolled her eyes to the ceiling. "I can't believe I'm admitting all this."

Her secrets were like a drug. She'd given me a little something, and I wanted more. Needed more.

My voice was gruff. "Don't be afraid to tell me what you're thinking. I want to know everything, even if I can't do anything about it." I leaned in closer to her on the bed. "I love when you open up to me, tell me things you don't tell anyone else. We've told each other some major secrets. And I think our mutual attraction might be the biggest secret we've kept from each other."

She nodded. "I'm losing my mind a little when it comes to you, Caleb. That's the truth. You make me feel all the things I try not to. Emotional things. Sexual things. I just *feel* so much. That's something I've always worked hard to avoid."

I let my thoughts escape me. "I feel it, too, Teagan. Every damn thing."

"So what now?" she asked. "What do we do with this?"

That's the question. "I don't know."

Sadness washed across her face, and she looked away.

"Look at me," I insisted. "Let me explain." I paused. "With you...it's so much more than a sexual attraction. I admire you and have so much fucking respect for you. I know how rare it is for you to open up to someone, to give your heart to them. I can't imagine letting you give any part of yourself to me because I'm leaving in a few months—not your heart or your body. It's not fair. So I've felt like I needed to resist what's happening between us with all of my might." My control was slipping away. "The thing is, I don't know if that's realistic. Because as quickly as three months will fly by, it's also an eternity when every second I can't kiss you feels like torture."

Her chest rose and fell. The next thing I knew, she'd leaned in and her lips were on mine—wet, plump, beautiful lips that tasted sweeter than sugar, the lips I'd fantasized about for so damn long. And now her hands were raking through my hair.

Groaning into her mouth, I let go, inhaling every bit of her taste, no longer caring about anything but this moment. Then again, I would've told myself anything just to be able to continue. *As long as you don't fuck her, Caleb, everything will be okay. What harm will kissing her do? Kissing never killed anyone. What's the danger in touching her, tasting her?* I was lying to myself, but I didn't give a shite right about now. Not a single bit, now that I knew what this felt like.

Pushing my tongue deeper into her mouth, I couldn't get enough. I needed to taste every inch of her. That thought made me worried that her family might walk in on us. But that wasn't enough of a reason to pull back.

Threading my hands through her hair, I realized firsthand just how much of it she had. I wanted to bury my face in it. I wanted to bury my face in a lot of places right now. Whenever I'd slow the pace of our kiss, Teagan would moan and speed up, as if to tell me I'd better not stop. So I'd kiss her faster and thrust my tongue harder. I did with my mouth what I wished I could with my body. This would have to be the limit.

No sooner than I'd had that thought, I found myself on top of her, pinning her beneath me as our kiss grew even deeper, more intense. My cock was so hard, it felt like it might break in half. Teagan's moans of pleasure were causing me to lose my mind.

Then her leg accidentally hit the end table. The noise scared the living crap out of me, because for a second, I thought someone had walked in. That was enough to force me up to lock the door. Not sure how we would explain the door being locked if someone came down, but it was better than getting caught.

As I returned to the bed, my dick stuck straight up through my gray joggers, still harder than a fucking rock. Teagan's eyes were fixed firmly on my groin, and that certainly wasn't helping the situation. Whatever it was we were doing, I was determined to keep my dick in my pants—where it belonged until I got back to England.

Teagan panted, looking hungry for me. As much as I wanted to resume devouring her lips—and move on to other things—that near-miss was a wake-up call. What if it had been Maura? She and her husband had been so good to me, opening their home and making me feel like part of their family. And this was how I thanked them? By messing around with their daughter? I needed to take a step back.

I returned to the bed, lying back against the headboard before turning to her. "We've crossed a dangerous line."

Teagan's expression bled disappointment. "I'm a big girl. I can handle it."

Running my hands through my hair, I said, "Yeah. Well, I'm not sure I can."

Her eyes brimmed with confusion. "What are you saying?"

"Just that we need to be careful." I pulled on my hair. "I don't even know what that means. I just don't want to fuck everything up by taking things too far."

She looked like she might cry. I was doing a horrible job explaining this.

"Teagan, you're the best fucking friend I've ever had. I've never told you that, but now you know. And there's about to be an ocean between us. I can't complicate your life and then leave. I won't do that to you. You mean too much to me."

That was the most ridiculous statement I'd ever uttered, because this was *already* complicated.

Her face crinkled in torment. "What do we do with the time we have left?"

"I don't know. I'm very confused. We just need to be careful."

"What does that mean?" she repeated.

Fuck if I know. "Maybe study upstairs instead of down here," I said, though it killed me. Our study sessions were my favorite part of the week.

Even as I said it, my hand traveled over to touch her hair. I ran my hands through the strands as she closed her eyes. It reminded me of what she'd done the night I slept in her bed. I'd fallen asleep as she massaged my hair.

I wanted to pull her toward me and claim her mouth again, but instead I leaned in and placed a single kiss on her forehead before forcing myself off of her bed. It might have been the most mature decision I'd ever made.

"I should go upstairs."

She wouldn't look at me as she said, "Okay."

Teagan seemed downright gutted, and there was no one to blame for that but me. I'd kissed her, led her on, and told her there wasn't a chance for us.

Nice work, arsehole.

CHAPTER
NINETEEN

Teagan

I suppose the one good thing about avoiding being alone with Caleb was that we were making a point to hang out together more outside of the house. He'd meet me at the aquarium after my internship and we'd walk around downtown, browsing the stores or getting something to eat.

As for our study sessions, we moved those upstairs to the spare living room, a space no one ever used because there was no television there. It finally had a use—as a cockblocker.

Caleb had also been picking up extra hours at the restaurant. He didn't say why, but I suspected it was to send money home to his mother. I knew he felt like he needed to help with his father's rehab costs. From what he'd told me, though, his mother had been having trouble convincing his dad to get help this time around, so he'd yet to enter a program.

One Saturday afternoon, I thought Caleb was at work, but instead he came to find me downstairs. He stayed in the safe space of the doorway as he asked, "Have any interest in going to Harvard Square this afternoon? I have the day off. Archie and Angela want to meet up there."

I didn't have to think about it. With the days until Caleb's departure dwindling, I'd take any opportunity to hang out with him, especially outside the house where things were "safe."

"Yeah. That sounds awesome. I haven't been there in a while."

"Cool. We'll leave at three, then?"

"Sounds good."

A giddy excitement came over me whenever I knew I'd be spending time with him. Even though we'd discussed setting a clear boundary between us, going out together always felt like a date—minus the physical contact.

Lately, I found myself being very passive aggressive, though. I'd wear clothing that clung to my body, put on a little eye makeup, and do my hair so it was long and sleek. I played up my sexuality, because as much as I knew he was leaving, I still wanted him to want me, and I still held out hope that he would kiss me again. That was an immature and selfish way of thinking, but I couldn't help it. I was completely smitten. I was tempted to tell him I wanted him anyway, even if he was leaving. Would it make me seem cheap to admit such a thing? Maybe I was kidding myself, thinking I'd be able to survive the outcome of that.

Caleb's eyes widened when he entered the foyer where I was waiting at 3PM.

"You look really beautiful," he said.

Chills ran down my spine. "Thank you."

His heated gaze trailed down my body, then up again and lingered on my eyes. "Shall we go?"

"Yeah."

Even walking alongside him made my body react. The entire way to the trolley line, I had the urge to grab his hand. But I didn't. Regardless of how I was feeling, I would never make the first move again. After all, it was me who'd kissed him that night. Technically, he'd never initiated anything.

It was chillier than I'd expected. The temperatures were forecasted to be on the warmer side, but apparently not mild enough to be without a jacket. I hadn't worn one because I didn't want to ruin the look I'd worked so hard to achieve—you know, the look I stupidly hoped would make Caleb lose control. As we waited at the trolley platform, he took off his hoodie and placed it around my shoulders.

"You don't have to do that."

"You're shivering. Of course I do."

"But now you'll be cold yourself."

"I'll buy something at one of those stands in Cambridge. Maybe a sweatshirt that says Harvard on it so people will think I'm an Ivy Leaguer."

Should I tell him? "I got into Harvard."

He shook his head with a smile. "That doesn't surprise me one bit. You're a genius. Why didn't you go?"

"The marine biology program at Northern was a better fit for me. Plus, I didn't get any financial aid and would've had to live there. It was just too expensive. In the end, I made the most practical decision."

"Still damn impressive to be able to say you got in." He pulled the drawstrings of the hoodie I was now wearing. "One of the things I admire about you is that you know what you want, and you don't make decisions just because

186

they seem right on paper. You go with your gut and your passion. You've always known you wanted to be a marine biologist, even though it may not be a common choice. I envy that."

Go with your gut. His words were ironic, because they reminded me of how I felt about him. He was leaving, and he wasn't right for me on paper, yet every moment I was with him felt right, despite the odds stacked against us.

"You'll figure out what you want to do," I told him. "So many people change their minds after college, and many don't end up using their degrees for their chosen career."

He laughed. "You always have a way of making me feel better when I'm feeling like a fuck up. How do you do that?"

I shook my head. "You're not a fuck up. Before you came, I barely left my room. You made me want to come out and live. I'd say you're a pretty good influence."

"Can't say I've ever been called a good influence before. Usually it's the opposite." He stared at me long and hard. "I need more fucking time here," he whispered. "But if I had that, it would only be harder to go."

I understood that to my core.

The trolley arrived, interrupting our conversation. There were no seats, and it was pretty crowded, which made sense since it was a sunny day. That meant more people would be traveling into the city to enjoy the nice weather.

As we stood together in a corner of the car, I remembered again my plan to buy his cologne after he left and spray it on my sheets. At one point, the trolley stopped short, sending me right into his chest. He held me there for a moment, placing his hand firmly on my back, right over my bra strap. Those seconds in his arms felt incredible. I looked up, and he looked down at me. The sexual tension between us was particularly high today.

Please kiss me.

But he didn't.

After he let go of me, even though the moment had passed, the ache of longing remained in my chest.

———

Once we got to Harvard Square, Caleb did as he'd promised, purchasing a Harvard hoodie, although apparently it wasn't for him; it was for me.

"You're the one who should be wearing this proudly. The girl who turned Harvard down. Badass."

Though I appreciated the gesture, I was reluctant to part with my current Caleb-scented hoodie. But when he handed it to me, I put on the new white and burgundy one with the Harvard logo.

He zipped it up, his long, gorgeous fingers grazing my chest like electric shocks.

"It looks good on you," he said.

We met Archie and Angela at a Chinese restaurant in Harvard Square. I knew Archie was coming to the end of his three-month stay in Boston, and given my vested interest in such matters, I was curious about what his leaving might mean for them.

Archie and Caleb shared a Scorpion bowl, and I sipped a Coke. Angela had a glass of white wine.

As we waited for our food, I finally garnered the courage to ask her. "So, I know Archie's leaving soon. What are you two gonna do?"

Angela brushed her long black hair to the side and seemed to shrug the whole thing off. "We'll play it by ear. We don't know if it's going to work long-distance, but I'd like to try." She looked over at Caleb and back at me. "What about you two?"

I felt flushed. "Oh...we're not together." I glanced at Caleb nervously.

"Are you kidding?" She turned to Archie. "I thought you said they were dating."

"No, I said Caleb *wanted* her."

I swore I heard a record screeching.

She cringed. "Sorry. You guys are just so cute together. And the way you look at each other... I assumed..."

I wasn't sure if it was the alcohol going to his head or what, but rather than ignore her comment, Caleb decided to address it head on.

"You're right, Angela. I've made no secret of my feelings toward Teagan. Every moment we're together, I'm trying harder not to want her. But I made a decision not to do anything about it, because I'm leaving soon. She's aware of that."

I was formulating my response when he added, "But many days—*especially* today—I feel like saying *fuck it*, because..." He turned to meet my gaze. "Well, look at her."

My entire body filled with heat as I stared into his eyes, wanting him.

She sighed. "Wow. Repressed feelings are so hot. I'd put my money on you losing the battle, Caleb."

I slipped my hand under the table and found his. He looped his fingers with mine and squeezed. We held hands for the remainder of our time at the restaurant.

I didn't know if Caleb's admission changed anything, but as we walked around Harvard Square that night, I was in sort of a daze, still thinking about what he'd said at the restaurant.

It was close to eleven by the time Caleb and I caught the train and then transferred to the trolley that would take us home.

There were plenty of seats, but Caleb chose to stand in the corner, so I stood across from him rather than sit. We stared at each other more blatantly than usual. His eyes looked almost pained, displaying the conflict swirling around in his mind.

"I want to kiss you so badly right now," he finally whispered.

I gripped his shirt as we swayed from the motion of the train. As I looked up at him, I silently begged for him to give in to his need. He leaned in and let out a frustrated breath before taking my mouth with his. Grabbing his shirt for balance, I felt my legs go weak as I succumbed to his lips. Our tongues collided, and our bodies pressed together. His hands were buried in my hair, which was probably the only thing keeping me from collapsing into a pile of mush on the trolley floor.

His hands left my hair and slid down my back, landing on my ass. The muscles between my legs pulsated as I felt his erection pressed against me through his jeans. I'd never been more turned on in my life. My panties were already wet. The way he worked his tongue around my mouth made me wonder what else he could do with it. And that only made me wetter.

"You're driving me mad, Teagan," he spoke over my lips.

I pushed my mouth against his, eager to taste even more of him, if that were possible. The heat of his breath, the feel of his body against mine was almost too much to bear.

A half-hour must have passed before we realized we'd completely missed our stop. We wound up at the end of the trolley line just as the conductor announced that it was the last car of the night. So we couldn't even take it back the other way.

"I've taken things too far in more ways than one tonight," Caleb said with a laugh.

After we got off the trolley, I wasn't even sure where we were. We sat together on a nearby park bench and held hands, looking up at the stars.

Maura texted to make sure I was okay, and I told her I was safe with Caleb. She didn't ask anything more than that.

Caleb noticed me looking down at my phone. "Was that Maura?"

"Yeah. I told her I was with you and I was safe."

He shook his head at the night sky. "She's gonna hate me."

"That's not true. She loves you." *I might love you, too.*

I moved to straddle him on the bench, and he adjusted so he was no longer pressing into me. But I could still feel how hard he was between my legs.

He buried his face in my neck and whispered over my skin, "I've never felt this way about anyone, Teagan."

His words touched my heart. "Neither have I," I panted, kissing his neck.

He pushed me back a bit so he could look at me. "I'm terrified of these next several weeks. I've tried so hard not to fall for you. But the harder I try to avoid it, the worse it is."

I moved down off of him, opting to sit next to him, and I placed my head on his shoulder.

"I miss being alone with you," I said. "Studying with you in my room, late night chats—all because you're avoiding the possibility that we'll cross the line. But in the meantime, we're losing precious time together before you leave." I turned to him and placed my hands around his face, bringing his eyes to mine. "I'm not gonna break, you know. Even if we lose control, I'll be okay."

He placed his hands over mine, lowering them to his lap. "How can you possibly say that? Are you really that strong? Because I know I will *not* fucking be okay, Teagan."

I felt sick. "At this point, I'm already going to be crushed when you leave. I've been falling for you for a very long time, even back when you were with Veronica."

"Yeah?" He smiled, seeming a bit surprised.

"Yes."

"I never considered staying for her. But for you, I want to stay forever. Before my mother told me about my father's relapse, I went to the school to see if there was a way I could extend my stay. But they told me it wasn't possible, that the program is only meant to be for one year. They confirmed that I have to go back."

"I didn't know you did that."

"Well, even if they had told me I could stay, I'd likely have to go back now. I can't leave my mother to deal with that alone." He blew out a long breath. "It just sucks."

Laying my head on his shoulder again, I said, "It does."

"I want to stay here. Please understand that."

"I know," I whispered.

"I don't want to stay away from you anymore. But we can't sleep together. Alright? I have to draw a line somewhere. But I'm done avoiding you. I want to spend all the free time I have left with you. And I want to kiss the hell out of you every chance I get."

I looked up at him and smiled. "It's a deal."

We fell into another kiss on that park bench and stayed there for at least an hour. We eventually called an Uber to take us home.

I didn't fully understand what difference it would make if we had sex at this point. My heart was already in so deep it was breaking. It didn't matter if Caleb was physically inside of me. He was already inside my heart and soul.

CHAPTER
TWENTY

Caleb

Every day I felt more attached to Teagan, and even though we were spending every moment we could find kissing and touching, I hadn't dared to venture below the waist. There was only so much we could do down in her room anyway with her family right upstairs. Consequently, my dick was so hard most of the time I was certain it was going to combust. I was the holdout, and I kept convincing myself I was doing the right thing, but with every moment we spent together, stopping felt less and less natural.

I'd taken on more hours at the restaurant, but today I had a rare Friday night off. And I really wanted to spend it with Teagan.

She normally got back from her internship about five-thirty on Friday nights. It was five forty-five, so I went downstairs to her room. It was empty, so I lay down on her bed and rang her.

"Hey," she answered,

"Where are you?"

"I have to stay late tonight—until seven. I get to help clean out some of the tanks, though."

"Only you would be excited about cleaning fish shit."

"I never said it excited me, but you know me so well."

"Indeed I do." I sighed, imagining the way she was probably smiling right now. "So you'll be back around seven-thirty? I miss your face."

"Yeah, another couple of hours or so."

"Shit. Alright. I guess I can wait here for you in your bed."

"You're in my room?"

"Yes. It's how I knew you weren't here."

"Don't go searching in my drawers or anything."

"Well, now that you've said that, you've got me curious. Please tell me you have a vibrator or porn in here somewhere."

"How else do you think I deal with my constant pent-up sexual frustration? It has to be released somehow."

Christ. I hadn't been serious, but now I might walk around hard all night.

"I have to go," she said.

"You can't just say something like that and hang up on me." I laughed.

"Goodbye, Caleb."

———

Restless and thinking about nothing but Teagan masturbating, I didn't feel like waiting for her to come home. So I took the train to the aquarium to surprise her. I figured maybe we could grab a bite to eat downtown after her shift.

When I entered the building, I was surprised to see her standing at the counter of the gift shop. A guy I assumed was that Jacob bloke who'd taken her out once leaned toward her, getting way too close for my comfort.

A rush of adrenaline coursed through my veins, though she was merely talking to him. In a flash I saw the future where I wouldn't be around for Teagan, a future where she'd go on to date other guys, fall in love, and have lots of sex—not with me. I couldn't control any of that from an ocean away.

She hadn't seen me yet. *Maybe I should just turn around and go home.* But that didn't feel right. What *did* feel right was interrupting.

"Are you off the clock?" I asked as I approached.

Teagan turned at the sound of my voice. "Caleb."

The smile on her face took away much of my uneasiness. She seemed happy to see me.

"Hi," I said, shifting to glare at Jacob.

"Jacob, this is Caleb."

"Hey," he said, looking like I'd rained on his parade.

Maybe I'd pissed on it. Either way, it was my pleasure.

"Hi," I muttered before turning back to her. "Are you done?"

"Yeah. Got finished early. Let me get my stuff."

As I waited for her, Jacob and I gave each other the evil eye. That stoked the flames of my jealousy.

When Teagan rejoined me, I took her hand and gave Jacob a smug look before we left. It wasn't my most mature moment, but I wasn't thinking clearly.

I waited until we were outside to do what I really wanted to. I backed Teagan against the wall of the building and devoured her mouth, shoving my tongue inside not so gracefully, more possessively. She didn't question it, though. Instead, she opened wide and let me have my way with her. She pulled my hair and moaned into my mouth. And now, finally, I had what I needed to calm my damn nerves.

After a few minutes, I reluctantly ripped myself away.

She covered her mouth. "What was that for?"

I gritted my teeth. "That was me bloody jealous as all hell."

"You know I'm not into Jacob."

"It's not really him that's bothering me—more the idea of him, future guys I won't be able to protect you from because I won't be here." I shut my eyes in an attempt to grab my bearings. "You deserve the world, Teagan. Someone who appreciates how amazingly smart, funny, witty, and caring you are. You're gonna make someone so happy someday."

I hadn't expected to say that, and I didn't like the bitter taste those words left with me. It was unnatural to say them, because I didn't want her with anyone else. I wanted her with me.

Her eyes shone with tears, and she echoed exactly what I'd been feeling inside. "I don't want anyone else. I want you."

What was I supposed to say to that? *Sorry? You can't have me?*

I wanted her so damn badly right now—in every way.

"I just wish we could go somewhere right now," she said.

I brushed a hair off her face. "Somewhere?"

"Somewhere away from everyone. Somewhere we could be alone."

My heart beat faster by the second because I knew I was readying to give her what she wanted. "If we were totally alone, that would be very bad. You know that, right?"

"Yes, I do," she answered immediately.

The raw sexual hunger in her eyes likely mirrored my own. I sometimes treated Teagan like an innocent girl when she was very much a woman—at least, in this moment she seemed to be. She needed me just as much as I needed her.

Pulling her by the hair gently toward me, I growled over her lips. "You want that, don't you? You want me to lose control."

The sounds of the city faded away.

"Yes. Very much." Teagan trembled.

I rubbed my hands over her arms. "Jesus. You're shaking."

"You've been so scared to touch me, Caleb. I'm scared I'll never know what it's like to be with you, that I'll always wonder. We're running out of time, and I can't focus on anything else. I feel like I'm going crazy."

Taking her face in my hands, I brought her mouth to mine again as my heart pummeled against my chest. As our tongues collided, I knew I'd finally reached my breaking point. For the first time since I'd developed feelings for her, letting go felt like the only choice.

When I released her lips, I took her hand. "Come on."

"Where are we going?"

"You'll see," I said.

She followed me down the street, our pace hurried. It was just a short walk to the Marriott Long Wharf Hotel.

When we arrived, I pushed through the revolving doors in a haze. My heart beat out of my chest as we approached the front desk. My ears pounded right along with it.

"Do you have an available room?"

Now it was up to fate. If they didn't have a room, that would be a sign from the universe that this was all a mistake.

The clerk clicked on some keys. "Just one night?"

Thump.

Thump.

Thump.

Was that my head or my ears?

I cleared my throat. "Yes. One night."

"One bed or two?"

I looked at Teagan. "One."

When she smiled at me, I calmed down a bit.

He tapped on the computer some more and then looked up. "Card and ID, please."

This is happening.

I squeezed Teagan's hand, still unable to believe how reckless we were being right now. *What is this life?* One minute I was picking Teagan up for maybe a quick dinner or a movie, and the next we were about to go up to a hotel room and fuck. It felt terribly wrong—yet oddly right at the same time. There wasn't any going back now.

"Here you go, sir." He handed me a key card and went on about a WiFi password and other things that were completely going in one ear and out the other. Who could concentrate on meaningless information at a time like this?

"Thank you," I said as we walked away.

My blood vibrated in my body. You'd think I was about to dive off a board at the Olympics.

Jesus. Why was I so nervous? I'd had sex plenty of times. But never had it mattered the way it seemed to matter now. Never had it mattered at all.

Teagan followed me to the lift, which was empty. When the doors closed and we were alone, I whispered in her ear. "Are you sure you want to do this?"

As nervous as I was, I silently begged for her to say yes.

She looked me straight in the eyes. "I'm sure, Caleb."

I squeezed her hand.

Well, it seems we've finally lost control.

But at least we'd lost it together.

I always carried two condoms in my wallet. I'd never had to use them so unexpectedly, but I thanked God I had them with me right now.

When the lift doors dinged open on our floor, Teagan took my hand as we went down the hallway. A couple of kids wrapped in towels skidded past us, returning from the pool. The bright orange carpet with blue designs almost seemed psychedelic in my continued fog. Perhaps all of my heightened senses were causing a distortion.

I pressed the key card to the door and pushed it open. Teagan was so close, practically stuck to my back as we entered. The heavy hotel door latched shut behind us. Then, everything happened in rapid succession.

We fell together onto the bed, a mess of hormones gone awry. Never more aroused in my life, I was so hard I thought I might explode in my jeans.

"Do whatever you want to me..." She spoke over my lips. "Just don't stop."

The raw need in her voice drove me even further into a frenzy. Teagan lay on top of me as I worked to pull her shirt over her head, no easy feat when two people refuse to break their kiss for even a millisecond. My tongue was so far down her throat, I hoped I wasn't choking her.

Teagan was grinding her pussy over my cock so hard I worried I'd come from the friction alone. I needed to be inside her before that happened.

Lifting my shirt off, I wanted nothing more than to feel her beautiful baps pressed against my bare skin. Her eyes fell to my chest, and I loved the way she looked at me, like she wanted to devour me.

Unclasping her bra, I threw it across the room. Then I unbuttoned her trousers. I used my feet to slide them down before ripping her knickers off. They were drenched.

"You're so wet," I rasped. "I can't wait to feel that beautiful pussy around my cock."

I needed to get the condom on before I was tempted to slip inside her with nothing.

Reaching into my back pocket, I removed the condom packages before unbuckling my belt and tossing it aside. I took off my trousers and slid my underwear down. My cock bobbed forward, and the next thing I knew, I could feel her wet pussy over my throbbing shaft. I ripped the condom package open with my teeth.

I started rolling it over my cock, but Teagan finished the job, sliding her little fingers down my shaft. It was surreal to feel her touching me.

"I need you, Teagan."

"Please," she panted before straddling me.

Someone likes it on top.

Within seconds, I'd thrust deep inside of her, her pussy so hot and wet—welcoming. She leaned down to kiss me, and we remained attached at the mouth as I began to fuck her. I hadn't meant to be so aggressive, but I couldn't control my pace when it felt so good. And she didn't seem to mind.

Someone wake me from this dream where Teagan is on top of me while I am balls deep inside of her. Then she broke the kiss, moving to an upright position. She began to ride me. *Teagan is riding me.* She rode me like there was no tomorrow while her beautiful, full tits bounced. I could've died in this moment and been perfectly fine.

She was completely uninhibited, the opposite of what I'd expected based on her lack of experience. I looked up at her as she thrust her hips, and it was almost impossible to keep myself from coming. By some miracle, I was able to control it.

"You're so beautiful," I murmured, gazing up at her in awe. I fucking loved her in charge. It was probably, in fact, the best thing that had ever happened to me.

No, it was most definitely the best thing that had ever happened to me.

She sped up her movements, and I nearly lost it.

"Fuck, Teagan. Easy, baby."

My hands went to each side of her, trying to slow the pace so I wouldn't come before she did. Then the most incredible thing happened. Teagan's eyes began to roll back at almost the same moment I could feel the muscles between her legs tighten around my cock. I could feel her orgasm on me. It was so intense that there was no question what was happening. And I simultaneously let myself go, coming so hard into the condom that I wondered whether the rubber could contain it all.

When Teagan collapsed on me, her breathing was erratic. We were both completely out of breath.

"I can't believe that just happened," she said against my neck.

I pulled her against me. "You're so fucking beautiful when you come, Teagan."

"I've never come like that. It felt amazing."

Hearing that absolutely thrilled me.

I squeezed her apple bottom possessively. "For someone who's avoided sex, you definitely seem to know what you're doing, love."

"You're the first person who's ever made me want to let go like that."

I cupped her face. "Thank you for trusting me enough to let go."

After I carefully pulled out of her, I got up to discard the condom. I took a moment to stare at her beautiful naked body splayed out on the bed as she waited for me to return. Her long hair practically covered half of her. She looked like a piece of artwork displayed in the finest museum—gorgeously curvy, classy.

"You're astonishingly beautiful naked."

Her eyes wandered over my body, immediately making me hard again. "You're so sexy, Caleb. I've always wanted you. I've dreamed about that body. I feel so high right now."

And with that, my dick was officially ready again.

I crawled over to her and kissed her lips. "What now? Tell me what you want."

"I want you again," she said, blushing.

"This time I want you under me." On all fours, I pinned her beneath me as I positioned my erection.

We fucked several more times in that hotel room. At one point I had to run to the concierge desk downstairs, which thankfully sold condoms. We ordered room service and talked all night—about our fears and dreams, mixed in with a little nonsense. I'd always felt close to Teagan, but now she'd infiltrated my soul in a way that was irreversible.

CHAPTER
TWENTY-ONE

Teagan

It was the worst possible time for him to message me.

Caleb: I want to eat your pussy again.
Caleb: I want to eat your pussy again.
Caleb: I want to eat your pussy again.

The texts wouldn't stop coming. The awful part? I was in church with my parents and Shelley. It was Easter, the only time I ever went with them. Caleb's phone was doing that thing where it sent the same text over and over, even though he'd only sent it once. Thank goodness I'd shielded the screen when I checked the first time. Given where I was, I felt like I should've ignited into flames or something.

After our night at the hotel in the city, Caleb and I had continued to have sex, albeit more quietly because of the need to sneak around in my room. It had been a couple of weeks now. We'd both decided it was better to enjoy the time we had left, rather than force ourselves away from each other. And we were addicted. I knew the chances of getting hurt were much higher this way, but I enjoyed him too much to stop. We enjoyed *each other*. It was the happiest I'd ever been in my life.

Caleb would sneak into my bedroom almost every night and go back to his room before anyone woke in the morning. There was a chance we could get caught, but I wasn't sure my parents would mind if they knew—better Caleb than someone they didn't know and trust. It's not like I wouldn't be having sex if I were living in the dorms.

But this was a lot more than sex.

———

Caleb slowly pulled out of me.

The second I didn't feel him anymore, a coldness came over me. I suddenly felt the past couple of weeks crashing down on us as we lay in my bed that night.

He must have seen that I was coming out of my haze. He pulled me toward him and whispered over my lips. "Talk to me, Teagan."

Looking up into his eyes, I shook my head. "I just...I don't know what we're doing."

He nodded, like this came as no surprise to him. "You're starting to regret it."

"*Regret* is not the right word."

Caleb shook his head. "I knew this would happen. It wasn't enough to stop us from being together, but I knew reality would set in. It was inevitable."

"You have a little over a month left. I thought I could do this with you until the end, but I feel like I'm getting in too deep. It might be time to stop."

He looked pained. "I don't want to leave you, Teagan. I hope you realize that."

"I know you don't." I considered a last-ditch proposal I knew I'd likely regret. It came out before I could change my mind about proposing it.

"There's still no way you could stay, right?"

Caleb buried his face in the crook of my neck and spoke over my skin. "I want to...so badly. I just worry about my mother. I suppose I could drop out and find a way to get a work visa or something—or maybe try to enroll in another program somewhere else. I'm not entirely sure I can do that, or that I'd be able to make it happen in time, though."

The fact that he was even considering staying filled me with what was likely false hope. "Do we have any other options?"

"I should have the answer, but I don't," he said.

"I just can't imagine never seeing you again," I cried.

"Sometimes I feel like I need to do something drastic so we don't have to be apart, but..." His words trailed off.

My heart beat faster as I continued his statement for him. "But?"

"The more I think about it, the more unsure I am that...being with me would be the best decision for *you* right now."

My stomach filled with dread. "The right decision for me?"

He placed his hand on my side and squeezed. "You're so young, Teagan. We both are. What if we turn our lives upside down for each other only to find it was a mistake?"

What was I thinking?

I truly regretted proposing he stay. Caleb not going back to England was a fantasy. He had too much responsibility back home, and we both needed to finish school. That had always been clear to me. It had just gotten clouded by my growing feelings.

"This doesn't have to be the end for us, Teagan. We need to take it one day at a time. Maybe you can take a trip to England, or I can come back and visit."

Visit?

The thought of only seeing him for short visits sounded miserable. It was hard enough now when he merely came home late from the restaurant. I knew deep down I could never handle a long-distance relationship. I didn't want to put that burden on either of us. This just sucked.

"If two people are meant to be, they find a way to be together," he said. "Even if not immediately. But I don't think it's wise for either of us to make any promises."

I felt my heart breaking. He didn't seem confident that we'd ever work out. I knew I needed to make a mature decision before I got hurt.

"Maybe we need to tone this down right now, then."

He swallowed. "You mean, stop sleeping together?"

"Everything."

While he looked disappointed, Caleb nodded. "If you think that's best."

"It's not what I want, Caleb. But we're getting down to the wire now. If you know there's no chance in hell of you sticking around, we should start weaning ourselves off of each other."

"Fuck." He turned to stare up at the ceiling. "That sounds painful. But I get it. I don't ever want to hurt you, and I'm afraid I already have. So if I can avoid doing more damage, that's what I need to do."

I turned his face toward mine. "I don't want you to think I will ever regret getting to experience everything with you. I absolutely won't. It would have haunted me if we didn't have this time together."

"I needed to hear that." He leaned in to kiss the nape of my neck. "This last month is going to be tough."

"Let's just take it day by day, okay? Try to get through it without hurting one another."

His voice was strained. "I never want to hurt you."

I forced a pathetic smile. "I know."

Caleb's brow lifted. "I assume this means I'm going up to my room."

I nodded sadly. "Yes. I think it's best if you do."

Caleb stole one final, chaste kiss before lifting himself off the bed. Even though my heart was broken, I knew this was right.

After he left, I couldn't sleep.

I was devastated.

———

Maura caught me in the kitchen after I went upstairs for breakfast the next morning. "You have a second?"

Opening the fridge, I said, "Sure. What's up?"

"I was thinking of planning something for Caleb's goodbye. Maybe a party or a dinner out? What do you think?"

I paused on my way to the carton of milk. Something about the word *goodbye* hit me hard. I knew he was leaving, of course, but hearing that actual word caused me to burst into tears.

I just wished it hadn't happened in front of Maura. She was already on to me, and now there would be no denying what was going on.

I wiped my eyes. "Whatever."

"Teagan, I know you've been sleeping with him."

I closed my eyes and continued to wipe my face.

"I've heard him coming up from your room in the early morning when he thinks we're asleep."

Not sure why I felt like being candid all of a sudden. Maybe because there was no sense in denying something so obvious. But I also needed to let it out to someone.

"We're not...doing that anymore. We decided to stop, so that neither of us gets hurt any more than we have to when he leaves."

"You care about each other." She smiled sympathetically. "I've always known that."

"I do care about him. So much. But we're trying to be mature. He has to go back to England. That's the end of the story."

She took a seat and gestured to the chair in front of her. As much as I didn't really want to, I sat down.

"I know he doesn't want to go back," she said.

"He doesn't, but that's not going to change anything. He has to. Things are not great back home. His mother needs him, and he has reasons for feeling responsible."

No way was I going to violate Caleb's trust by telling her about his home life. But I wanted her to understand.

"I've always suspected there was something back home that wasn't right."

"Anyway, I don't mean to blow off your idea about a going away party. I just don't know if I can handle it."

She stared down at the table. "Maybe Dad and I will take him out to a nice dinner. That way it can be low key, and you can decide if you want to come. No big goodbye party."

There was that word again. *Goodbye.* It cut like a knife.

I nodded but doubted I'd be able to sit through any kind of event that celebrated his leaving.

"You know..." she said. "When I was around your age, before I met your dad, I had a boyfriend who had to move overseas for a job. His name was Alvin."

"Interesting name."

"Yeah. He was an interesting guy, too." She grinned. "Anyway, we tried to make it work, but eventually it just became too difficult. It was hard to lose him. I remember feeling like he'd chosen the job over me, and ultimately that resentment was what did us in." She sighed. "He was my first love, so I can relate to what you must be feeling."

I wanted to be irritated with Maura right now for prying, but her words had a calming effect. Her relationship with this guy had ended, and eventually she met my father, who I knew she was head-over-heels in love with. *It doesn't have to be the end of the world when a relationship ends.*

"Thank you for sharing that with me."

Still, I refused to open up any more. My feelings were so raw. I'd fallen in love with Caleb and couldn't help feeling like his leaving was an abandonment, even though that wasn't fair and I knew better.

———————

Caleb: This staying away business is fucking hard. (And so am I.)

Caleb and I had been doing a great job distancing ourselves from each other. So I wasn't sure how to respond to his random text without telling him how sad I was. I chose not to respond at all.

Then he texted again.

Caleb: I fucking miss you, Teagan. Don't even respond, alright? I know this isn't helping. But I'm feeling very weak right now, because I'm right upstairs and can't see you, touch you, kiss you, be inside of you. So since I can't do those things, here I am texting you. Which I HATE. Because I can't stop thinking about you. If you take anything away from our time together, I want you to know this: You, Teagan Carroll, are the smartest, funniest, most unique person I have ever met. The weeks where we let go of our fears and allowed ourselves to experience each other to the fullest were the best weeks of my life. I want you to know how much it means that you gave yourself to me. I'm sorry I have to leave. You have no idea how much.

His text hurt my heart. Because as beautiful as his words were, they didn't change the fact that he was leaving. The more minutes that passed, though, the more unnatural it felt not to return his sentiments, so I gave in.

I let go of everything. The floodgates opened.

Teagan: Is this the part where I get mad at you for writing out your feelings instead of talking to me when I'm right downstairs? Didn't you tell me never to do that? (Kidding.) I'm glad you didn't come down here, because I wouldn't be able to control myself. And we know how that would have ended. I don't know what to say to your kind words, except that the pleasure of knowing you and experiencing being with you was all mine. I have no regrets about anything, Caleb. None.

A few minutes later, he sent one more text.

Caleb: <3 <3 <3

CHAPTER
TWENTY-TWO

Caleb

My last days went by in a blur. Too fast. With only three more nights left, the Carrolls were supposed to be taking me out to dinner. I knew Teagan was working late at the aquarium and wasn't planning to join us. And I was fine with that. Or at least I told myself I was. Because I knew it would be hard for her.

About an hour before we were scheduled to leave for the restaurant, Maura caught me blankly staring out the living room window.

She came up behind me. "How are you holding up?"

I turned around and forced a smile, certain she could see right through me. Then I just admitted the truth. "Not well."

Maura placed her hand on my arm. "I'm sorry. I know. Your leaving is going to be tough on all of us. I really do wish there was a way you could stay."

Lorne had run to the store with Shelley, and I'd always been tempted to open up to Maura about my past. We seemed to be home alone at the moment, so maybe now was a good time to do that. It would probably be my last chance.

Bracing myself for the emotions I knew would ensue, I said, "I don't talk about it very often, and I assume Teagan never told you how my sister died?"

"No," she answered, her face kind. "She would never say anything if you told her not to mention it. She's very protective of you."

We moved over to the couch and took seats across from each other. With my head in my hands half the time, I spent the next several minutes telling Maura about what had happened with my sister and how it related to my relationship with my father.

"This explains a lot," she said, placing her hand on my knee. "I understand better now why you don't want to go back home, but also why you feel you need to."

"My entire life, I've felt indebted to my family for what I did."

Maura's eyes were moist. "I'm so sorry, Caleb. This is devastating to hear."

I let out an exasperated breath. "Anyway, I just—I guess I'm telling you because I need you to know just how much it's meant to feel loved and respected here."

Maura wiped her eyes. "Nothing you told me changes how I feel about you—not in the least."

"You sound like Teagan."

"Well, she cares about you very much. And you care for her, too, don't you?"

"I love her."

Those words came out so easily, without even having to think about them. I'd felt those words trying to burst from me for a very long time.

Maura seemed stunned. But it was the truth. I *had* fallen in love with Teagan.

"Please don't tell her I said that," I added. "It will only make leaving worse. I haven't said those words to her because as much as they're true, I don't feel like I'm the right person for her at this point in time. I have a lot of issues I need to work out within myself and my family. I just have too much baggage right now."

"I'm certain she feels as strongly about you. One thing to keep in mind, when someone loves you they'll take every part of you, baggage and all."

I struggled with accepting her statement. "But I also feel like sometimes a person needs to respect the one they care about enough to let them go, to not bring them into their suffering. I need to work out so much before I could ever be the person Teagan deserves." I stared out the window. "She's so incredibly smart and special and unique in every way. Teagan needs someone with his shit together. And I'm not that person yet, Maura."

"I really do hope things surprise you when you get home," she said after a moment.

I knew better. Things at home would be as bad as they always had been, perhaps even worse.

"Thank you for listening," I said.

"Anytime. And I hope you'll come back and visit us. There will always be a place for you in this family."

———

A little while later, Lorne, Maura, Shelley, and I piled into the Subaru and drove to dinner. The Harborside Restaurant downtown was as classy as you could get. There were fish tanks everywhere, and it reeked of seafood—fresh seafood, but nevertheless, it was pungent. The restaurant overlooked Boston Harbor.

I'd worn the one pair of nice trousers I owned, but still felt underdressed.

I ordered the lobster because, well, when in Rome...

Shelley, who wasn't a big seafood lover, ordered steak while Lorne and Maura ordered the stuffed halibut.

The food hadn't arrived yet, and I was buttering a piece of bread when I looked up and saw her standing there. She looked flushed—but beautiful. Absolutely beautiful.

Teagan.

"You came!" Shelley shouted.

Teagan gave a wobbly smile. "Yeah, I couldn't miss it."

We looked into each other's eyes, and I felt my heart clench. Her showing up, even though I knew it was painful for her, meant so damn much to me. Perhaps I didn't realize how much until it happened.

Teagan took the chair next to me. It was as if we had been saving it for her, even though it was clear from the looks on everyone's faces that no one had expected her to show.

"Nice that you could make it, honey," Lorne said.

She looked at me. "I brought a change of clothes to the aquarium just in case I could get out in time."

Maura flagged down the waitress to bring Teagan a menu. Just like she had when we went to dinner in the North End, she ordered the mackerel, which I thought was hysterical, because once again that was what dolphins eat.

"My Dolphina," I mouthed.

She smiled and reached under the table to grab my hand. I linked my fingers with hers. It felt so incredibly good to be touching her again after several days of distance—painful but good.

When the food arrived, we were forced to let go of each other. I suppose it would have been hard to break apart a lobster with one hand, but I was willing to try.

During the meal, everyone mostly ate in silence.

Then, while waiting for dessert, Lorne asked, "So, might there be even a small part of you that's happy to be returning home, Caleb?"

I shrugged. "I've missed my mum. It will be nice to see her. And I know she's looking forward to having me back. But I haven't missed home at all and am not looking forward to returning."

"What's been your favorite part of Boston?" Shelley asked.

Uh, that would be your sister. "That's a tough question, because there have been so many things. But you guys have definitely been the best part of my time here. Your family dinners, your overall hospitality—I won't forget any of it."

To my utter shock, Shelley started to cry. I got up from my seat and gave her a hug. She was such a sweet girl, and I truly loved her. Apparently, she loved me, too.

Teagan looked like she was holding back tears.

Thankfully, the dessert arrived just then.

After we left the restaurant, we all took a walk along the Charles River. I could hardly believe I was just a few days from leaving my new family behind.

The following evening, with two nights left, I decided to make sure I was all packed. I didn't think I'd have the mental energy to deal with last-minute organizing on my final day, so I needed to get everything put away before then.

I wanted a keepsake that would remind me of Teagan, so I took her *Ten Secrets* book and slipped it into my suitcase. I hadn't brought much with me, but I was returning with an extra suitcase filled with things I'd purchased here. The s'mores maker Teagan had bought me for Christmas was also safely packed away.

I knew Teagan was home tonight, and I wanted nothing more than to hang out with her, but I was terrified of what would happen if we did—that we'd undo any progress we might have made by avoiding each other recently.

Then the perfect idea hit me, a way we could be together in a less intimate setting.

A half-hour later, after returning from the store, I ventured down to Teagan's room, stopping short of entering.

She'd been reading a book and closed it when she noticed me.

I lifted the paper bag I was holding. "It's my second-to-last night, and there's no way I'm leaving without making s'mores one more time with you."

I never expected her to start crying. She'd managed to hold her composure—in front of me, at least—up until this moment. My heart felt heavy. I put the bag down and wrapped my arms around her.

I held her and whispered, "I'm going to miss you so much."

After a few seconds, she backed away and wiped her eyes. "Let's do it."

"Yeah?"

"Yeah." She forced a smile. "Let's roast the shit out of those s'mores."

———

Wanting every second of this night to last, I took my time building the fire in the yard. Teagan was quiet as I lit the wood and prepared the sticks. Once the fire got going, we mostly stole glances at each other through the flames while we roasted the marshmallows.

She was the first to speak. "It seems like just yesterday we were out here doing this for the first time."

I handed her one of the marshmallow sticks. "That was the first night you ever opened up to me. A lot has changed since then. I never imagined what an important part of my life you'd become."

She deflected a bit. "What's the first thing you're gonna do when you get home?"

I stared into the fire and smiled. "Hug my mum. Depending on how tired I am, I might take her out for a late-night dinner or breakfast, catch her up on all the amazing things I experienced in Boston. Then I'll go to my room and crash while undoubtedly thinking of you and wishing I were back here."

"I do want to keep in touch, okay? I know we won't be *together*, but I'll always care about you. I will always want to know you're okay—even if it's hard. I don't think I've made that clear."

I smiled, though part of me felt sad. "I can't imagine a world where I never spoke to you again, Teagan. I need to know you're okay, too. Alright? It might be painful to talk all the time, but let's vow to never lose touch."

With that commitment would come the inevitability of seeing her move on without me. I couldn't think about that right now.

Despite making the first s'more and devouring it, I had no appetite for more. As I started to prepare another one, my stomach turned sour at the thought of my impending departure. Plain and simple, being out here was about spending my final moments with Teagan; it wasn't about the damn s'mores.

Putting down my stick, I moved to wrap my arms around her as she leaned her back against my chest. I kissed the top of her head and breathed her in. I wondered if I'd ever feel this peace with anyone else—and wondered if by some miracle Teagan and I might find our way back to each other one day.

CHAPTER
TWENTY-THREE

Teagan

The night before Caleb's departure felt like a bad dream. I wanted to spend his last night with him, but would it be harmful to go to that risky place, knowing he'd be gone tomorrow? Regardless, I kept wishing he would come down to my room. He never did. At the same time, I could've easily gone upstairs. But I didn't.

We'd done an amazing job not crossing the line. When we made s'mores last night, he'd just held me. Then we went to our separate rooms. But the fact remained that I only had this one night. I might never see Caleb Yates again after tomorrow. Was I missing an opportunity to experience one more moment with him? Should I risk hurting myself more in order to be with him one more time?

The longer I sat in bed, the more the urgency in my chest grew. In the end, I knew it wasn't going away unless I went to him. It was past 1AM, and I had no clue if he was even awake.

Grabbing a robe, I tiptoed up the stairs, willing myself to be silent so as not to alert my family. My heart nearly stopped as I peeked up into the kitchen. A shadow moved, but I looked again and realized it was Caleb. We met at the top of the stairs. Apparently, he'd been coming to see me just as I'd broken down and decided to go to him.

We crashed into each other simultaneously. There were no words, just a tidal wave of emotions I could feel emanating from him: longing, sorrow. Our feelings poured from each of us into the other.

Caleb placed his hands around my face and took my mouth in his. Our breaths were frantic, desperate. It felt unlike any other kiss I had experienced with him. Quite suddenly, he lifted me off my feet and cradled me in his arms. Then, he carried me back down the stairs to my bedroom.

As he placed me on my bed, he hovered over me. "I really tried to stay away, Teagan."

Practically unable to speak, I nodded. "I need you tonight."

He buried his mouth in my neck, kissing me so hard I knew there would be marks tomorrow. My fingers raked over his muscular back. He devoured my neck before ripping off my cami and sucking hard on each of my breasts until my nipples were sore.

Desperate to have him inside me, I grinded my body over the heat of his engorged cock.

His breathing became erratic before he gripped my shorts and pulled them down. I worked to slide them completely off my legs. He yanked my panties so hard I thought they might have ripped. He pulled them off before inserting two of his fingers deeply inside of me.

Caleb bit my bottom lip. I was so turned on I nearly forgot how miserable I was supposed to be. He was rougher than usual, but I reveled in his need to claim my body. It made me painfully sad that this might be our last time. That meant tonight needed to matter.

"Please, Caleb," I begged.

He looked at me, his eyes drugged with lust.

"I need to fuck you hard, Teagan. Is that alright?"

Grabbing his ass, I pushed him against me. "Yes. Please."

He lowered his pants, and within seconds I felt his hot, slick cock against my leg. It was wet at the tip, and my legs quivered with the need to feel him inside of me.

"You mentioned once you were on the pill, even though we used protection?" he whispered.

I panted. "Yes."

"Can I have you without a condom tonight?"

Heat sparked through me, and I nodded, spreading my legs as he entered me almost immediately. The skin-to-skin contact took my breath away as he filled me.

"Teagan...you...this feels so amazing. Christ. Being inside of you like this—it's the most incredible feeling ever."

Swallowing his words with my kiss, I moaned over his mouth as he moved in and out of me. I knew we were too loud. Thankfully my bed didn't squeak much, but someone could easily hear us if they came down to the kitchen. I'd have to hope that didn't happen. Being with him tonight was worth the risk of getting caught.

"I never want to forget how this feels," I breathed.

His voice was shaky. "Why the fuck didn't we do it like this sooner?"

I bucked my hips, meeting his thrusts. "Because we're stupid?"

We laughed over each other's lips, and he pounded me harder, as if to punish us for losing any opportunity to have amazing sex like this.

"Fuck, Teagan... I'm losing it," he groaned.

I nodded vigorously, letting him know I was ready, too. Almost immediately, I felt his body quake and the warmth of his cum filling me. Our bodies rocked back and forth together until we came down from the high.

Still inside of me, Caleb showered my neck and breasts with kisses. I'd never felt more loved by anyone in my life, though I knew love couldn't be what this was. He just had me fooled in the moment.

When he finally pulled out, I tightened my grip on him. "Please don't leave me tonight."

"I won't, baby. I promise. I'll be here all night."

Pulling on his hair, I began to kiss him again, and over the next several minutes, I could feel his erection growing for a second round. The muscles between my legs contracted, immediately wanting him again.

And so we made love all night. It was almost morning by the time we fell asleep.

When the light came through my window the next day, it felt intrusive. Today was the day I would lose Caleb, and the sun was a most unwelcome sight.

Caleb stirred and turned to me. He kissed me passionately before he asked, "Are you okay?"

"No," I said.

"Neither am I. And that was the dumbest fucking question ever, wasn't it?" He sighed. "Can we just stay in this spot forever?"

My chest constricted. "I wish."

We lay together until the clock dictated that we force ourselves up.

To my surprise, when we ventured upstairs to the kitchen, it was empty.

I suspected Maura knew we might need some privacy and had arranged for everyone to leave the house for a while. My suspicions were confirmed when she sent me a text .

Maura: Just FYI, we went to the city to the farmer's market. We won't be back until at least ten. Love you.

"Someone texted?" Caleb asked.

"Maura. She said they won't be coming back until ten."

He looked surprised. "Really..."

"Yeah."

A few minutes later, as I buttered a piece of toast at the counter, I felt Caleb come up behind me. He kissed my neck softly, and the hairs on my skin rose to attention.

His erection pressed against my ass, and I felt the need for him again between my legs.

The next thing I knew, he'd lifted my shirt and moved my underwear to the side. He entered me in one rough movement. I gasped at the feel of him inside of me, and with both hands gripping the counter, I closed my eyes in ecstasy as Caleb took me from behind. We'd make the best of these last minutes together. Instead of wallowing, we'd go out with a bang.

———————

Of course, all good things must come to an end, and ours had arrived.

Things were quiet and somber the rest of the morning as my family reappeared and Caleb gathered the last of his things and packed them into my father's Subaru. The entire family would drive Caleb to Logan Airport. As much as I didn't want to say goodbye in front of them, I also figured it might be less painful if I didn't totally lose my shit. So, it would be better that they would be there. I'd have to keep myself under control.

The ride felt surreal. Caleb and I had probably never said less to each other, but there simply were no words to describe how we felt.

When we got to the airport, Maura said, "Why don't we all say goodbye to Caleb at the curb? And then, Teagan, you can walk him inside."

So much for using my family as a buffer.

I got out of the car and watched as Maura hugged Caleb tightly. Tears streamed down her cheeks. My dad patted Caleb hard on the back. Caleb looked almost numb, as if he were just going through the motions of saying goodbye to them. Last was Shelley, who started bawling when he took her into his arms and lifted her up. I felt my first tear fall. Caleb's eyes shut tight, but he didn't cry.

I followed him to the outdoor station where he checked his luggage, and then we entered the sliding glass doors to the airport. Hand in hand, we walked until we reached the point where I could no longer accompany him.

We stood facing each other as he brushed the hair out of my face.

He swallowed. "This is one of the hardest moments of my life."

I closed my eyes and started to cry.

He wiped my tears with his thumbs. "Teagan, look at me for a moment. I need you to know something."

My tears blurred my vision as I looked up at him.

"Don't ever believe you're not worthy. You are, bar none, the most amazing human being I have ever known. I need you to understand that my leaving has *nothing* to do with you not being enough to keep me here. Just the opposite. *I'm* not enough for you right now. I have so many broken pieces. Please never doubt whether you were enough to make me stay. Alright?"

I nodded through my tears. "I know your life back home is complicated. I understand why you have to leave. I just hope you know you can count on me if you ever need me. I will miss you every single day, and I will never forget all of the things you did for me—teaching me the importance of appreciating my family, making me feel beautiful, helping me come out of my shell. I've grown so much just from being around you, Caleb. You might think you're broken, but you helped put me back together."

And there it was. The first tear fell from his eyes, proof of how hard leaving was for him and perhaps my biggest proof—although too late—of how much he cared for me.

Wiping his cheek, he spoke with a strained voice. "Take care of yourself, Teagan." He placed one more long, hard, torturous kiss on my lips before he ripped himself away and headed toward the escalator.

I stood in the same spot watching him until he reached the top. He turned back one more time and saluted me with a kiss. Then he was gone.

CHAPTER
TWENTY-FOUR

Teagan - Three Months Later

Though it still felt warm and summery in Boston, the new school year had started, and it was strange not to have my internship at the aquarium anymore. I was currently applying for a new one next semester. I'd heard about an opening with a research project that involved managing a database of environmental data and creating a photo catalog for various types of whales and other marine life—not the most exciting gig, but it would be something to add to my resume.

I was spending a typical afternoon back in my room after class when Kai came to hang out, as she often did when she got home from school.

"Have you heard from Caleb?"

Why does she have to bring him up?

"No."

"Really?"

"No. We haven't spoken much."

My anger flared. Didn't she realize this was a sensitive topic? Caleb and I weren't supposed to be in *regular* touch with each other. That was never the plan. We were just supposed to not *lose* touch and check in from time to time.

"Don't you think that's odd?" she asked.

"Not really. We're not together," I said defensively. "We decided it would be best not to suffer through a long-distance relationship. I think if we were talking every day and stuff, *that* would be odd."

She didn't seem to buy that. "So that's it? He's just gone from your life?"

I sighed. While I knew things had to be the way they were if Caleb and I were going to move on with our lives, every day that I didn't hear from him hurt. And I hated that I felt this way. But I understood. I understood why he was giving me space—and why I also had to give him space. Aside from the first couple of weeks after he left Boston, I had only spoken to him a handful of times. He always sounded kind of down when we talked, like it made him sad or something. So I'd stopped trying to initiate it.

"It's for the best," I said.

She tilted her head, studying me. "Are you just saying that, or do you mean it?"

"What does it matter? This is the way it has to be. Did his leaving hurt? Yes. But he's gone. There's nothing I can do about it. So I have to try to find a way to move on."

An impish grin spread across her face. "I think I might have just the thing, actually."

"Uh-oh. What?"

"Luke's brother is back living at home. He graduated last year and is staying with their parents for a while until he can find his own place. He's really cute *and* single."

Luke was a guy Kai had been dating for a few months. This was the first I'd heard that he had a brother.

"What's his name?"

"Ethan."

"Okay. Nice name," I said, still uninterested.

"Why don't the four of us go out this weekend?"

I knew that would probably be good for me, but I hesitated. "I'm not sure."

"What's the hold up?"

"I'm just not sure I'm ready to start seeing anyone."

"Okay, but you're wasting time."

"I don't want to rush into anything."

"You're only young once. You can't be hung up on some dude who left for England and is never coming back."

"I never said I was hung up on Caleb. What makes you think that?"

"It's your eyes. You don't see it, but whenever I mention him, they change. I can't explain it, except to say I can see your sadness."

Blowing out a long breath, I realized I might have been more transparent than I thought. Caleb's name felt like a knife to my heart, a reminder that he was out there somewhere, no longer part of my life, and I might never see him again. After he left, I'd realized even more how much I cared about him.

She hopped up from her seat. "I have to run. Late for work. But think about this weekend, okay? I'll send you a link to Ethan's profile so you can look through his photos and tell me what you think."

No way.

I rolled my eyes and pretended to play along. "Okay."

I don't know what made me check Archie's Instagram that night. Caleb's friend was also back living in England now. My understanding was that nothing ever became of his relationship with Angela from Boston. They'd just cut ties, apparently.

Okay, I know why I checked Archie's Instagram.

Kai's bringing Caleb up earlier had opened up some kind of emotional wound. I'd spent the rest of the day thinking about him—more than usual. I knew Caleb never posted much on his own accounts, aside from stupid memes. I'd be more likely to see something about Caleb through Archie's page. I'd checked there before, and most of the time, there were just shots of Archie out and about on the town or various meals he'd enjoyed. But when I checked tonight, I hit the motherlode.

I started shaking as I looked at the most recent photo he'd posted. *My heart.* God, my heart. It felt like it might burst out of my chest. Or maybe it was breaking. My eyes stung with tears. I wiped them away so I could examine the photo. Next to *my Caleb* was a gorgeous brunette with her arm around him. She kissed his cheek as he flashed a sly grin. There was nothing hesitant or regretful about his expression. He didn't look like he had a care in the world. Archie had captioned it: *At least someone is getting some tonight.*

Jealousy mixed with pain mixed with hate roiled inside me. Okay, it wasn't quite hate—because can you hate someone if you still love them? *Three months.* Was one summer enough time to have mourned our relationship?

I felt everything rising up in me, and I barely made it to the bathroom in time to vomit out what felt like my entire soul.

After I came up for air, I noticed my phone was still open to the photo. Exiting Instagram as fast as I could, I threw my phone across the room. My hands trembled. It was an odd sense of despair, because in the back of my mind, I also knew I had no right to be upset. Caleb and I had never agreed to keep our relationship going. He was one-hundred-percent free to pursue anyone he wanted, to do whatever or *whomever* he wanted—and yet I'd hoped he'd pine for me a bit longer. I had certainly continued to pine for him.

But that stopped now, whether I wanted to do it or not.

CHAPTER
TWENTY-FIVE

Teagan - Two Months Later

"**Y**ou okay, baby?"

Ethan and I had just been messing around in my bed. We hadn't had sex yet, but we'd done everything else. Unlike other guys I'd dated before Caleb, I actually found Ethan attractive. We'd been having an amazing time together, for the most part. Ethan worked as a computer programmer in Cambridge. He'd moved out of his parents' house into his own apartment near work, but often came to Brookline to hang out with me when I had to get up early and didn't feel like venturing to his side of the city. He was not only charming and funny, but super patient. He had his shit together, and I really liked him.

Once again, though, I had to explain to him why I'd become closed-off right at the point where it would have seemed natural to have sex.

"I'm sorry. I don't know why...but I'm just not ready."

He looked worried. "You know I'll never pressure you, right?"

"That's one of the things I appreciate about you." I sighed. "I want you to know it's not you, okay? The last relationship I was in hurt me pretty badly, so I feel like I need to go slow this time."

I'd told Ethan everything about Caleb, so he knew exactly whom I was referring to. Even though Caleb had moved on, I still couldn't. Ethan probably wished he could strangle Caleb.

I had to give it to him, though. Ethan was always great about moving on from my awkward rejections.

He changed the subject. "Hey, I wanted to talk to you about something. Luke and I were thinking of going camping up in New Hampshire. What do you think? Just Luke, Kai, you, and me."

"Like in tents or a camper?"

"My dad's camper. It's old, but it has a bedroom in the back, and the four of us can fight over that. There's plenty of room to crash in the main area, though. What do you say?"

I couldn't think of a reason to say no. "That sounds super fun. Yeah. Let's do it."

"Cool." He smiled. "I'll get lots of booze, and we can buy stuff to make s'mores by the fire."

As soon as he said *s'mores*, I totally lost my train of thought. Caleb's face smiling through the flames as we made s'mores in my yard swam before my eyes.

Damn you, Caleb, and your gorgeous smile still haunting me.

Jesus. I felt like I might cry. What was wrong with me?

"Be right back," I said as I escaped to my bathroom, closing the door and leaning back against it. I let myself have one good cry as the feelings I'd been suppressing came out to play for a moment. I grabbed my phone off the sink and did something I knew I'd regret. I looked up Caleb's Instagram. But when I typed in his profile name, nothing came up. Panic set in. Had Caleb deleted his Instagram account? Or had he blocked me somehow? *Why?*

I also checked Facebook, the only other social media account he had. That page, too, was totally gone. *What's happening?* Why would he delete his social media accounts?

If I didn't come out of the bathroom soon, Ethan would think something was wrong. So I returned to the bed and lay down next to him. As he fell asleep, I tossed and turned, obsessing about Caleb's disappearance and feeling like I was losing my mind.

———

The following day, I had to make sure Caleb was okay. So I dialed his number. When there was no answer, I left a message.

"Hey...uh...it's Teagan. Long time no speak, right? Call me crazy, but I need to know you're okay. I happened to be on Insta, and I noticed your account was gone. Your Facebook, too. Just wanted to make sure everything was kosher. Can you call or text me to let me know? Anyway, hope all is well. Bye."

My stomach churned as I spoke, but after I hung up, I felt a ton better. At least I had initiated contact.

———

When two days passed and Caleb hadn't called me back, I felt a little desperate. I'd also tried emailing him, but the only account I had was his university email, and he might not have checked that. I didn't want to contact Archie, but I sent him a DM on Instagram anyway.

> **Hey, Archie! It's Teagan in Boston. Quick question—I was wondering if everything is okay with Caleb. He's not answering his phone and I noticed he took down his social media pages. Just wanted to know if you've heard from him. Thanks! Hope all is well!**

After a few days, my message to Archie remained unread. I wasn't sure if he checked his messages, and I realized I didn't even know his last name, so I couldn't look him up anywhere else in order to reach him.

It had gotten to the point where I couldn't eat or sleep. As a last-ditch effort, I Googled Caleb's mother's name and the address I had for him in England.

I knew his mom's name was Poppy and his father was Lionel. I found a listing for a Poppy Yates at the address Caleb had given me before he left.

That's it.

My heart pounded as I dialed. On the third ring, a man with a deep English accent answered.

"Hello?"

My body straightened, and my heart began to race. "Hi...is this Mr. Yates? Lionel?"

238

"Yes. Who's this?"

I cleared my throat. "This is Teagan Carroll. I'm a friend of Caleb's. He stayed with our family when he was in the States. I was wondering if you could tell me how to get in touch with him."

"Caleb isn't here. He's away for the weekend."

A mix of relief and confusion washed over me.

Okay. He's alive. He's fine. That's all I needed to know.

"Ah, I see. Do you know if he has a new phone number?"

"No. He has the same phone, as far as I know."

Caleb's dad wasn't very forthcoming. Based on how Caleb had described him, this didn't come as a shock.

"I see." Feeling helpless, I pulled on my hair. "Okay... well, would you mind telling him Teagan called? Ask him to call me back when he has a chance?"

"Alright," he said after a pause.

"Okay...well...thank you. Hope you have a nice day."

When he didn't say anything further, I hung up. He wasn't the friendliest person, but at least I knew Caleb was alive and breathing. That was the most important thing, right? And he hadn't changed his phone number, so that meant...he'd chosen not to respond to me?

———

Kai popped open a beer as Ethan worked to light a fire.

It was a beautiful fall night and perfect for camping. We'd spent a good portion of the day leaf peeping; it was peak season for that in New Hampshire. Thankfully, our camper was heated, and even had WiFi, so we were definitely *glamping*. That was the way to do it, if you asked me.

"So, who's gonna get the bedroom?" Kai asked.

"I say we flip a coin," Luke replied.

"I say Teagan and I get it, considering I'm the one driving your ass home tomorrow. That means I need the better night's sleep."

"Somehow I don't think sleep is what you have in mind," Luke cracked.

Ethan's cheeks actually turned a little red. I realized he might not have told Luke we hadn't had sex yet. Probably wasn't great for his ego to admit his girlfriend had been putting off sleeping with him. Kai knew the deal, though, and quickly changed the subject to her sister Andrea's wedding, which was in a couple of weeks. I'd be helping out at the ceremony. Ethan would be going as my date.

After Ethan lit the campfire, I was pretty proud of myself for keeping it together while building my s'more. I'd accepted that Caleb was *choosing* not to respond to me, and therefore I'd decided not to regard him with the sentimentality I once had. In any case, I was happy to enjoy the s'mores rather than cry into them. Small victories.

In the end, Ethan and I won the bedroom in the camper that night. I ended up giving him a hand job and making him come before he could try to have sex with me. I felt terrible about the whole thing. I was starting to hate myself for treating him this way. A man could only take so much. But the bigger question was: why? Why wasn't I ready? He'd given me more than enough time. But I couldn't make it happen. I only hoped I didn't lose a great guy in the meantime.

CHAPTER
TWENTY-SIX

Teagan

Despite having grown more comfortable expressing my feminine side, I still hated having to put full makeup on. But Kai had specifically asked me to wear it for the photos at her sister Andrea's wedding. Andrea had asked me to hand out programs, which meant I'd have to smile and nod a lot. This entire night was going to be out of my comfort zone. Not only did I allow Kai to do my hair in large, loose curls that were *so* not my style, but I'd put on one of Maura's super fancy dresses. I couldn't remember the last time I'd gotten really dressed up.

I opened the drawer where I kept my old makeup, and my heart nearly stopped. There was a yellow envelope amidst the mess of lipsticks and other junk. On the front it said: *Dolphina.*

How long had this been in here? I never opened my makeup drawer. I kept a few lip glosses and an eyeliner on top of the sink, but I guessed I hadn't gone for anything beyond that since Caleb left.

My heart pounded as I carefully opened the envelope and read what was inside.

My beautiful Teagan,

First off, hello again. You're probably wondering why I left this in your makeup drawer, which you never open. I guess I figured that would allow enough time to pass before you discovered this note. Perhaps you were able to get over my leaving by now, and that's why this is the appropriate time to remind you that no matter where I am, no matter how many days or months or years have gone by, I can assure you I have not forgotten you. I can also assure you that I still think about you all the time.

If I've done something to make you think otherwise, please get that out of your head. I hope that by the time you're reading this, you've moved on from me, from the sadness my leaving caused you. But if for some reason you haven't, take this letter and place it close to your heart. Close your eyes and feel me with you. Know that as I'm writing this, I feel so much in my heart for you. And I dare not say that four-letter word, only because it's not fair. That doesn't mean I don't feel it.

I'm confident that no matter where I am or how many months or years go by, what I feel for you won't change. Our lives might change, but I will always carry these feelings in my heart. If you've opened up this drawer for your makeup, maybe you're going somewhere special or out for a night on the town. Whatever it may be, please do one thing for me: don't ever settle, Teagan. Don't EVER settle. You deserve the world. I hope as you're reading this, you haven't grown to hate me, for leaving or otherwise. I hope you remember me in a positive light. But whatever the case may be, know that wherever I am, a part of you is with me.

Fondly,
Caleb

P.S. You really don't need the makeup at all.

I clutched the letter to my chest, once again feeling what he'd told me to feel. *Him.* THIS—this was the way it was supposed to feel. Caleb told me not to settle. I'd been trying to figure out why I couldn't sleep with Ethan. Plain and simple, being with Caleb—knowing what it felt like to give not only your body but your heart and soul to someone—had made it impossible for me to accept anything less.

Even if I couldn't be with Caleb, this letter reminded me what it should feel like to truly want someone in every way. Just reading his words had made my soul come alive.

It wasn't right to keep stringing Ethan along. Whether I wasn't into him enough or I still loved Caleb, I couldn't quite determine. But in any case, Caleb was right. I shouldn't settle. It wasn't fair to me or Ethan.

Obviously I didn't bring it up at Kai's sister's wedding, and then in the days that followed, I put off addressing my feelings with my boyfriend. I did almost everything I could to distract myself from having to deal with the inevitable. Don't ask me why one of those distractions included Googling my birth mother. I'd never considered looking for her, and certainly didn't care to meet her. But suddenly, I became curious. There was no doubt that since Caleb left, I'd felt very lost. Maybe seeking information on her was an attempt to find my bearings? I wasn't sure, but I typed "Ariadne Mellencamp" in the search bar.

My father had said he would support me if I ever decided to find Ariadne. I wasn't looking to meet her, though, just to get more details on her life. But what would I do with that information? If I knew she was alive or where she lived, how would that change my life? I wasn't sure, but hit the search button anyway.

A plethora of addresses associated with Ariadne came up: Miami, Florida, to Los Angeles, California, to London, England. There only seemed to be one listing for her name—same person, just different locales. She was one of a kind, alright, and I don't mean that in a good way.

An image search pulled up a photo of her from six years ago. She was apparently part of some adult dance troupe in Los Angeles. She looked more haggard than I would have thought for someone in her mid-thirties at the time. She had some wrinkles around her eyes. Maybe it was just an unflattering photo—or perhaps she took no better care of herself than she had her abandoned child.

My dad had also mentioned that she loved to smoke. In any case, seeing her was still like looking into the future at myself.

I thought seeing her face after all these years might have triggered some emotion in me. But all I saw when I looked at her photo was a self-centered person who seemed dead on the inside. Perhaps she lived with a lot of regret. Or perhaps the idea of her having an actual heart was just a fantasy I'd created.

The one feeling that did arise from looking at this photo was *love*—not for the woman in the photo, but for the woman who'd picked up all the pieces Ariadne had shattered and left behind.

Shutting my laptop, I ran upstairs in search of her. Maura sat in the living room, writing out some bills at the corner table. I stopped in front of her, and she looked up.

"What's up, Teagan?"

Without saying a word, I leaned in and pulled her into the tightest hug.

"Oh my..." she said, clearly caught off guard.

"I'm so sorry, Maura."

"For what?"

"For being an asshole the past fifteen years."

She gripped me tighter. "Oh, sweetie. I never thought that."

"It just hit me."

"What did?"

I looked into her eyes. "That you're my mother. You've been my mother all along. I resisted it because I was too busy feeling sorry for myself to appreciate the fact that when my birth mother left, God sent me someone better."

Her mouth dropped. "Teagan," she said. "I love you so much."

I responded in the only way that *finally* felt natural. "I love you, too, Mom."

CHAPTER
TWENTY-SEVEN

Caleb

My room was completely dark and the window open, letting in a cool breeze. I'd ruined a perfectly calm evening by opening a can of worms I'd likely never be able to close. Why had I decided to look her up? It was the biggest mistake I could've made tonight.

It had been so long since we'd spoken. I needed to explain things to Teagan. But before I reached out to her again, I wanted to get the lay of the land. I'd hoped to see a glimmer of a smile, some reassurance that she was okay, that she was happy. I got far more than I'd bargained for.

I kept staring at the photo. Teagan had been tagged by her friend Kai in a series of snapshots taken at some sort of campground. She sat between the legs of a tall bloke, whom I'd consider good-looking, but not good enough for her. She was smiling and seemed quite content, leaning back into his chest. To add salt to my wound, in one of the shots, they were making fucking s'mores.

Wow.

As hard as it was to look at these photos, a small part of me was relieved that Teagan had moved on. Unfortunately, a bigger part was shaken to see the proof. That's precisely why I should have never gone online. You'd think after not having social media for two months, I'd have realized there was no benefit to it. My life had been much better without it. And I certainly would've been better off had I never gone back on.

I continued to stare at Teagan's beautiful face in the dark until my mother interrupted my thoughts from the doorway.

"I made potato and leek soup. Care to join me for some?"

Her words barely registered.

"Caleb?" she said after a moment. "Is everything alright?"

With my head still basically in my ass, I muttered, "Hmm?"

"Why are you sitting in the dark?"

Closing the laptop, I stared out at the streetlights. "I meant to turn the light on. But I got a bit distracted, so I stayed in the dark."

She moved over to the foot of my bed. "Everything alright?"

I looked up at her. "Not really."

"You want to talk about it?"

Blowing out a long breath, I debated. I'd never told my mother how close Teagan and I had become. I hadn't wanted Mum to feel guilty about me having to leave the US. At the moment, though, the feelings punching at my chest needed to come out somehow.

"Remember the older girl from the family I lived with in Boston?"

"Sure." Mum blinked. "Teagan was her name, right?"

"Yeah."

"Everything okay with her?"

"She's doing great, apparently." I sighed. "It's me who's not so hot right now."

"Did something happen between you and her while you were there?"

I nodded. "We...were rather serious toward the end."

Even in the dark, I could see the surprise on my mother's face. "You never mentioned it. Why?"

"What was the point in telling you? I didn't want you to worry or feel like I resented having to come back home."

"I remember you saying you and she didn't get on too well when you first moved there. Funny how things can change." She smiled.

"We became very close. For the first time in my life I had a connection with someone that ran much deeper than physical. She and I felt very similarly about our place in the world. We were able to help each other through things." I leaned back against my headboard and crossed my arms. "I confided in her about Emma."

"Really?" My mother's eyes widened. "Well, now I know you trusted her. That's not something you open up about very easily."

I nodded. "Yeah."

"Well, I had no idea, Caleb. I'm sorry you had to end things with someone you cared for. She wasn't able to come to England, even for a visit?"

I'd often wondered what Teagan might have said if I'd asked her to come to the UK. But ultimately, I knew why I hadn't.

I shook my head. "You know the mental space I was in when I first came home. Asking her to leave her life behind to come over here with me when I was a mess— that wouldn't have been fair."

"Fair to whom? I bet she would have gone anywhere you asked if you'd told her you were in love with her." She tilted her head. "Is that what I'm understanding? That you fell in love?"

In silence, I nodded.

"Oh, Caleb." She sighed. "What did you find online tonight?"

I exhaled a long breath. "I saw some photos of Teagan looking happy with some guy. It seems she's moved on. It's what I hoped would happen and hoped would never happen at the same time."

"If you're upset, why don't you call her?"

I laughed almost angrily. "I won't dare do that now. I left her in shambles. She deserves happiness."

"She's only with him because you left."

"Exactly. I *left*. In her eyes, I *chose* to leave her. That's not something she should ever forget."

"A lot has happened in the months since you've been home, son. You should tell her."

"Telling her won't make me any more attractive to her—just the opposite."

"But it will explain why you lost touch, why she hasn't heard from you. Do you really think that you're that replaceable? She probably assumes the lack of communication means you didn't care about her, when that isn't the case at all."

"What's the point? It's not like we can be together. I'm not likely able to get approval to go to the US anymore.

She'd have to dump this new guy and leave everything she knows to follow me—a bloke who's already abandoned her—across the pond. How does that make sense?"

My mother placed her hand on my arm. "Love doesn't make sense, my boy. People have done crazier things for love than move across an ocean."

Pressure built in my chest. On one hand, I knew she was right, and I needed to fight. But the seeds of doubt, of self-loathing, were growing. "I miss her."

"You love her?"

I closed my eyes and nodded. "I do."

"You never told her?"

"Not in those words, no."

My mother looked stricken. "You've spent a good portion of your life trying to punish yourself for what happened with Emma. It's time you stopped sabotaging yourself. If you're in love with Teagan, you should tell her and let her make the decision as to whether she'd like to try to make things work. It's likely she never suggested coming to England because you never gave her the option, am I right?"

"You would be right."

"Why would a girl offer to move for someone who never told her he loves her?"

I didn't have an answer. I'd always told myself I'd find my way back to Teagan. But seeing her happy with someone else made me second-guess everything. Regardless of what I wanted or what my mother believed, I knew contacting Teagan now and disrupting her happiness wasn't the right decision.

So, I wouldn't.

CHAPTER
TWENTY-EIGHT

Teagan

As I stared into the lights of the tree, I could hardly believe it had been a year since last Christmas. It seemed like yesterday that Caleb and I were exchanging gifts down in my room. Playing with the snail necklace around my neck, I wondered what he was doing tonight. Wherever Caleb was, I hoped he was happy.

I knew Christmas was hard for him. I'd been more tempted tonight than ever to contact him again—especially since his social media pages were back up. Whatever had caused him to remove them remained a mystery. The whole thing seemed bizarre, but he'd made a decision to cut ties, and I had to trust he had a good reason.

Since ending my relationship with Ethan, I hadn't dated anyone else. I knew now that I really shouldn't settle. As hard as it was to leave a decent guy, I knew it was the best decision for me and also for him. Ethan deserved a girlfriend who could give him all of herself, something I hadn't been willing to do.

My dad sat next to me on the couch as we waited for the neighbors to arrive for our annual Christmas Eve party.

With an eggnog in hand, he asked, "How's my girl?"

"Hey, Dad."

He tilted his head. "You look down."

"I'm okay. Just thinking about stuff."

"Would *stuff* happen to have an alter ego named Caleb Yates?"

My father was definitely more astute than I'd given him credit for.

"He's crossed my mind tonight, yeah."

"Maura told me you haven't heard from him in a long time."

"Yeah. At first I thought there might be something wrong, but I called his house. His father said he was away for the weekend. Then all the social media pages he'd taken down reappeared. He still hasn't bothered to contact me, so I'm guessing he felt it best to cut ties."

"It's hard when someone you care about does that."

Ah, yes. My father could relate to this feeling. "I know you understand what this is like."

"Yeah." He sighed. "But you know, a wonderful thing came out of Ariadne disappearing. Not only did she leave me with the most beautiful gift—you—but she left the door open for me to meet the true love of my life."

I smiled. "That's true, isn't it?"

"And of course, Shelley became the other wonderful result of that situation."

"It's hard to imagine life without that rug rat." I laughed.

"Yep." He grinned. "Things will work out the way they're supposed to. You have to trust in that."

I really wanted to believe it. "Thanks, Dad. I'll try."

As much as I knew the right thing was to stay upstairs and mingle with all the arriving guests, I found myself going back down to my room for a while, though I told myself I would rejoin them later.

Lying on my bed, I closed my eyes and tried to clear my mind, which had been focused on Caleb all night. Fondling the snail necklace, I ended up nodding off.

I had no idea how long I'd been asleep when my phone rang, waking me up.

The number on the screen was one I didn't recognize. Typically, I wouldn't have answered, except this number was unique: it was a UK number. When that sank in, my heart nearly skipped a beat as I picked up.

"Hello?"

His voice was low and gravelly. "Teagan…"

It took a few seconds for it to register. He'd only uttered my name, but it was the most beautiful sound.

"Caleb?" It came out in a whisper. My voice was weak, my body was weak—everything felt weak.

"Yeah, it's me."

"Oh my God. It's so good to hear your voice."

"It's good to hear yours, too. Merry Christmas."

"Merry Christmas." I put my hand over my heart. "Am I dreaming? Is it really you? I've been so worried."

"You have?"

"Yes, of course. How could I not? You disappeared—except you didn't. I knew you were okay, so I just figured you didn't want to talk to me. But I still worried. I even called your house and—"

"You called my house?"

"Yes."

"When?" His voice took on an edge.

"Several weeks ago."

"What happened when you called?"

"Your father answered. He said you were away for the weekend."

Caleb let out a long breath. "Fuck. I'm sorry. There's so much I have to tell you, Teagan."

My voice cracked. "Why didn't you return my call to your cell? That was the reason I called your parents' house."

"I didn't get your call, love."

"You didn't?"

"No. My phone was lost after a very drunken night. I never got it back. I never knew you called me, and my father never told me you called the house." I could feel his frustration over the line. "Teagan, I'm so very sorry you were worried about me. Do you have some time to talk? I know your holiday party must be happening."

It was laughable to think I would ditch this phone call for the party—or anything else in the world.

"Caleb, there's nothing more important right now than talking to you. Please tell me what happened."

"Alright." He paused. "When I first got back to the UK, I was in a bad place. Not only was I missing you, but my father's drinking was out of control. We fought constantly. I handled it by leaving the house, going out every night, getting plastered, and trying to forget what was happening at home."

My stomach sank. "Oh no."

"It was the worst possible thing I could've done, and so irresponsible."

In silence, I let him continue.

"One of those nights, I came home and found my father getting physical with my mother. I lost it and intervened. The neighbors called the police, and my father accused me of assault. My mother refused to tell the police my father had been attacking her because she didn't want him to go to jail. So she told them he and I had argued, that it was a family issue."

"Shit."

"Things only got worse after that. I couldn't live under the same roof with him. I was a mess, and my own drinking got out of control, I'm ashamed to say. I ended up getting into a fight with someone at one of the clubs here. I was arrested and held for a few days until my mother could bail me out. That was the lowest point. I realized then that I needed help—not just for my drinking but for all the issues that led to it."

"Wait. You were arrested?"

"Yeah. But instead of jail time for assault, I was sentenced to community service and a stint in rehab. I spent two months in a facility that not only treats substance abuse, but also its underlying issues. When you get there, they take your phone. I had just replaced the old one when they took the new one away. They don't want you having outside distractions. And I deactivated my social media accounts to make it easier during that time. Everything happened so fast. I didn't want you to worry, so I chose not to tell you any of what was happening. But I neglected to consider that you might notice my accounts missing. I didn't know you were alarmed. I'm so sorry, Teagan."

Holy shit. He was right that I would have been worried, but here I was thinking he'd been having the time of his life and had chosen not to contact me.

"Oh my God, Caleb. This explains everything. It all makes sense now. I thought you didn't want any contact with me because you'd moved on. I saw a photo of you on Archie's page. A girl was kissing you, and I just thought—"

"What? Fuck. Teagan, that meant nothing. That was just some girl at the pub. I don't even know who she was. I swear, nothing happened. We were out, and she was hanging all over me. Archie must have snapped a picture. I was drunk, but not too drunk to realize where I was and what I was doing. I haven't been with anyone sexually since you, never took things that far."

He hasn't slept with anyone?

It felt like I'd let out a breath I'd been holding since our conversation started. I could feel tears forming in my eyes—a mix of relief and utter sadness for all he'd been through.

"Wow."

"It's so good to hear your voice, Teagan."

I wanted to jump through the phone. My skin crawled with an intense need to see him.

"You're better now? The program helped?" I asked.

"I'm sober, yeah. And the therapists there did delve into my past a lot, my issues with my dad. I wouldn't say I'm fixed, but talking about things with a professional on a regular basis has definitely helped. I still have work to do, though."

"I'm so proud of you."

"Anyway...my therapy is sort of related to the reason I'm calling."

My heart raced. "Okay..."

"I needed to work on myself before I could begin to truly give myself to anyone. Part of why I didn't fight harder for us before I left was because I didn't feel like I deserved to be happy, or that I deserved you." I heard him take a deep breath. "Are you happy, Teagan? Be honest. I know you're with someone."

With someone?

"I'm not...with anyone. What made you say that?"

"You're not?"

"No."

"But you were. I saw a photo online."

"For a couple of months, yes. But I broke it off with him after I found your letter in the makeup drawer, and it reminded me that I should never settle. He was my boyfriend for a while, but we never had sex," I added.

"Wow. I just assumed..." Caleb sighed. "So let me get this straight... The guy in the photos Kai posted from the campsite—you're not with him anymore?"

"I broke up with him."

"You're single."

"Yes."

"Hang on a second."

There was some fumbling, and then I heard Caleb yelling away from the phone. "Yes!" It seemed to echo. He did it again. "Fuck yes!"

"Oh my God. Did you just scream outside? I heard it echo."

"Absobloodylutely, Teagan. If you had said you were happy with some other guy, I might not have told you what

I am about to say. I might have kept it inside forever. And that might have killed me. But the truth is, now I can say it—and I have so much to say."

I sniffled. "Say it, Caleb. Please, say it."

"I've been staying away from contacting you because when I logged back into my accounts and saw you tagged in those photos, I believed you were happy. I didn't want to disrupt your life, because that wouldn't have been fair. So I stopped myself from calling you. But not reaching out to you has been slowly eating away at me. I asked the universe to give me a sign that I should bite the bullet. I never thought I'd get it, but I finally did."

"What was it?"

"Well, I should back up a bit. My father moved out. It was a long time coming. He's living with one of his brothers now, but that's a story for another day. Anyway, I confessed to my mother recently how miserable I'd always been through the years at Christmas. This year, it's just the two of us, and we decided to do something we've never done: take a drive to Nottingham and stay somewhere else, maybe get some takeaway and enjoy each other's company away from home and all the bad memories there. I'm calling you now from Nottingham, actually."

That made me smile. "Your mom is with you?"

"She's upstairs in the room. I'm outside the hotel at the moment. I came out here to call you. Anyway, all day I've been thinking about last Christmas, how amazing it was to spend it with you and your family. All day I've wanted call you. But I still hesitated."

"What finally made you do it?"

"My mother and I started looking at the hotel's listing of nearby restaurants, and a lot of them weren't even open tonight, but there was one Chinese place that was: Bo Cheng's. Bo Fucking Cheng's, Teagan! I swear."

"Oh my God." I laughed hysterically. "Oh my freaking God! How is that possible?"

"In that moment, I knew I'd received the sign I needed, and I had to call you, even if it meant disrupting your happiness. Because there's so much I need to say." He exhaled. "First off, I love you. I love you so much. I never said it because I was afraid, but I've loved you for a very long time."

I closed my eyes and let that sink in. My voice cracked. "I love you, too."

"Listen, I'm likely stuck here in England because of my arrest record. It's now going to be very difficult to get a visa to come to the US. So, I have to ask you a question."

"Okay..."

"Would you be willing to come here? Whether it's after the school year, after you graduate, or just whenever you can—assuming I can't get there—I don't care. I'll find a way to pay for your ticket."

Emotions flooded through me, but I had no doubt about my answer.

"Yes! Yes, I will. Of course."

"You mean that?"

"Yes. All you had to do was ask. I don't even have to think about it. We'll figure something out."

We were going to be together again. And there it was: the best damn Christmas present I could have received.

———————

Now that I knew Caleb wanted me in England, I couldn't get there fast enough. The day after our phone call, I told Maura and Dad about everything Caleb had told me and my plans to travel to London at the end of the school year.

Then the following week, I went to the student services office to inquire about transferring for my last year to their partner university in London. I'd definitely have to finish my junior year here, but they said they'd look into it for me. Basically, it would be the opposite of what Caleb had done. If it wasn't possible, I'd take time off or figure something else out. It didn't matter, as long as we could be together. There was nothing I wanted more than to be with Caleb.

Caleb wanted to pay for me to get there, but he and his mother had depleted their funds paying for rehab. I didn't want him to have to sell his soul for my ticket. Anyway, I needed not only travel money, but a means to stay in England. And I was determined to get both. As of now, I could stay in the UK for up to six months without any kind of special visa. We'd have to wing things beyond that. I had some savings, but that wouldn't even cover the cost of my plane ticket. I'd started spending my free time researching work possibilities in the UK online.

Maura came to find me in my bedroom after I'd returned from school.

"Hey. I came for an update," she said. "Did you have any luck in talking to Northern about transferring next year?"

"They said they needed to talk to some people at the university in England to see if it would be a possibility. So I have to wait."

"Do you think you'll go even if you can't transfer?"

"Yes. I know that for a fact. I only have a year left, and I could always come back and finish later or figure something else out. I can't last another year away from him now that I know he wants me there."

"That's very romantic." Maura smiled. "And there's something I'd like to give you, Teagan, to make this easier."

I sat down next to her. "Okay..."

"I had planned to wait until you were a bit older, but I feel like this is the right time."

Maura pulled a small box from her sweater pocket. "Before I show it to you, I should preface this by saying that I think your father was completely insane when he bought this. But everything works out for a reason."

"What is it?"

Maura opened the box, revealing a large, square diamond that looked fit for a queen. It had smaller diamonds all around the center stone. It was breathtaking.

"Did my father buy that for you?"

She shook her head and chuckled. "No."

"No?" My forehead crinkled in confusion.

"He bought it for Ariadne."

My jaw dropped. "What?"

"Yeah. It was a last-ditch effort to get her to stay. She wore it for a while, but gave it back to him before she left. At least she had the decency to do that. To this day, I'm still shocked she didn't keep it."

My mouth dropped. "You want to give this to me? I'm not sure I can take this."

"Oh, yes you can." She looked down at the ring. "Listen, after your father and I were in love, he showed me this ring and told me we would sell it and pick out something else. At that time, we'd just gotten on our feet financially, so it didn't make sense to spend that money on myself. Still, it also didn't feel right to trade it for cash, either. So I asked him if it would be okay if I saved it— either for you or for a rainy day if the family ever needed it."

"He was okay with that?"

"You know your dad. As long as I was happy... He let me hold it for safe keeping. I always knew in my heart I'd give it to you because it was the last thing Ariadne left you—the only thing she left. This ring never seemed like mine. In my mind, it was always yours."

I stared at the sparkling diamond. "Wow."

She smiled. "So, what I'd like you to do is sell it and use the money to pay for your ticket to England and living expenses for as long as the money lasts. A ring like this should represent love. In selling it, you'll be able to be with the one you love and have money to support yourself for a while."

So overcome with emotion, I could hardly speak. "Are you sure?"

"There's nothing I have ever been more sure of."

I took the diamond and held it in between my thumb and index finger. The overhead lights reflected into the stone. It was gorgeous. But it was so...gone. So freaking gone. I needed that money, and I wasn't going to fight it. I'd owe Maura big time.

I wrapped my arms around her. "I'll never be able to repay you for this."

"No need. As I said, this has always been yours anyway. Knowing you'll get to be with Caleb makes me so happy. That's worth more than this ring could ever be."

CHAPTER
TWENTY-NINE

Teagan

Even though Caleb and I talked on the phone almost every day now, it wasn't the same as getting to be with him. The remainder of the school year progressed slowly and painfully. What got us through was knowing each passing day brought us one step closer to being together. But it was finally over.

I hadn't been able to get into an exchange program through Northern University, so I'd decided to take the next year off to figure out my life. That started with hopping on the first plane to the UK once classes ended.

"Can you take me in your suitcase?" Shelley asked.

It was two days before I was set to leave for England, and I had a long way to go with my packing.

I smiled. "You know, I never thought I'd say this, but I really wish I could."

Sometimes you don't appreciate something until you're about to lose it. My sister and I had grown a lot closer over the past year. She'd come to my room to talk about boys she had crushes on. I'd helped her with her homework. Sometimes, she and I just chatted about random things. But we were part of each other's lives. And now, after we'd finally found a groove, I was moving to England for at least six months.

"I'm gonna miss you so much." Shelley tried to sneak something into my carry-on.

"What's that you just put inside my bag?" I asked her.

"It was supposed to be a surprise." She fished it out and handed it to me.

It was a silver bracelet that said *sister* and had two intertwined hearts on the charm. My heart swelled.

"You know, it should be me giving you a present, not the other way around. So often you've been a better sister than I have," I told her. "I owe you a lot of lost time, and now I'm leaving."

She hugged me. "It's okay, Teagan. Just send me pictures and special candy we can't get here or something."

I squeezed her and chuckled. "That's supposed to make up for years of being a crappy big sister?"

She shrugged. "Are you coming back?"

"I hope so. But I don't know what life has in store right now. I'm just going to see what happens."

———

My flight was a red eye, so it was approaching everyone's bedtime when we got in the car to drive to the airport. My parents had been amazingly supportive, so it surprised me when my dad seemed nervous on the way.

"I can't believe I'm supporting my daughter dropping out of college," he said. "I must be nuts."

Maura placed her hand on his knee as he drove. "No. You're not nuts, just an old romantic."

"I promise to finish school, Dad," I said from the backseat. "I just need to do this right now."

"You promise that if things aren't going well there, you'll come right back?" he asked.

"Yes. Of course. I'm not gonna stay anywhere I'm unhappy."

I had no idea how things were going to go on Caleb's turf. My parents provided a safe and loving environment with no stressors. In London, I'd be living with Caleb and his mother. I had no clue if she would like me; I'd only spoken to Poppy Yates briefly over the phone. There were so many unknowns. But this trip would make or break Caleb and me.

When we arrived at the airport, my parents and sister exited the car to bid me adieu at the drop-off platform.

"You give Caleb a big hug for us, okay?" Maura said, tears filling her eyes.

"I will. Thanks for everything, Mom. I love you."

She squeezed me tightly. "I love you, too."

Next my father took me into his arms. "Sweetheart, remember I'm just a phone call away. You get on the next plane home if you're anything less than over the moon there. Okay?"

"Okay, Dad. I promise I won't hesitate to come back."

Shelley was full-on bawling when we embraced. "I love you, Teagan."

"I love you, too, Shell Belle."

During our hug, I reached into my pocket and took out something I'd bought her. It was the same bracelet she'd given me, except in her favorite metal, gold.

"Now we have the same bracelets to always look down and think of each other."

She placed it around her wrist. "Thank you, Teagan. I wanted to buy myself one when I got yours, but I couldn't afford it."

I jingled the charm on my matching bracelet. "Thank you for mine. I'll wear it all the time."

"Me, too," she said as we hugged again.

I blew my family one last kiss before walking through the sliding glass doors. As I made my way up the escalator to the gate, butterflies swarmed in my belly. It was just me now. *Wow. I'm really doing this.*

———

After I made it through customs at Heathrow, I looked around frantically for signs of Caleb.

When I finally found him, he was holding a bouquet of...I wasn't sure. *What is that?*

We rushed forward as if in a race to get to each other.

Caleb wrapped his arms around me before I could figure out what he was holding. Not that it mattered. I wanted to be wrapped up in him like this forever. His familiar smell engulfed me, and he squeezed me so hard, I thought I might break. It felt so good to be in his arms again.

"I feel like I've been holding my breath for a year," he said against my ear.

When he finally let me go, I got a look at what he was holding.

I covered my mouth. "Oh my goodness. What did you do?"

"It's a charred marshmallow bouquet." He flashed a crooked smile.

He'd wrapped a purple ribbon around a bunch of toasted marshmallows on sticks.

"That has to be the most creative thing I've seen in a long time."

"Only the best for you, my love."

He handed me the bouquet before pulling me in for a deep kiss. We stood for an indeterminate amount of time in the middle of the crowded airport, sucking face, completely oblivious to the crowd of people around us.

"Can I tell you something?" he whispered.

"Yeah?"

"I'm so fucking nervous."

"Why?"

"Because I want things to be absolutely perfect for you here, and I know they won't be."

"What do you mean?"

"I want you to be comfortable. Our flat is small, Teagan. It's nothing like your house back home."

"Please don't worry about that. You know it doesn't matter to me."

"I know. I'm just not sure you realize how different things are going to be."

Unsure how I could convince him, I spoke louder. "I don't care about that, Caleb. I came here for you, not for the roof over my head or anything else. I don't want anything but you."

He let out a long breath before reaching over to place one more kiss on my lips. I'd thought I'd never be with him like this again. That seemed unfathomable now.

Caleb's neighborhood in Stratford was really cute. It was a market town with over eight-hundred years of history and happened to be where William Shakespeare was born. It was apparently easy to get to and from London from where he lived. The downside was that it wasn't the safest area at night. Caleb made it clear he wouldn't trust me walking alone after dark. I wanted to tell him his concerns were probably unwarranted, but then again, I hadn't listened to Maura when she'd warned me about Syd's Theater and look what happened.

Caleb and Poppy's second-floor apartment was inside a narrow brick house. My heart pounded as Caleb helped me carry my bags up the stairs to their place.

As soon as the door opened, Caleb's mother came rushing toward us.

"My goodness, you're back faster than I thought. I wanted to put some makeup on." She reached out to me. "Teagan, welcome."

As we hugged, I said, "It's so amazing to finally meet you, Mrs. Yates."

"Please call me Poppy," she said.

Caleb looked a little nervous as he stood with his hands in his pockets, observing my interaction with his mother.

A few moments of awkward silence ensued as his mother took me in. I couldn't tell what she was thinking.

Stupid American girl?

Boy, I would think my son could do better?

So, this is the girl who wanted to steal my son and keep him in the US?

Then she finally said, "I can see why my son is so smitten with you. You're absolutely lovely."

Caleb smiled over at me. I didn't know what to say, but relief flooded through me.

"The feeling is mutual," I said. "And you're lovely as well."

"I made some lunch, if you're hungry," she said.

The only thing I was really hungry for at this point was Caleb. But given that we were now home with his mother, I had no clue when we would be able to properly "reunite." But I knew I should eat, and there was no way I could refuse her offer.

"Lunch sounds wonderful."

I followed Caleb and his mother into the small kitchen. A large pot of something was boiling on the stove. Through a window leading out to a fire escape I could see a clothing line with various shorts and shirts blowing in the wind. Then next to the sink was the washer.

"There's the famous kitchen washing machine I've heard so much about."

His mother seemed confused. "What's that?"

"Mum, would you believe in the States they have a designated room for laundry? It's brilliant."

She laughed. "I hope being here isn't a rude awakening for you, Teagan."

"Your place is cozy and intimate. I spend most of my time down in my basement bedroom back home anyway, so this is just my speed."

Caleb seemed unable to stop staring at me. I, of course, noticed this because I couldn't stop staring at him.

When his mother turned to tend to the soup, he mouthed, "I want you."

He looked ready to devour me, which caused a stir in my body.

"I want you, too," I whispered, certain my face must have turned fifty shades of red with his mother right there.

She interrupted our flirting when she approached the table holding two steaming bowls.

"Smells delicious."

"It's my mum's famous potato and leek soup."

"I can't wait to try it."

After we finished the wonderful soup, Caleb's mother boiled some tea and put out cookies. She was doing everything in her power to make me feel comfortable, which I appreciated.

The topic of conversation turned serious during our tea, though.

"You've come an awfully long way, Teagan—uprooted your life. That's a testament to how much you truly care for my son."

"There's no place I would rather be," I told her. "Caleb made a huge impression on my life in a short amount of time—not only in what he taught me about appreciating what I have, but the way he's persevered through many tough things, always wearing a smile when I know it's not always easy for him."

His mom nodded. "It's been a tough year in this house. My husband and I are estranged for the first time in years, and Caleb going to rehab was not something we saw coming. It's been very hard. But seeing the look on his face when he found out you were coming to England—that's something I'll never forget."

I reached for Caleb's hand under the table. "Thank you for sharing that. It only solidifies for me that being here is right. All he had to do was ask, honestly."

I hadn't expected to feel so at home here, and I must have been more relaxed than I realized as a huge yawn overtook me.

"You must be tired from the trip," Poppy noted.

"Yeah, I definitely am."

I had no idea where I was going to be sleeping. Caleb and I hadn't discussed it. The apartment was small, so there weren't a lot of choices.

I decided to bite the bullet. "Where will I be sleeping?"

Caleb looked at his mother and back at me. "With me."

"We don't have a lot of space," Poppy added. "And I'm not born yesterday and thinking having Caleb sleep on the couch will change anything that happens when I'm not here." She smiled. "Just be careful and hold my boy at night if he has a nightmare."

Wow. "I promise I will."

When I started to clean up, Poppy shooed me away.

"You go rest. I've got this. You'll have plenty of time to help over the next six months." She winked.

Caleb took me by the hand and led me to his room, which was thankfully on the opposite side of the house from his mother's bedroom. That would make things a little less awkward.

The décor in Caleb's room was simple, and it was clean. Like in his room back in Boston, he had workout equipment lying around. The window that overlooked the street was cracked open. The bed was full-sized with a gray blanket on top, and a burgundy throw rug lay on the floor.

Caleb sat down on his bed and gestured for me to come toward him. He buried his face in my abdomen, kissing softly over my shirt before lifting it off of me and returning his mouth to the bare skin of my stomach.

"I've missed this body so much." The feel of his words vibrating against my skin sent shockwaves through me.

Looking down at the massive bulge straining in his jeans, I felt the muscles between my legs twitch in anticipation. I couldn't wait to feel him inside of me again.

Caleb continued to slowly undress me, taking his time as much as I wanted him to hurry.

"We need to be very quiet," he whispered.

The last thing I wanted was his mother to hear us having sex. It was bad enough she knew damn well what was going on in here. But nothing could have stopped me from needing to have him right now.

When Caleb lowered my pants, he noticed my lacy underwear. He'd never seen me in something like that, but I'd bought them in case I ended up in this very situation upon arrival.

"Fuck, Teagan. Are you trying to kill me right here and now with these knickers?"

He sat on the edge of the bed and unbuckled his pants before pulling them off, along with his underwear. His beautiful, hard cock sprung free. It glistened at the tip, so ready. I had the urge to lick it, so I knelt and took him into my mouth.

Caleb let out the sound of starvation being satisfied, a low, sexy groan. "Fuuuuck," he added after a moment. "You need to stop that."

I knew if I continued, he would come, so I let him go, because I really needed him inside of me.

I marveled at his perfect body, which was even more carved than before. I still couldn't believe he was mine. When I'd first met Caleb, he'd seemed so out of my league, the idea of being with him like a dream.

He flipped me around and rested his weight over me. We'd had sex several different ways in the past, but Caleb seemed to like being dominant, which made that my favorite position, too.

He spread my legs and pushed inside of me slowly until he was balls deep.

The sound I made must have been a little too loud, because he placed his mouth over mine. "Shh, baby. Shhh."

"Sorry," I whispered.

Caleb began to move slowly. It was intense, and I could tell he wanted to move faster and harder, but the bed would most definitely have made too much noise. Having to hold back was excruciating. With every thrust into me, I wanted him more and more, harder and harder. After I started to grind my hips a certain way, Caleb lost control.

"Shit," he groaned, and I felt his warm cum spill inside of me. "Christ. I love you, Teagan. I love you so much."

"I love you, too," I said as an orgasm ripped through me.

It was the first time he'd told me he loved me in person, and with that, I knew I was exactly where I needed to be.

CHAPTER
THIRTY

Caleb

Waking up to the sight of Teagan in my bed was definitely weird—but in a good way. She'd been absolutely knackered last night, so I quietly got up without waking her to let her sleep in.

My mother was in the kitchen, sipping tea as I entered.

"Morning, Mum." I scratched the scruff on my chin.

She set her cup down. "How are things?" Her expression held a bit of a smirk.

It was definitely awkward as fuck that she knew Teagan and I had been shagging in there last night. But I suppose the sooner we got used to this arrangement, the better.

Still, I couldn't quite make eye contact. "Things are good."

"She's very sweet. I look forward to getting to know her better—without smothering her. Don't worry. I remember what you said about her needing her space. Lord knows we don't have a lot of it. I'll let her come to me."

"Thank you," I said. "I appreciate that."

Sitting down, I grabbed one of the breakfast biscuits my mother had baked and poured some tea from the pot on the table.

As happy as I was that Teagan was here, we had a lot to work out. I was set to re-enroll in classes this autumn, and she needed to find work, or at least something to keep her busy while she was here.

One of my uncles owned a flower shop and had promised a job for her. That was far from exciting, but at least it would be something. I prayed she didn't resent the fact that I was returning to school while she couldn't right now. She'd essentially hung her life up for a while to be with me, and I hoped she didn't regret that.

There was also something else bothering me, something I'd been keeping from her. I didn't know when the right time to divulge it would be. Now was too soon. She hadn't even acclimated to being here yet. At the same time, it couldn't wait too long.

"Are you stressed?" my mother asked. "Just take it one day at a time. She came for you, not for any other reason."

"I still struggle sometimes, Mum—feeling like I don't deserve to be happy."

She nodded. "It's hard to break out of the habit of destructive thinking. Maybe you need to stop worrying about whether you deserve something and just accept it as a gift."

"What if I slip up again?"

"You mean start drinking?"

"Anything—push her away, start drinking again, just mess up somehow. She came all this way. I don't want to fuck it all up."

"You realize that questions starting with *what if* are futile, don't you?"

I blew out a breath. "Yeah."

My mother had been so supportive. I knew it wasn't easy for her to be living away from my father after all these years, and wondered if it was only a matter of time before he ended up back home again. That was definitely not something I wanted while Teagan was living with us.

"Do you think you and dad will work things out?"

My mother looked away. "Over the past few months, I've learned it's possible to love someone and not be able to have them in your lives. Things were toxic for so long, and I'd just accepted it. Deep down, your father has a good heart, but he doesn't know how to deal with his own child. And to be frank, you're more important to me than he is." She sighed. "There are lots of other things that made it impossible to live with him, too—like the way he treated me. So right now, I think it's best if things stay the way they are."

My mother's happiness mattered to me more than my own, more than anything. If she was happier with my father not living here, I needed to accept that—and perhaps be grateful for it.

"It's a new era for us, Caleb." My mother reached across the table for my hand. "You know it's okay if you're not perfect, right? Even if you handle things wrong from time to time, as long as you treat the people you love with respect, most of the time they won't leave if they love you back. Your father stopped respecting me. And that's why I had to leave him."

I nodded. "Understood."

It made me proud that my mother had the courage to stand up to him.

After I drank my tea, I went back to my room to see if Teagan was still asleep. To my surprise, she was standing in the middle of the hallway, wrapped in a towel after having apparently come from the shower. Water droplets streamed down her arms, and her hair was damp. I wanted to rip the towel off of her, but that wouldn't have been wise.

She'd been standing in front of a photo of Emma and me taken when we were toddlers. My mother had taken down most of the photos of Emma over the years so as not to upset me. But as part of my most recent therapy, we'd been advised to put some back up.

Teagan held her towel closed over her breasts as she continued looking at the photo. "I'd never seen her before."

I placed my hands on her shoulders as I stood behind her.

Expelling a long breath, I said, "That's my beautiful sister, Emma Louise."

She reached up to touch my hand.

My mother came down the hall to get to her room and saw us standing there.

"You've found my Emma," Mum said. "She's our little angel, always guiding us."

Teagan turned to my mother. "She was so beautiful."

I swallowed, feeling the pain creep up my throat to choke me. I tried my best to stay strong.

"Caleb normally refuses to look at any photos of her. I think you being here is giving him strength, Teagan."

My mother patted me on the back before continuing toward her room.

Taking Teagan's hand, I led her into our room. *Our room.* That still sounded strange.

Closing the door, I prompted her to lie down next to me. Still wrapped in her towel, she curled into my arms.

"For years, we couldn't have Emma's photos out. It was too much for me. But recently we put them back up, and I've been dealing with it, but I haven't actually looked at her face until just now." I kissed the top of her head. "My mother is right. Having you here is so good for me. It's the happiest I've been in a long time."

She rested her head on my chest. "It feels so surreal to be in England with you. I'd always had this idea in my head about what it looked like here, the dynamic between you and your mother. I know things are a lot different now that your dad is away, but there's a serenity I wasn't expecting. There's a lot of love here, too—and a lot of pain that lingers. I can feel it all, everything that lies within these walls. I'm just so happy to be here, to have an opportunity to experience a new life, new adventures. But really, it wouldn't matter where I was as long as I can be with you."

This girl—this beautiful woman—breathed life into me every second we were together. I needed to find a way for us to *stay* together for more than just these next six months. I needed her forever.

———

A week after Teagan's arrival, the information I'd been keeping from her became hard to contain.

In the months before Teagan's move, we'd spent a lot of time on the phone. She'd told me she'd decided to

Google her birth mother, Ariadne. She'd explained how that led her to realize how important Maura was in her life. I loved hearing that she'd finally given Maura the credit she deserved.

She'd also told me that according to the addresses listed, Ariadne had lived for a time here in the UK. That didn't come as a surprise, since Teagan had always described her birth mother as a wanderer and world traveler. I remembered her telling me Ariadne had convinced Lorne to quit his job for a time and travel with her all those years ago.

I hadn't thought much about the Ariadne-UK connection until one night I visited my uncle. Frederick is a cop, and I knew he had access to certain information beyond what a general Google search would provide. For shits and giggles, I'd given him the name *Ariadne Mellencamp* and asked what he might be able to find out about her time here in England.

A listing in Brighton had popped up. That was a little under three hours away from here. More notable was the information that came along with it: the names of other people at that residence. Were they connected to Teagan as well? I'd immediately regretted seeking that information because now I had to share it with Teagan.

CHAPTER
THIRTY-ONE

Teagan

A week into my new gig at Caleb's uncle's flower shop, I felt like I was getting adjusted. It had taken me a while to figure out the difference between geraniums and carnations and other flowers, but once I'd set up a labeling system, I started to get the hang of it. Working under the tutelage of Caleb's Aunt Noreen, I took my time making the various arrangements. It was a peaceful job, overall; not too rushed and perfect for someone still learning the ropes.

The shop was not too far from where we lived. My favorite part of the day was when Caleb would come by to accompany me home after his summer classes ended. I was definitely envious, but I'd decided to focus on other types of learning during this time. Caleb and the world around us had much to teach me, I knew.

The bell dinged as he entered the shop. Noreen had left me alone for the last half-hour of my shift.

"Hey, baby." I ran from behind the counter to wrap my arms around Caleb's neck. "How was your day?"

"Good." His smile seemed forced and a little...off.

My heart pounded. "Is everything okay?"

"Yes. But there's something I want to talk to you about. Mum is working late, so we can be alone for a bit. Let's go home, alright?"

A rush of adrenaline hit me. "Is it something bad?"

"No. Please don't worry. It's just something I need to talk to you about."

The walk home was strange, to say the least. Caleb looked down at the sidewalk the whole time, and I felt nauseous. Things had been going so well here. I should've known the other shoe would drop.

Once inside the apartment, Caleb took a seat on the couch and I planted myself next to him. His legs bopped up and down.

"What?" I urged, unable to take it anymore.

"I did a stupid thing."

My nerves made my throat dry. "Okay...what?"

"My curiosity got the best of me, and I investigated something I had no right to." After a long pause, he continued. "When you told me your birth mother had lived here at one time, I had my uncle who's a cop look into it further. He found the address where she lived and some other information."

I felt my eyes widen.

"I know—it was stupid of me. I never thought anything would come of it."

I took a deep breath. "Come of it? What did you find?"

"A man called Stuart Erickson and a girl called Emma Erickson were listed at the same address as Ariadne. Of course, that naturally gave me the chills because Emma was my sister's name. Stuart was listed as forty-four years old and Emma as ten."

Shock consumed me as I said nothing.

"We don't need to do anything with this information, Teagan. Searching her name was stupid. And now I've uncovered something that doesn't have to mean anything—if you don't want it to."

What was I supposed to say? I took another breath. "I do agree it was unnecessary for you to look into her name."

"Of course. I know. It was just a dumb curiosity. I never meant to hurt you. Please tell me you don't hate me for it."

Of course I couldn't hate him for it. He'd impulsively searched her name and came up with unexpected information that wasn't meant to be hurtful. But now that I knew about it, it wasn't something I could erase, nor did I know how to handle it.

I exhaled. "I don't hate you. I'm just a little perplexed... and unsure of what to do with this."

"We don't have to do anything with it." He examined my face. "Or, if you want, I can grab Mum's car when she gets home, and we can take a ride out there, scope it out. Brighton is only a few hours from here."

Now my curiosity began to stir as well. Who were Stuart and Emma? Was Ariadne still living in England? Based on the number of addresses I'd found listed for her over the years, my gut said she was long gone. But I was just as impulsive as Caleb had been.

When we got to the address in Brighton and knocked on the door, no one was home. It was a small stone house and impossible to see inside because the shades were drawn.

"Doesn't look like anyone's here," Caleb said. "Let's just go. It wasn't meant to be." I could tell he felt guilty for dragging me into this.

Just as we'd gotten back in our car, lights approached in the distance.

We froze, waiting to see what would transpire.

My pulse raced as I watched a man and girl exit the car that had parked in the driveway right in front of us. As I caught sight of her face, I realized not only did she look like Ariadne, she looked like *me*.

Immediately, I knew.

I turned to Caleb. "She's my sister."

———————

It was nearing 8PM now, and Caleb and I were still parked outside the house, unsure what to do.

"Look at me," he finally said. "We need to make a decision. You don't have to go in. But if you do, I'll be right here by your side. This is your choice. You don't have to do anything you don't want to."

"I'm pretty sure if I turn around and leave now, it will haunt me. I have to confirm it."

"Then you have your answer. We should go in."

Blowing out a shaky breath, I opened the passenger-side door. Caleb followed, and we headed up the small set of stairs to the front door. With a trembling hand, I rang the doorbell.

The man opened. "Can I help you?" He had brown hair with gray on the sides.

"Hi...uh...I'm looking for Ariadne Mellencamp."

His expression changed, and his eyes slowly narrowed. "Who are you?"

"My name is Teagan Carroll. I'm visiting from the United States. Ariadne is my birth mother, although I've never met her. I understand she might live at this address?"

I knew she wasn't here. If she were, I probably wouldn't have come to the door. This visit wasn't about Ariadne. It was about the little girl.

It took him a few seconds to respond. "How old are you?"

"Twenty."

Caleb grabbed my hand and squeezed it.

The man stepped out of the way to let us through. "Come in."

The smell of something toasting registered. Normally, that would have made me hungry, but I was too nervous.

The girl appeared behind him. "Who are you?"

Her green eyes were the same as mine. Her thick, light brown hair—also the same as mine—had been gathered in a side ponytail.

"My name is Teagan. Nice to meet you."

"That's a nice name."

"What's your name?" I asked.

"Emma."

I swallowed. "Hi, Emma."

Her father turned to her. "Emma, can you go to your room for a moment?"

She protested. "Why?"

"I need to discuss something with our guests."

"But—"

"Emma, just do what I asked. Please."

After she reluctantly disappeared into her room, Stuart led us over to the couch in the living room. Caleb sat next to me and held my hand while the man took a seat across from us.

"You've been looking for Ariadne?" he asked.

"Not really," I told him. "I accidentally stumbled on this address as one of her previous residences. When I saw there was a child living here, it made me curious, and I came to see her. I don't have any interest in meeting Ariadne."

He nodded. "Ariadne hasn't lived here in a very long time. We haven't seen her in years."

This story sounded familiar. A feeling of dread grew in my chest. When he seemed hesitant to continue, I decided to tell him my story.

"My father was Ariadne's college professor two decades ago. He fell in love with her. She convinced him to travel the world with her, paying for everything. She got pregnant with me and wanted to terminate, but my father convinced her to stick around long enough to have the baby. She left soon after I was born, and I've never met her. Nor do I care to."

Stuart stared at me a moment. "You look just like her."

"I know. I look just like Emma, too. Is she—"

"Yes. Ariadne is her mother."

My heart swelled in my chest. Emma was my sister. *My sister.* I had another sister, and I'd had no idea all this time.

I braced myself. "What happened?"

He shook his head and laughed a little. "Well, like your father, I was sucked in by her charm, her mystery, her beauty. Ariadne was traveling alone when I met her on a park bench. That night, I took her home with me, and we lived together for two years. We opened up a café that sold organic tea, coffee, and snacks down the road. We were blissfully happy until she got pregnant. She admitted at that point that she wasn't ready to settle down. And like your father, apparently, I did everything in my power to convince her to keep the baby, to stay and raise it with me."

Feeling a mix of disgust and sadness, I said, "I know where this story is going."

"You do know. Because you've lived it, my dear."

"She left after Emma was born?"

"Soon after, yes. Woke up one morning to find a note from her. She apologized for having to leave, saying Emma would be better off without her in our lives."

"Was that the last time you saw her?"

He nodded. "I didn't bother chasing her down. She knew where to find us if she changed her mind, but she never came back."

Horror rushed through me as I thought of another little girl experiencing the same abandonment I had, at the hands of the same person.

"What does Emma know about her mother?" Caleb asked.

"I've never had the heart to tell her that her mother chose to leave."

"My father felt the same way for a long time. Never wanted to hurt me," I said. "How did you explain it to her?"

"I told her Ariadne was sick and had to leave to get better. Technically, that's the truth. I do believe that woman is mentally ill in some way."

"Will you tell her the full story someday?" I asked.

He looked conflicted. "Yes. I think so. I've just been waiting for the right time. But it never feels right to lay that on her."

"I understand. My father chose to tell me the truth when I was a little older than Emma. I definitely appreciated his honesty, and it helped explain so much. I was lucky to have a really supportive stepmother, though."

"That's the one thing we're definitely missing here. I've had women come and go, but no one willing to take on the responsibility of mothering my daughter." He sighed. "Ariadne's leaving also left us in financial shambles. Without her around to help with the café, it inevitably closed. I had to find other work and childcare for Emma. It's been a difficult ten years, but I don't regret a second of it. My daughter is the best thing to ever happen to me."

I couldn't help but smile at that. "You sound like my dad."

"He and I surely have more in common than we know. And I have to say, I don't know you very well, but it's clear he and your stepmother did a wonderful job."

"Thank you." I smiled with pride.

He turned to Caleb. "I'm sorry. We've been ignoring you."

"No need to apologize. I'm just happy we had an opportunity to meet you. My girl has lived far too long feeling like she was alone in her situation. I do believe we were meant to find you. It's funny how things work out sometimes." Caleb turned to look at me. "I thought Teagan's coming to the UK was solely to benefit me, but now I see it's bigger than that. Fate had other plans."

Stuart rubbed his hand over his face. "I'd love for you to get to know Emma, but I'm not sure what I want to say about who you are quite yet. Maybe we could wing it for a while until I figure it out? I'd like to tell her the truth about her mother before we explain your relation to her, if that's okay."

I smiled, hoping he knew there were no hard feelings about that decision. "Of course. There is no rush at all. As long as she can find out the truth at some point, I'm good with that."

"How long are you here in England?"

That question gave me anxiety. But I answered with what I knew.

"I've been here a few weeks. My plan is to stay for the six months I'm allowed and then figure it out from there. I came to be with Caleb. I have one more year of school left that I have to finish, but being with him for now is more important."

"Young love is definitely powerful." He grinned.

"Maybe we could come out here on the weekends—or every other one—if you'll allow it," Caleb suggested. "We could take Emma for ice cream, or the four of us could just hang out from time to time."

A voice came from behind us. "Can I come out now?"

Stuart looked up at her. "Sure, my love."

She pointed to Caleb. "I know she's Teagan, but what's your name?"

"Caleb. Nice to meet you, lovely."

"Who are you people?"

Caleb chuckled. "We're new friends of your dad."

"Teagan might be someone who can look after you when I have business to take care of from time to time," Stuart added. "How would you feel about that?"

Her eyes went wide. "Like a new babysitter?"

"Yeah. Occasionally."

Instead of answering, Emma came over and wrapped her hands around my cheeks. "You're so pretty."

I thought I might lose it. She had no idea who I was, but based on how she was looking at me, maybe there was some kind of innate connection. It was like looking in the mirror—not only because of our looks, but because of our shared experiences.

I finally found the words. "You're so pretty, too."

In that moment, I knew I'd been given another purpose in life: to make sure Emma felt less alone—loved— to make sure she understood that her mother leaving was not her fault.

Growing up, I'd always wished for an older sister. Lord knows I'd done a shitty job with the little sister I'd had for so many years. But I'd changed. Here was my chance to *be* the big sister I'd always wanted. I would never take family for granted again—any of them.

CHAPTER
THIRTY-TWO

Teagan

It was nine in the morning when the phone rang. Caleb and I had the day off from classes and work, so we'd slept in. Startled by the ring, I picked it up.

"Hello?"

"Hello...Teagan? It's Stuart."

Emma's father hadn't contacted me since our visit over a week ago. My family had been flabbergasted when I told them about Emma. My father was particularly emotional about history repeating itself, with Ariadne abandoning another child. But overall, they seemed happy that I'd found my long-lost sister. I hadn't been sure yet whether to celebrate the discovery, though, since Stuart hadn't made it clear when he planned to tell Emma the truth. For all I knew, that could be years away.

I sat up against the headboard. "Oh, hello. How are things?"

"Good, good. I, uh, wanted to let you know I spoke to Emma."

"Spoke to her? You mean, about Ariadne?"

"Yes. I was careful not to tell her that her mother abandoned her per se, but I explained that I'd recently learned her mother had a daughter twenty years ago. So she knows she has a sister."

I gripped the sheets. "What was her reaction?"

"She cried, actually. She said she never dreamed she'd have a sister."

I closed my eyes. Then opened them. "Wait—did you tell her it was me? The girl she met last week?"

"Oh, yes! I told her it was you. She knows, Teagan. That realization made her even happier."

Warmth washed over me. "I'm so happy she felt that way."

"When can you come out again?"

"Anytime you want me," I answered.

"This weekend?"

Caleb began to stir next to me.

"Hang on one second." I whispered, "Caleb...any reason we can't drive out to Brighton this weekend?"

He blinked his eyes open. "No reason I can think of."

I turned back to the phone. "We can come!"

"Brilliant, then. See you soon."

———

Emma was sitting on her bed reading a book when Caleb and I approached her room the following weekend.

I knocked on the door. "Hey, Emma."

She set the book down and looked up. "Are you really my sister?"

Nodding, I sat at the edge of her bed. "I am."

Caleb smiled and took a seat on the ground in the corner of the room to give us some space.

"Why didn't you tell me sooner?" Emma asked.

"Because we thought it would be best for you to meet me first, then talk to your dad. I hope that's okay."

She shrugged. "It is." Then a smile lit up her face, and all felt right in the world. This girl was essentially me, a decade ago. But she didn't have a mother figure like I did. That made me thankful for Maura all over again.

Picking at some lint on her bedspread, I asked, "Do you have any questions for me?"

"Is Caleb your boyfriend?"

I looked over at him and laughed.

"Yes, he is. That's why I'm here in England. I'm visiting him."

Her expression dampened. "Are you leaving?"

"I may have to for a while, but I'll be back."

Something about the look on her face told me she had little confidence in that. After all, like me, this was a girl who'd been trained by Ariadne to expect abandonment.

"How do I know you'll be back?" she asked. "My mother left and never came back."

I squeezed her hand, unsure what to say.

When Caleb noticed my struggle to answer, he chimed in. "Teagan is a woman of her word, Emma. She told me she would come visit me, and she has. She would never say anything she didn't mean. She's not your mother. She's your sister. And she understands more than anyone in this world what it feels like not to have your mother around. You can trust her, okay?"

She smiled at him and then at me. "Okay."

I brought her into a hug. "Come here."

Over the years, I'd never been a hugger. I could count on my fingers the number of times I'd initiated such contact with my family. But when it came to this little girl, it felt right.

"I can't believe I have a big sister." When I released her, she asked, "Do you have any other sisters and brothers?"

"I have one sister. She's my dad's child with my stepmom. She's really cool, and she'll want to claim you as her own. I think you're gonna become her new favorite."

"What's her name?"

"Shelley."

Her next question took me by surprise. "Do you know why our mum left?"

I shook my head sadly. "No, honey, I don't."

"Dad says she's sick, but I don't know if he's just saying that."

"There are all kinds of sicknesses, Emma. I feel like our mother is sick in the head. And that's why she left. I've learned over the years not to take it personally. But it's hard. I know. I know exactly what you're going through."

Caleb stood and walked over to the bed. He sat next to me. "You know, Emma, when I first met your sister, she was struggling with many of the same thoughts and feelings you are. You're both very lucky to have each other now. Because a shared experience is always easier than going through it alone. No matter where Teagan is, you'll never have to feel alone again."

Emma smiled shyly. "I'm so happy she found me."

"Actually..." I corrected. "Caleb found you."

Her eyes widened as she turned to him. "You did?"

"Yes." He glanced over at me and grinned.

"How?"

"The magical Internet, lovely. I'm so happy it worked out."

"Thank you, Caleb, for finding me."

He looked a bit choked up. "Of course."

I took his hand. "You're really lucky to have a good daddy, too, Emma. Just like I did. We're both lucky."

"What's your dad's name?" she asked.

"Lorne."

"That's a funny name. So is Teagan a little, although I like it."

"Well, Emma is a beautiful name."

I looked at Caleb.

"My sister's name was Emma," he told her. "She passed when we were little."

"Really? That's so sad."

"Yeah. I miss her very much." He took a deep breath and said, "You and your sister are so lucky to have each other."

"I can be your new sister Emma, if you want."

My heart melted, and Caleb smiled from ear to ear. "I would love that." He looked at me. "The three of us can be like a family. Your dad included, of course."

"You're not *like* a family. You *are* my family," she said, reaching out her hand to me.

I held on to her for a long time. "You know what else, Emma? Someday you'll meet someone, like I did with Caleb, and the fact that our mom wasn't around will mean even less. Because that person will love you enough to make up for it all. In the meantime, you will have us to make up for it, okay? No more going through this alone. We're a team now."

"Do you like s'mores?" Caleb asked.

Emma crinkled her nose. "What are s'mores?"

"Oh, I forgot—you're English like me," he said with a laugh.

"S'mores are an amazing treat," I explained. "People light a fire outside and make them."

Caleb never wasted an opportunity. "Why don't I go to the store and buy the stuff to make them right now? I'll check with your dad first to see if he'll allow us to light a fire."

And so, that evening we introduced my little sister to s'mores. It was the start of what I knew would become a family tradition, and the start of an entirely new future I never could have anticipated.

CHAPTER
THIRTY-THREE

Teagan

I was nearing the halfway point of my stay in England. Now that summer was over, the reality that my days here were numbered had started to creep in. The beginning of the fall semester meant Caleb's schedule of classes was heavier, so he was around less. That only gave me more time alone to worry about the future.

Caleb had to stay in the UK to finish school, but I had a couple of choices to make. I could go back to the US and finish my last year of school there, or I could figure out a way to come back here sooner. Either way, the consensus seemed to be that I would be returning to the States, at least for a while, after this trip ended. Unfortunately, although I did miss my parents and Shelley, this was not at all what I wanted.

I loved spending time with Emma, and even the job at the flower shop was starting to grow on me. Arranging bouquets had a meditative effect I hadn't been anticipating. I was going to miss it.

But most of all, I was deeply in love with Caleb and couldn't imagine having to separate from him. I felt at home here with him and Poppy. His mother had become one of my favorite people. Caleb would often need to study, so his mother and I would sit in the kitchen and talk or venture out shopping together. She'd taught me how to cook a few things Caleb loved. As much as I hated being away from my own family, Caleb and Poppy had become my family, too. The thought of leaving them—and especially now Emma—had me panicked.

But Caleb and I were handling the unknowns of my impending departure much like we'd handled things for a time before he left the US. We were having lots of sex and not talking about anything upsetting, as if the inevitable weren't looming. While that helped us to enjoy each moment, it didn't prepare us for the heartbreak of another separation.

One day, Caleb surprised me with a trip to Nottingham, a place he'd always said he wanted to show me before I left.

We spent the day walking around Nottingham Castle and the big cathedral. We also visited City of Caves, a historical underworld of sorts beneath the city.

Then Caleb pulled up in front of Bo Cheng's, the restaurant he'd called me about last Christmas, the one that had signaled him to finally reach out to me again.

"I totally forgot about this place," I said as we exited the car to head in for a late lunch.

"We couldn't come to Nottingham without noshing at Bo Cheng's, love."

Caleb and I went inside and enjoyed the most deliciously decadent Chinese food I'd eaten in a long time.

As we were paying the bill, he announced, "I have a surprise for you."

I perked up. "What?"

He reached across the table for my hands. "We're not going home tonight."

"We're not?"

"I booked us an evening at a local cottage. I got a good deal."

"Oh my God. Really?" We'd be alone at night for the first time since my arrival. "We can screw as loudly as we want!"

He wriggled his brows. "Damn right."

We arrived at the cottage twenty minutes later. It was just a short distance from the city center and totally exceeded my expectations. The small, Victorian structure had an old-world charm on the outside and featured a lovely courtyard out back, but it was more modern on the inside. The living room was bright and inviting with yellow walls and cozy furniture.

Caleb wasted no time starting a fire in the fireplace, and the house was soon warm and intimate. It felt like a dream to stay in this oasis with him overnight. Aside from our night at that hotel in Boston, we'd never been totally alone.

We planted ourselves on the ground in front of the flames.

Resting my head against Caleb's chest, I let out the thoughts that had been on my mind all day. "I'm so scared to leave you."

I turned around to gauge his reaction.

He looked really...tense, like something was on his mind.

It took almost a full minute for him to respond. "I... think we should get married."

"What?"

"I think we should get married—soon. Then we can start the paperwork to switch your status over to a spousal visa. It's the only way to guarantee that it will be easy for us." He wrapped his legs around me as he looked into my eyes. "But here's the thing, I would want to marry you even if the distance weren't separating us. Because there's no one else I'd rather spend my life with. You're everything to me. I don't want to lose you because of stupid rules and regulations. Life is too short. Be with me. Marry me, Teagan."

My heart pounded so hard. He had no clue that I'd prayed he would come to this conclusion. In my head, it seemed like an extreme possibility. But in my heart, I knew it was the only way we stood a chance at being together without complications. I just never thought he'd go for it so soon. But there was no part of me that didn't feel ready to commit to him.

"I will absolutely marry you."

He beamed. "Yeah?"

"I can tell you were nervous to ask me, but I've been hoping you would."

He slipped his hand into his back pocket and took out a ring box. His proposal had seemed so impulsive, but apparently he'd planned this.

"I was afraid to take this out. I felt like I needed to feel you out first, to confirm you didn't think my suggestion was too crazy. But now that I know we're on the same page, this is me getting down on one knee."

Technically, since we were lying on the ground, he stood up on one knee. I sat up and placed my hand over my heart.

PENELOPE WARD

"Teagan, you've made my life brighter from the moment you yelled at me through your keyboard. And it's only been better from there. You're the best friend and lover anyone could ask for." He opened the box and looked down at the sparkly round diamond set in a gold band. "This ring was my nan's. She gave it to my mother some years ago and asked her to give it to me only when Mum was certain I'd found the one. My mother didn't hesitate to hand this over when she realized how worried I was about you leaving England. She helped me come to the conclusion that I should take the risk of asking you to marry me, that the worst that could happen was you'd say no." He looked up at me. "Teagan, my love, once again, will you be my wife?"

"Yes!"

We fell into a long kiss, rolling around on the carpet in bliss.

"When is this happening?" I asked.

"The sooner the better. We can book an appointment at the Home Office tomorrow to see what we need to do. If all goes well, we can get everything sorted before your six months is up."

Hope filled me. "And then I'll never have to leave?"

"That's the idea."

My mind began to whirl. "We have a little wedding to plan!"

"It'll be fun. Emma can be your flower girl—bridesmaid, whatever. We'll keep it small. Someday we'll have a real one in Boston with all of your family and friends. Maybe fly Mum over, too."

My heart leaped for joy. "That sounds like a plan. I don't need a big wedding. I'd rather use the money for our

303

future house, wherever that may be. And I kind of want it to be here. I want to be here for Emma—living here."

Caleb smiled wide. "That makes me incredibly happy. You know I don't want to leave my mother. But I want to make something very clear. If you don't want to stay here forever, you come first. I would go absolutely anywhere you wanted me to because I can't live without you."

The following morning over breakfast and tea in the adorable cottage kitchen, Caleb got a bright idea.

"I wonder if I could call Bo Cheng."

I chuckled. "Why would you want to do that?"

"I want to thank him. If he hadn't given up his room in your house, I wouldn't be blissfully happy right now. God knows where I would be without you, Teagan." Caleb hugged me and kissed behind my ear. "Do you still have access to the student directory at Northern?"

"Yeah, since my attendance is on hold, I'm still considered active."

I logged into the student portal from my phone and searched for Bo Cheng's name. It came right up, and I recited the number for Caleb as he entered it into his phone. He put the call on speaker.

Someone answered. "Hello?"

"Bo?"

"Yeah."

"Bo Cheng?"

"Yes." He sounded like we'd maybe woken him up from a nap.

"You don't know me. My name is Caleb Yates, but I owe you a huge thank you for...well, for your allergies."

Covering my mouth, I cracked up as he continued.

"If you hadn't been greatly allergic to Catlin Jenner, I would've never met my girl, Teagan. We wouldn't be in England right now planning a future together. She wouldn't have found her long-lost sister, and I might never have tasted s'mores or Hot Cheetos in my life. You, Bo Cheng, and your allergies are magical, my friend. You've changed our world."

The next thing we heard was...a click.

My mouth dropped. "Did Bo Cheng just fucking hang up on us?"

Caleb snorted. "It seems he did."

EPILOGUE

Caleb

The Carrolls gathered around the computer screen while Shelley spoke to Emma on Skype.

"I'm trying to get my parents to come to England next summer. Then we can finally meet!"

Maura leaned over her shoulder and chimed in. "It's not definite yet. But it's very likely, sweetie. We can't wait to meet you."

Emma jumped up and down in her seat. "Yay! I'm so excited!"

Stuart peeked out from behind Emma in the background. "Would love to see you all here."

Not only had my wife's little sister gained an older sibling, it seemed the entire Carroll family had accepted Emma as one of their own. They'd often Skype with her, even when they weren't Skyping with us. And Emma seemed overjoyed to have an adopted American family.

Emma also spent quite a bit of time at home with us in Stratford whenever Stuart had plans. My mother had really taken to her. Given that she had my sister's name, I knew spending time with Emma was also healing for

Mum. It was all very cosmic. I'd always known Teagan and I were meant to be together, but finding Emma made it seem so much bigger than that—bigger than us—like all of this was meant to happen in exactly the way it had.

Teagan and I were in the midst of our first visit back to Boston together since getting married almost a year ago. A couple of weeks after our engagement at the cottage in Nottingham, Teagan and I had a small civil ceremony with just my mother, Stuart, and Emma in attendance. Teagan wore a single flower in her long, flowing hair and a simple white dress. I'd borrowed a suit from my uncle, which happened to fit. It wasn't the fanciest of affairs, but it hadn't needed to be. Stuart had connected the Carrolls in live via his computer so they could watch the entire thing from the US.

We'd spent the weeks after the wedding dealing with the paperwork that would allow Teagan to stay in the UK as my wife. Between finding Emma and getting married, the past year had been a whirlwind in the best possible way.

Things were better than ever, but certainly not perfect. My relationship with my father remained estranged, although when I'd brought Teagan to meet him at my uncle's house after we were married, he'd been at least cordial to her. Mum had remained strong and hadn't taken my father back. It seemed for the time being his drinking was under control, but without living under the same roof with him, we couldn't be completely sure.

I'd been doing well since my days in rehab, but I recognized my need to continue therapy. So I'd gone back to seeing someone every other week. In fact, having that consistent outlet and seeing all of the good that was possible because of it helped me decide on a career. I'd changed my major to psychology and hoped to become a counselor myself.

Teagan would finally be starting her last year of school once we returned to England. Her plan was to continue working at the flower shop while she finished off her marine biology degree at my university. Even though she helped Mum a bit with the rent, she hadn't had to spend all of the money from the ring Maura gave her, so she'd put the remainder of it in the bank to use toward school. Hopefully, after graduation she'd find a suitable job reasonably close to home. Yes, we still lived with my mother, but we were saving up for our own place. As Teagan had originally proposed, we'd opted to forego the big wedding in Boston in order to use that money toward our future house. We were thinking of possibly settling closer to Brighton, near Emma and Stuart. So many decisions to make, but we'd be making them together.

As nice as it was to be back in the Carrolls' house in Brookline, we got so much attention here that I missed my alone time with Teagan. Her family had missed her so much, they wanted to spend every waking minute with us. Back home, my mother kept her distance, even in our small house.

After we hung up from the family Skype call with Emma, Maura announced, "Dinner's in ten, guys."

I whispered in Teagan's ear, "We actually have ten minutes alone? Let's escape." Pulling her by the hand, I led her down to the basement, where we'd been sleeping.

"Ten minutes isn't that much time," she said.

"I assure you, ten minutes is all I'll need." I winked. "Maybe five."

Anytime Teagan and I were alone together downstairs, it made me feel nostalgic. Our lives had changed so much since the days we used to study in this room together. If you'd asked me then if I ever believed Teagan would be living in England with me, I would've thought you were crazy. But if you'd asked me whether I thought we would end up together someday, somehow the answer would have been yes. I hadn't known how that was going to happen, but when I left Boston, I knew in my heart it wasn't the end.

And I was about to prove that to her.

"If I told you I always knew we'd end up together, would you believe me?"

"You mean from the time you met me?" Teagan brushed her hand along the hairs on my arm as we lay across from each other on the bed.

"Not quite that long. But when I left Boston to head home, I knew we'd be together again. At the time, I just didn't know how to make it happen."

She laced her fingers with mine and stared down at our wedding rings. "I don't think I had as much faith as you did. But I was definitely in love with you when you left, and that wasn't going to change."

"You said you found the letter I left you in the makeup drawer. I assume you never found the other one."

Her eyes went wide. "There was another one?"

"Yes. But you weren't meant to find it."

I stood and walked over to the corner of the room. I moved the carpet and lifted one of the floorboards. There it was—the letter I'd hidden the day before I left Boston. Teagan had been showering when I'd snuck the letter into its hiding place, but I'd spent the previous week scouring the room for a secret spot. When I happened upon the loose board, I figured it was my best bet.

I waved the envelope in the air.

"Oh my God. That's been there the entire time? Under the floor?"

"Yep. Guess I picked a good place for it, eh?"

She hopped up and ran over to me. "What does it say?"

I opened the envelope and unfolded the paper before reading her what I'd written.

Dear Teagan,

If you're reading this, one of two things has happened. Either we're together again, and I'm personally delivering this letter (which is my hope), or by some twist of fate you found it before I got to you. If it's the latter, I'm sorry. It means I haven't found my way back to you. That wasn't my intention.

Of course there's always the chance my plan was foiled—maybe something happened to me and someone is finding this years later, after you've moved out. That would be unfortunate. If you're reading this and you're not Teagan Carroll, please see that she gets this, wherever she is. She needs to know I've always loved her and never intended for us to be apart forever.

In the event that I'm lucky enough to be with you right now, Teagan, I hope you can see this letter as proof that even as I was gearing up to break your heart and go back to England, somehow I knew we'd be together again. I just needed to fix my messed-up parts before I could give you my all, because you deserve every part of me.

I hope you see this letter as evidence that I've always believed in us. And I'll never stop.

As I write this, I may be about to venture "home." But from probably the moment you held my hand while I freaked out in that dodgy theater, I've known that home would always be wherever you are.

Love, Caleb

P.S. Not bad for a love story that started in the loo.

ACKNOWLEDGEMENTS

I consider myself the luckiest gal in the world to have readers all over the world who continue to support and promote my books. Your enthusiasm and hunger for my stories is what motivates me every day. And to all of the book bloggers who work tirelessly to support me, please know how much I appreciate you.

To Vi – Forever my partner in crime. Hopefully you don't get tired of me singing your praises. Each year our friendship becomes more invaluable to me. I couldn't do any of this without you. The best part of this career has been our collaborations and getting to work with my friend each and every day.

To Julie – My late-night watch dog. Thank you for your friendship and for always inspiring me with your amazing writing and attitude.

To Luna –Thank you being there day in and day out and especially this year for being such an inspiration. The best is yet to come.

To Erika –Thank you for always brightening my days with your daily check-ins and virtual smiles. It will always be an E thing!

To my Facebook reader group, Penelope's Peeps – I adore you all. You are my home and favorite place to be.

To my agent extraordinaire, Kimberly Brower – Thank you for everything you do and for believing in me long before you were my agent, back when you were a blogger and I was a first-time author.

To my editor Jessica Royer Ocken – It's always a pleasure working with you. I look forward to many more experiences to come.

To Elaine of Allusion Book Formatting and Publishing – Thank you for being the best proofreader, formatter, and friend a girl could ask for.

To my assistant Brooke – Thank you for hard work in handling Vi's and my releases and so much more. We appreciate you so much!

To Letitia of RBA Designs – My awesome cover designer. This cover is one of my favorites that you've designed. Thank you for always working with me until the finished product is exactly perfect.

To my husband – Thank you for always taking on so much more than you should have to so that I am able to write. I love you so much.

To the best parents in the world – I'm so lucky to have you! Thank you for everything you have ever done for me and for always being there.

To my besties: Allison, Angela, Tarah and Sonia – Thank you for putting up with that friend who suddenly became a nutty writer.

Last but not least, to my daughter and son – Mommy loves you. You are my motivation and inspiration!

ABOUT THE AUTHOR

Penelope Ward is a *New York Times, USA Today* and *#1 Wall Street Journal* bestselling author.

She grew up in Boston with five older brothers and spent most of her twenties as a television news anchor. Penelope resides in Rhode Island with her husband, son and beautiful daughter with autism.

With over two million books sold, she is a 21-time *New York Times* bestseller and the author of over twenty novels.

Penelope's books have been translated into over a dozen languages and can be found in bookstores around the world.

Subscribe to Penelope's newsletter here:
http://bit.ly/1X725rj

OTHER BOOKS
BY PENELOPE WARD

OTHER BOOKS BY PENELOPE WARD
& VI KEELAND

CPSIA information can be obtained
at www.ICGtesting.com
Printed in the USA
BVHW031250290820
587587BV00002B/321